REMISSION

OFELIA MARTINEZ

READING CACTUS
PRESS

Library of Congress Control Number: 2021902911

First Edition

ISBN 978-1-954906-006 (hardcover)

ISBN 978-1-954906-02-0 (paperback)

ISBN 978-1-954906-01-3 (eBook)

REMISSION

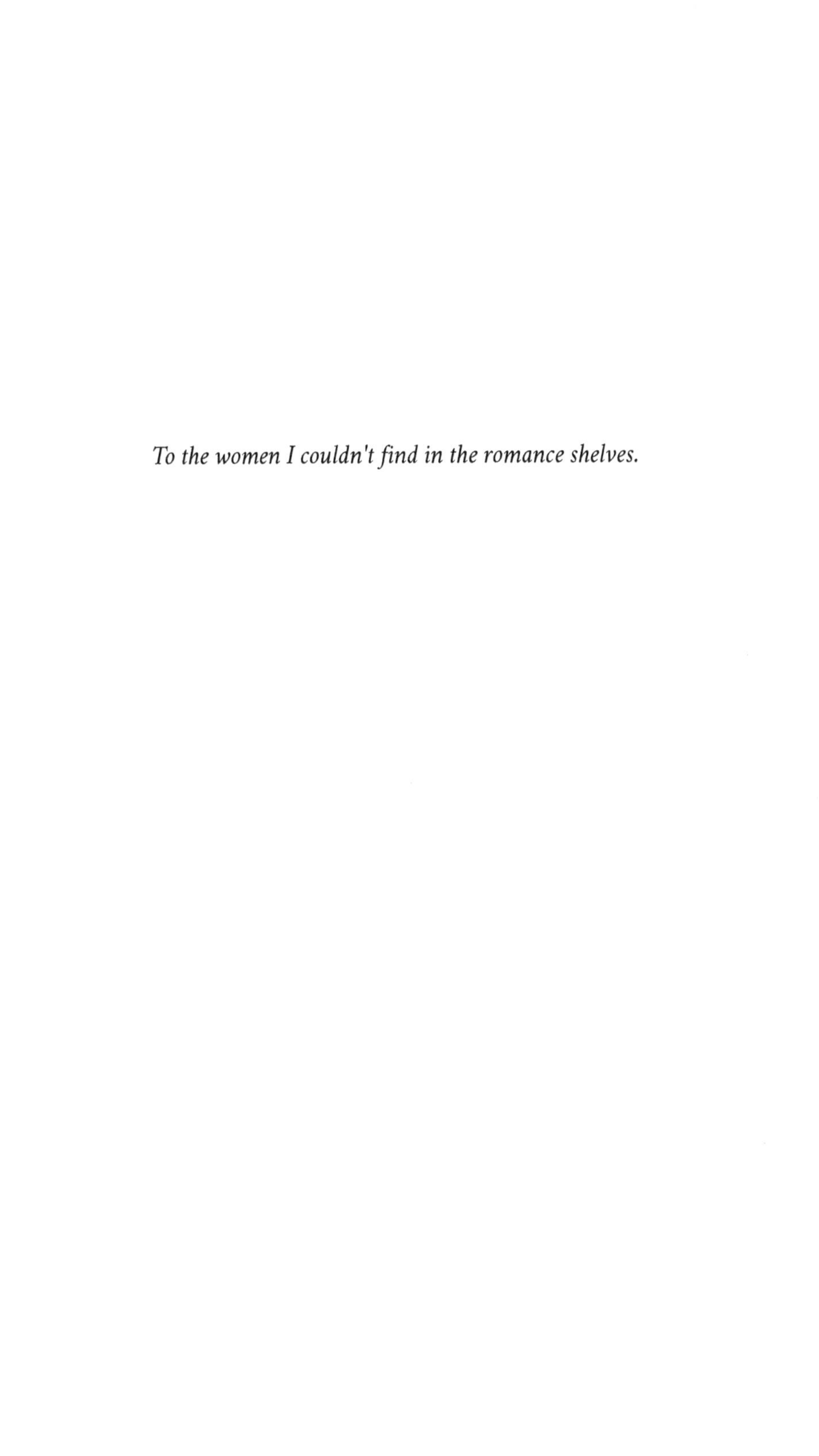

To the women I couldn't find in the romance shelves.

SATAN IN THE AUDIENCE

The interview was going well, and I hadn't barfed or passed out once. As we neared its conclusion, the muscles in my legs relaxed, and I uncrossed my legs, taking a taller posture in my chair. The question-and-answer bit, my favorite part, was next. Reaching young girls and women wanting to become doctors was reason enough to put myself through the stress of getting on stage to lecture at universities.

"Dr. Carolina Ramirez, everyone. Can we all please give her a round of applause?"

The packed auditorium erupted, and my cheeks would have been tomato-red had I not prepared with extra layers of makeup. I was thirty-five years old, for crying out loud. I should've been over stage fright by this point in my career.

"Please, that's enough. Thank you," I said, waving down the audience.

"We would like to thank you so much for being with us today," said the interviewer. "Before we turn it over to the audience, I would like the students here today to know that when you signed on for this guest lecture and interview, you did so only on the condition that there would be extensive time for a Q&A."

"That's right. It's a standard request on all of my speaking contracts."

"Why is that important to you?" The young journalism student interviewing me smiled as she asked. She let the note cards rest on her lap, a sure sign the interview would soon be over. During the course of the interview, she had collected a constellation of sweat droplets on her upper lip and continuously wiped her hands on her black slacks. I had done hundreds of these interviews, and on this occasion, the interviewer seemed more nervous than me. I smiled reassuringly at her as if to say, *We may both be nervous, but we are in this together.*

"If I'm honest, if I could, I would skip the lecture and interview, and instead take each of you for coffee to talk one-on-one. Sadly, unless I clone myself, time does not allow that luxury."

"If anyone could manage *that,* surely it would be you," the interviewer said.

I laughed. "No. For now, I'm still going to focus on my oncology research and my patients. I will always follow my passion. Let's leave the cloning to someone else."

"We have a few people with microphones in the audience. Please raise your hand if you have a question for Dr. Ramirez."

I placed my hand in front of my forehead to block the blinding spotlight, so I could see the person asking the first question.

The young woman couldn't look up at me as she clutched my book in her shaky hands.

"Dr. Ramirez, I loved your book—" Her voice cracked a bit.

"Thank you. What is your name?"

"Araceli."

"Hi, Araceli," I said with an encouraging smile. "It's nice to meet you."

"You too, Dr. Ramirez," she said, giggling. She tucked a strand of hair behind her ear and fidgeted with the book. "Your book is mainly about research. Honestly, a lot of it went over my head, but I couldn't stop reading. You made it seem . . . accessible . . . but you also talked about how you struggled to advance your career in this field. Why was it important to include that in a book that would have otherwise been a dry and boring publication about research?"

"Thank you, Araceli," I started. "That is a huge compliment to me. I worked really hard to make my book readable to anyone, even those not already in the medical community, hoping it might spark an interest in medicine. We need more soldiers in the trenches. But to answer your question, I was writing to my younger self, which means I was writing to any young woman intrigued by medicine but too intimidated to pursue it. The many female doctors who came before me made it so much easier, but it still is really, *really* hard to become a doctor. It's harder if, like me, you are a woman. Even harder if you are a minority. Even harder if you grew up with little money or opportunity. The list goes on and on. I want women in my same circumstances to know that it *is* possible. It won't be easy, but I swear to you that you will find mentors to help guide you in your career as a doctor."

"Thank you, Dr. Ramirez."

"Oh, before we go to the next question, Araceli, I see you have my book with you. If you'd like me to sign it, please stay after the Q&A. I'd love to chat with you some more."

Araceli smiled as though she had won the lottery, and I wondered if one day the letters M.D. would follow her name.

The next girl's name was Stephanie. She was much more self-assured, though she asked a more basic question.

"Why did you get into medicine?" she asked.

I hid my judgment because I would never embarrass someone publicly like that, but I always dreaded that question, and to my annoyance, it was the one most frequently asked. It was a simple question, but I didn't like sharing that truth, so I always gave a partial answer, which was not the same as lying. Not really. "Anyone who gets into medicine wants to save lives. If that is something you are interested in, then medicine is for you." I smiled, dismissing her more quickly than I had Araceli.

The microphone went to the next person, who was, unfortunately, sitting directly below the position of the spotlight, leaving me completely blind and unable to make out a face. I adjusted in my chair and craned my neck, trying to see the person, but it was no use.

"Hello," the voice said. This time it was a man.

"Hello." I smiled. "What is your question?"

"Your first grant," he said, and my blood went cold.

That voice. I knew that voice as well as I knew human anatomy.

"You got your first significant grant at a very young age. Most doctors are fellows or attendings before receiving that kind of research funding, but you were only a resident," he said.

My heart launched itself against my ribs, and, I swear, my poor lungs were caught in the crossfire because I couldn't breathe. The words were getting in, but I wasn't computing—not yet. I squinted, trying to make out the face that I knew in my bones belonged to the voice, but the lights were too bright. I had to give up.

I steeled my spine. *Fake it till you make it,* I reprimanded myself. *Feel confident. Be confident.* "I'm sorry," I said. "I'm not hearing a question in there."

"Please forgive me," he said. His accent had gotten softer over the years, but that voice was undeniably his. "My question is—where did you get the inspiration for your first research grant?"

The bastard. He was goading me. Here. In front of all these people. Fine. I could play his game. I could give as good as I took.

"A researcher was working in the sub-specialty of cancer research I was interested in at the time. I read all of his research, and I found a way I could improve upon his work."

"Isn't that plagiarism of someone else's research?" he asked.

"That is actually a misconception," I fired back. "All medical advances are built on the foundations laid by research before them. A mentor once told me that research was a dance. One doctor takes a step forward, and the next doctor picks up the lead, spinning the research into a twirl, pushing it further." I grinned and challenged him with a raised eyebrow before realizing he was probably too far away to make out my facial expressions.

"Sounds like a wise mentor," he said.

"He had his moments," I said, and just like that, our banter was back. "Medical research doesn't necessarily mean living in a laboratory like a mad scientist inventing new medicine, though it could certainly involve that. A lot of research, mine included, is about adjusting existing medications and protocols into new modalities. There are drugs that are used now for one thing but were originally intended for something else. I haven't invented any of the medications or radiology methods in my research. Other scientists did that long before me. But what I *have* done is change dosing and experiment with different combinations of medications. A lot of my research also involves psychological components—how much can a patient take mentally before it becomes too much?" I sat back, pleased with my answer. He wouldn't publicly ruffle my feathers—he had already taken enough.

I hadn't heard that voice in over seven years, not since he left town after nearly destroying my career. Despite my hatred of him, the familiar back and forth we had always shared returned, and I resented the excitement that simple fact brought into my body.

"Thank you, Dr. Ramirez. If I may, a second question, or rather a request—"

"Sure."

"I also have a copy of your book here with me. Would it be okay if I also stayed behind to get a signature?"

"Of course."

The last thing I wanted to do was speak with him, let alone sign his book. And what business did he have buying my book anyway? I took a deep breath; this was the worst possible time for my hatred of Hector Medina to rear its head.

I answered about twenty more questions. The entire time, I couldn't see him but knew his glare was glued to my skin. I managed, somehow, miraculously, to concentrate on the questions, but I know I wasn't one-hundred-percent on my A-game. Luckily, my B-game was also rather spectacular. When the interview wrapped up, I took a break backstage to gulp an entire water bottle in hopes of cooling off and calming down.

After the auditorium emptied, I came back on stage to meet with Araceli, as promised. The spotlight was turned off, and I was aware of the second figure in the room only by my peripheral vision, but I refused to look at him.

I sat on the stage, my legs dangling off the edge as I took Araceli's book. I chatted her up for about ten minutes to get to know her a little better so my dedication could be personalized. She left with a dazed look, as though she might swoon, and I grinned like a fool after her.

I didn't see him move so much as I sensed him approaching, drawn to him like the pull of a magnet that had always been there between us, binding us together. That hadn't changed, and alarms started blaring in my brain.

"That was very kind of you, Dr. Ramirez," he said.

Crossing my arms, I finally turned to him as he walked over

to me, his steps a loud echo in the empty auditorium. I liked this position of power, sitting on top of the stage like a queen waiting for her peasants to come up to her from below. I smiled and clung to that image to give me the strength I would need to deal with the person I hated the most in this universe.

"Dr. Medina," I said. "How . . . *nice* to see you."

"Please call me Hector, Carolina," he said, his voice trying to soothe me like a child. The nerve.

"That's 'Dr. Ramirez' to you, *Dr. Medina.* Let's keep this professional."

He finally stood in front of me, and I reveled in this view from the higher vantage point. He looked up to meet my face from several feet below. Letting out a breath, he handed me the book. I arched an eyebrow.

"I wasn't kidding," he said. "I would very much like a dedication."

"You are kidding." I scoffed.

"No, Carolina. I'm serious. I'm very proud of you."

Proud? That gave me pause. Why would the man who nearly ruined my career be *proud* of me?

Disbelieving, I snatched the book from his hand. I opened the cover to the third page, which had the most blank space for a dedication. I smiled devilishly. I couldn't resist:

To the Devil himself—
> *You couldn't pull me down to hell with you.*
> *Hate always,*
> *Dr. Ramirez*

Jumping off the edge of the stage, I landed squarely in front of him and handed him the book. Standing on his level, I hated the height difference. I was tall, but he still had a good three inches on me. He encroached on my space too much with his height. I damned him for looking more handsome than ever. In the seven years since I'd seen him, his impossibly good looks had actually improved. His dark-brown, tanned skin glowed even more. What had once been salt and pepper hair was now nearly white at the temples, and his face was a bit rounder. He'd gained weight. The good kind. He was broader at the shoulders than he'd been back then, and I hated myself for noticing he'd clearly been working out. The man was like freaking wine.

He opened the book to read the inscription and laughed.

"That's funny, huh?" I said.

What in the world was happening? I didn't understand any of this. Why was he here? Why was he happy, smiling of all things, and *proud* of me? Nothing made sense, but I would be damned before I'd ask him.

"I will treasure this forever," he said, clutching the book to his chest. "I see you remain judgmental and critical of me."

"I see you remain tactless and careless," I shot back.

He laughed, and I noticed the sparkle in his eye. A sparkle I knew well, but it was so much brighter now.

I slung my purse over my shoulder, ready to get going and forget this crazy day ever happened, but Hector grabbed my wrist as I turned to leave.

"No, Carolina, wait." I looked at his hand on my wrist at the same time he did, and we both froze. We only connected for two, maybe three seconds, before he withdrew his hand, but those seconds electrified us. Nine years since the first time I'd touched him. Seven since the last time I'd spoken with him. I couldn't believe my body still reacted to him the same way after all this time.

"I'm sorry," he said.

"It's okay," I said, palming my wrist with my other hand to calm the fire on my skin.

"Can I please take you out for a drink, or coffee perhaps?"

I was speechless, so I could only shake my head.

"Please, Carolina. I have so much I have to say to you."

He said my name in nearly every sentence like he was pleading. I took too long to answer, and he pulled off his glasses to clean them. I knew that tell well. He was thinking. He wanted to find an argument that would persuade me to have drinks with him.

"Even if I wanted to," I said, "which I don't, I can't. I have a flight to catch."

"How about in Kansas City?" he asked, hopeful.

My entire body stilled. "In Kansas City?"

"Yes. Tomorrow. That little café on Westport Road you liked so much. Wait, is that still open?"

"It-it is, but you're going to be in Kansas City?"

"Yes. Does five sound okay to you? Tomorrow?" He smiled, and in that moment, he looked like a little kid.

"Why?" I asked, closing my eyes, seeking patience from within. "Why are you going to be in Kansas City? Please don't tell me you're coming back."

"Is the idea so terrible?"

"I-I, um, I have to go."

"Okay, but please. Meet me tomorrow. Five p.m."

I finally nodded. I would at least have to find out why my nightmare was back in my hometown. Then I ran out of the building as fast as I could because there was no air left in the vast auditorium.

NINE YEARS AGO

CHAPTER 2

THE RESEARCH GOD

"Ugh." Valentina, my twenty-four-year-old patient, rolled her eyes and turned away from me as I entered her room and looked at her chart on the laptop in the hospital's computer cart.

"Well, it's nice to see you too," I said.

"I fucking hate you," she said.

"No, you don't. I'm your favorite doctor." I smiled at her, looking up from her labs, which were good enough to widen my smile even further.

"You keep saying that, but you're not really my favorite doctor. You only think that because I'm your favorite patient," Valentina said.

"I have no favorite patients. I love you all the same."

She drew her finger in her mouth, pretending to gag.

"Are you really going to be sick?" I asked, only slightly concerned.

"No, but you look disgusting. It should be illegal."

"What should?"

"For doctors like you to walk around in front of patients like me."

"Doctors like me?"

"Yeah, you, strutting in here in your pencil skirt, white coat, with your—with your honey skin, amber eyes, and legs for miles. Flaunting all that in front of pale skeletons like me. It should be illegal for you to be that perfect."

I snorted. "I'm not perfect, Valentina. Far from it. And you are not a skeleton."

"I am. I'm a skeleton of my former self . . ." She trailed off, her gaze miles and miles away.

I hated seeing her so defeated. Damn it, Valentina. We knew. We knew the fight we had ahead of us. She couldn't give up on her treatment now. She wanted to be aggressive, and we'd only barely started. I was disconcerted by how low her spirits were so soon after beginning treatment.

It's only the start. She is in a bit of shock, just adjusting. I made a mental note to, if she was still in this mood in a few weeks, explore adding psych to her clinical team.

I sat on the chair next to her and brushed a long strand of hair away from her forehead. She smiled, though it was weak.

"But seriously," she said. "Why are you all dolled up? And hey! You weren't at rounds this morning," she complained.

"I wasn't at rounds because I'm off today. And I'm not dolled up."

Valentina arched an eyebrow. "So, *that's* how you dress on your days off?"

"What? This is professional!"

"No hot date? I'm disappointed. Remember, I have to live vicariously through you!"

I laughed at that. "No hot date. I'm here for a meeting. I get a new boss today, and the people upstairs are having a bit of a welcome thing for him."

"You dressed like *that*, and put on all that makeup, for a new boss? I smell something fishy. Give it up, Ramirez." She spoke with the authority of a coach.

"*Doctor* Ramirez. It cost me to get my degree, so you best show respect. I'm just trying to look professional. My new boss is kind of a big deal. I thought I should put my best foot forward."

"A big deal?" she asked, not buying it.

"Yes, and you should think he's a big deal too."

"Me?"

"Yes, you. It was *his* research that led to the clinical trials that make your treatment as effective as it is right now."

"Oh my god, is he that guy you won't shut up about? What's his name?"

"Medina. His name is Dr. Medina. And it's his research I won't shut up about. Not him."

"You clearly have a lady boner for him."

"Valentina!" I scolded her, and she pulled the bedsheets over her chin as if she weren't a grown woman.

"I'm dying," she said in a little girl's voice.

"You are not dying," I said, pulling the sheets back down. "Don't be a martyr."

"Is he hot?" she asked.

"Ew, Valentina, I've never seen him, but he is probably old. So unless you like bald and big-nosed with uncombed Einstein-like hair, which is how I've been picturing him, then yeah, he's probably hot."

She giggled back into her bed, and I felt lighter having left her in better spirits as I headed to the conference room.

Even if he did look like the troll of my imagination, I was still very nervous about meeting my godlike professional hero. Especially because I thought I'd never get to meet him in my life. His giving up a job at the FIHR, the Federal Institute of Health and Research, to come work here was like a miracle. It was such a coincidence that he would end up at my hospital, of all places. It would be like telling the average person they were going to meet Brenner Reindhart—from the best rock band of all time, *Industrial November*—and that he would be their boss.

I scanned the faces in the room eagerly. About half the staff were there early, and I smiled when I saw Sara, predictably standing by the lunch spread.

"Thanks for the heads up, Caro," said Sara, my best friend at the hospital. "This stuff is way better than what the nurses get at our meetings. *We* need the sustenance," she said, though the last word was muffled by the large piece of cantaloupe in her mouth.

"You're welcome." I gave her a side hug.

When we parted, Sara glared at me up and down. She put a hand on her hip and waited to swallow the bite she was chewing before speaking. "You look *really* nice," she said.

I pinched the bridge of my nose. Not this again. "It's not that weird," I snapped.

Sara laughed. "Yeah, honey. It is. Thanks again for the tip," she shouted as she left, a plate full of food shamelessly in her clutches.

Sara did have the right idea. My stomach rumbled at the sight of all the food. I had been so nervous all day that I hadn't eaten a bite, but now in my doctor's coat, and in the hospital— my favorite place in the world—I felt calmer, which in turn made me hungry.

As I piled fruit onto a plate, three doctors entered the conference room. I didn't have to see his face to know one of them was Dr. Braxton Keach. He was handsome, with black hair and blue eyes, but anything pleasant about him ended with his pretty-boy status. I swear Dr. Keach carried the stench of evil wherever he went, and I could sense his presence well before he made himself known. Though really, it was the excessive body spray that reminded me of so many of my high school memories. He didn't seem to understand that most of his patients were severely nauseous most of the time.

While we were both vying for the same prestigious fellowship offered by the hospital, my distaste for him didn't stem from friendly competition. No. It was the way he looked down on his patients and treated them as inferior. His disdain was subtle, so much so that it wouldn't be actionable in court, but I recognized his prejudiced behavior because he often turned it on me. For everyone else in the department, he turned on the charm. It made my teeth grind that no one else saw him for what he was.

Adding to my ongoing dislike of Dr. Keach, no one else noticed his double-face. Not only was Dr. Keach classically handsome, but he could bullshit like the best of them. The few other female residents in the room gravitated to him the minute he walked in and giggled like little girls. I rolled my eyes and wished I could sit them down and remind them they were doctors and should behave better. But Dr. Keach's presence would likely still prevail. Add to his handsomeness the fact that he was wealthy—from one of the most prominent families in Kansas City—and that meant everyone turned a blind eye to his more-than-lacking skills as a physician and his superiority complex. The result was a honey-tongued devil. But I knew.

"Dr. Ramirez," he said with his oily voice.

"Dr. Keach." I turned to the front of the room, my plate in my hand, ready to find another friendly face, any face, but he spoke before I could make my escape.

"Isn't this funny," he said with amusement in his eyes.

I didn't want to take the bait, I really didn't, but it was my day off so I could leave after the meeting. It was probably better to deal with it now than at my next shift when I would be trying to work.

"What is?" I said, indulging him.

"Last time we had a meeting like this was a year ago. You

remember. The Chief of Oncology was handing you a bouquet of flowers. The youngest resident to get a ten-million-dollar grant."

"I remember," I said. "Your jealousy is showing, Dr. Keach."

He laughed. "No, not jealous. Don't you find it weird?" he asked as he grabbed a wrap from the table and placed it on his plate. "Now, the chief has brought in Dr. Medina, the very man whose research you based your own grant on."

"Is there a point to this little speech?"

He shrugged. "I don't know, Ramirez. If I were you, I'd be a little suspicious. He did just come in kind of stealing your thunder. Seems like the chief traded up. You think he'll give him a bouquet of flowers too?"

He grinned, and I clenched every muscle to restrain myself from punching him in the face. I admired Dr. Medina. I wanted to learn from him. This was the best opportunity of my career, and Dr. Keach wanted to twist it into something it was not. This was what he did. He constantly tried to make this program difficult for me. He had wanted me to quit from the moment he'd met me, and the more I pushed back, the madder I made him, and the more he tried.

"Not everyone is as twisted as you are, Dr. Keach. Some of us are here to cure cancer. We have bigger fish to fry."

"Do you hear yourself?" he asked. "You sound like a child. Cure cancer? *You?*"

"Maybe not today," I said. "But I'm one step closer than I was yesterday." I turned away from him and waved goodbye with my napkin, showing how little respect I had for him.

I walked over to join colleagues I liked better. I was ready to drum up conversation with them when the back doors to the conference room opened, and chief Stuart stepped in, followed by a tall, dark, and handsome man. My eyes immediately widened. It couldn't be Dr. Medina. Could it?

The man who followed him wore a navy-blue suit with a

crisp white shirt and a grey—almost silver—tie. His black hair, thick and wavy, was meticulously combed back. He had a little bit of salt in his pepper-colored hair, which made the contrast to his deeply tanned skin much more noticeable. His strong brow shaded his eyes, so I couldn't see his eye color, but his face was chiseled except for a full bottom lip. I could sense the chiseled shape of his jaw despite the salt and pepper-speckled beard.

My lips parted, and my gaze followed him the rest of the meeting. He stood to the chief's right, scanning the faces as if he were looking for someone.

"Thank you, all," the chief started, "for being here. We'll make this quick. You know from my email last month that we have a new attending on staff. Please help me welcome Dr. Hector Medina."

Every doctor not holding a plate of food clapped. The noise snapped me out of whatever trance I had been in, and I found myself closing my mouth, which had grown dry. I needed to stop. Not only was he my boss, but I wanted him to be my mentor; *if that* weren't enough, the glistening gold band around his ring finger put me in check.

The chief continued. "We are fortunate to have him. He left a leadership position at the FIHR for an attending position here. That's a demotion if you ask me." The chief brought a hand to Dr. Medina's shoulder. Dr. Medina looked on the room with confidence and a smile that made my knees a little bit weak, though I'd never admit it to anyone. "But his decision also speaks to his character. He wants to refocus on patient care and rejoin research from the trenches, but I'll let him speak more about it himself. Dr. Medina, would you like to say a few words?"

"Thank you, Dr. Stuart. It is an honor to work with you and to be at this hospital with such great eager and young minds." His voice was deep and severe, and it carried a bit of a Spanish accent. "That's why I took this demotion, as you called it. I want to find new inspiration for my research, and the best source of inspiration I've ever had has been my patients. I know I will be a boss to most of you. To you, I say, I am a tough boss, but I am a fair boss. I look forward to working with you and, more importantly, learning from you."

He paused to look through the faces in the room as if he was searching for someone he knew. He took so long in his visual assessment that we all looked at each other, hoping to find the source he was seeking. Not settling on anyone in particular, he continued.

"I've been following research coming from this hospital for over a year now, and let me tell you, I've been impressed. That is why I chose Heartland Metro Hospital as my new professional home. There is one trial going on now that fascinates me. The grant proposal came across my desk at the FIHR a couple of years ago."

Oh no, I thought. If he was about to say what I thought he was, I was going to be sick. Two years ago was exactly when I first submitted my research proposal. Was he here to check up on my trial? Or worse still, did he intend to take back his work? I set my plate back on the conference table and straightened my jacket, hoping I was wrong but preparing to be right—the story of my life.

"If I remember correctly," Dr. Medina said, "the trial is underway now, and it deals with changes in cervical cancer treatment protocols in women under thirty."

I felt the moment when everyone turned to look at me, and I closed my eyes. *Traitors. The lot of you.*

Dr. Medina zeroed in on me. He planned it beautifully. Once he mentioned the trial and those few specifics, everyone pointed right to me. I envisioned a giant red arrow with blinking lights floating above my head. Perfect. *Well played, Dr. Medina. Well played.*

He kept his gaze on me for the remainder of his little speech.

"Imagine my surprise when I read this grant proposal and found that it continued precisely where my research left off before I left for the FIHR. It was as though someone cloned me and left half of me behind to keep the research going, only much later, of course," he said and laughed at his own joke about his old age, though he could barely be pushing forty. It wasn't that funny, but everyone still joined in with a burst of nervous laughter. Suck-ups.

"I'm guessing you are Dr. Ramirez?"

Oh, how could you tell? I cleared my throat and instead said, "Yes, Doctor. Carolina Ramirez. It's a pleasure to meet you."

"Do you have a patient to see after this meeting?" he asked. His eyes narrowed.

Shit. Shit. Shit. "No, Doctor. I'm available."

Dr. Keach snickered next to me. *Shit.* Why did I have to phrase it like that? Real smart on my part.

"Perfect. Meet me in my office when we are done here. No, uh, actually, wait for me. I'll need you to first show me to my office." Everyone in the room laughed in earnest, then. I simply nodded.

Dr. Medina talked about his mission and vision for the residency program now that he was at the helm and his strong direction toward innovative research. I stopped listening. I was equal parts excited to work with him and petrified he was here to take over my trial. Why else would he leave the FIHR? It was all beginning to make sense. I worked so hard on the trial, and the results so far had been promising. For me to lose control of it now would be a devastating blow.

Dr. Medina glanced at me frequently. He would turn his attention to someone else, then return to me. I felt like I might be sick and suddenly was very thankful I hadn't eaten.

The meeting ended after Dr. Stuart said a few closing remarks, and everyone trickled out of the room and back to work.

Before departing, Dr. Keach didn't miss the opportunity to get in one more dig. He leaned in close and whispered in my ear, "What did I tell you?"

Fuck off, I thought, but only glared in response. Dr. Keach left, and then Dr. Medina and I were alone.

"Lead the way, Dr. Ramirez."

I nodded and opened the door for him.

"Thank you."

We got on the elevator, and, simply to have something to say, I informed him, "Your office is on the seventh floor." I kept my eyes glued to my hands the rest of the elevator ride. I paid no attention to who got on or off the elevator, and the three floors up seemed to take ages. My back started to break into a sweat.

We got off the elevator, and I led him to his office where I opened the door and gestured for him to go in.

"Thank you, Dr. Ramirez. Please, take a seat."

The view from his corner office was spectacular. The sea of lush, green treetops concealed the bustling metropolis below as if the hospital were the solitary structure for miles. Of course they would lay out the red carpet for him. I'd kill for this office and this view.

I heard shuffling behind me, and I turned to look at him. He closed the door to his office, hung his suit jacket on the hook by the door, and then took his tie off.

"I hate these things," he said. "They are always trying to strangle me." He looked at the tie like it was his personal enemy, and I smiled at how he took offense at the strip of fabric. I then remembered I was in danger of losing control of my trial, and the smile was wiped away.

As he walked to the chair, he rolled up his sleeves. He sat down, and looking at his desk, he filled his cheeks with air. He let the air out slowly and grunted. "Well, this is stupid," he said.

I looked at the desk, not finding anything wrong.

"Um, you don't like the desk?"

"No, the desk is fine. But such an American thing to do."

"What is?"

"This view. It's perfect, and then you place this monstrosity of a desk in here facing away from the view."

"I'm sure we can call facility services, and they can rotate things around for you."

"Yes, yes. That will be great." He looked up, smiling at me, and I found myself relaxing. He was so strange and inconsistent, not to mention manic with his shifts in attention.

"You are probably wondering why I wanted to speak with you."

"I assume to . . . take away my clinical trial?" I said with a wince.

"Take your trial? Why would I do that?"

"You don't think I ripped off your research?"

"Is that what you think?"

I thought about that. I never had in the past, until freaking Keach said it.

"No, Doctor. You made suggestions for future steps, sure, but I definitely took those and ran with them in a different direction," I said.

"Then why the doubt?"

"I had no doubts, to be honest, not until it was suggested to me—"

"By whom?" he cut in.

I looked up at him, and his face showed genuine concern. "It doesn't matter," I said dismissively. "But if that's not why you called me into your office, then I am curious."

"I didn't want to say it in front of your peers and make things tough for you, but I'm only here because of your research."

My jaw dropped. Had I heard him right? I shook my head, blinking. Keith Richards basically just told me he sought me out because of my guitar solo. I could have died right then and there and been happy about it.

"Excuse me?"

"Where you took your grant. It was brilliant. Well, don't get too cocky. It was brilliant *for a resident.*"

Was this man trying to tease me? My hero. Teasing *me*? Here for *me*? I must be dreaming. And had my boss just called me cocky?

"We can do great things together, Dr. Ramirez. You are wrapping up year one of the trial, right?"

He said *together.* I relaxed in my chair, realizing my earlier fears were unfounded. They had to be. I wrote them off as parasitic ideas deposited by one Dr. Keach.

Dr. Medina was here to mentor me.

"Yes. It's a five-year grant."

"I have a feeling it will be successful."

"We won't have statistically significant data until at least the conclusion of year three."

"Yes, yes, I know. But I'm confident. You should be too."

My heart swelled with pride. If my mother could be here now, she would be so happy. I refocused my attention before my eyes became watery at the thought. I couldn't very well cry in the presence of my boss.

"I would like to propose that we write your follow-up grant together. Dr. Ramirez, what you are doing with this trial reminds me of why I got into medicine in the first place."

"I'm honored, Doctor. I honestly don't know what to say."

"Say thank you. With my name as a co-investigator, you will get as much funding as you want. Once we get year three data, I want us to write a proposal for lifetime follow-up with the patients from this trial. We can design other trials as well if you'd like, but that's the one I'm most interested in."

"That would be amazing. Thank you."

"That is all, Dr. Ramirez." He opened his laptop, dismissing me as if he hadn't just changed my life.

As I turned the knob to the door, he called after me. "Oh, before I forget, Dr. Ramirez, if anyone asks, just say I wanted to be brought up to speed with your trial." He put his index finger to his mouth conspiratorially before saying, "Our little secret for now."

CHAPTER 3

DAY OFF

Sunday mornings off were a rarity, even more so when those mornings off aligned with Sara's, which meant I would inevitably be coerced into going on a run with her.

She ran in front of me, fast little thing that she was, and I couldn't help but stare at her cute little behind. Her short, blonde ponytail bounced with her stride. We often laughed together because we both knew people always wanted something other than what they had, especially when it came to a body. I'd kill for a tiny body like hers, and she wished for my Amazonian physique complete with muscular thighs. I wished my hair was blonde like hers, and she lusted after my thick, dark brown hair.

I was stronger and could lift way more than she could, but her low body weight made her fast. So fast. I could barely keep up with her on our runs.

When we finished, we splayed out on the grass and

stretched. Sara took her earbuds off and pulled mine down as well to grab my attention. The weight of my hair pulled the hairband loose, so it was sliding down my ponytail. I took it off and regathered the ponytail, tightening the hairband more securely.

"What are the chances I could persuade your dad into making *chilaquiles* for us?" She grinned so wide it was hard to deny her, but I had to. At least this once.

"Rain check?"

"Um, okay. That's a first. I'm guessing you don't want to go elsewhere for breakfast, either?"

I shook my head and brought my water bottle to my lips, buying time from having to answer.

"Caro? What is it? Should I be concerned?"

Damn her and her closeness with my family. Dad loved her like a second daughter, and he'd never say no to her if he could help it, especially if she was asking him to cook for her.

Sara basically lived with Dad on her days off. I think the only reason he survived me getting through med school was that she kept him company when I was studying nearly twenty-four hours a day.

"Fine," I said finally. "I haven't told Dad, okay? I don't want you to be a nosy ass and spill the beans before I have the chance to talk with him."

"What on earth are you talking about?"

Sitting on the ground, I massaged my calves and tried to answer nonchalantly. "I haven't told him Dr. Medina is my new boss."

"I didn't know that was something to tell him." She crossed her arms in front of me.

"Okay, I'm going to tell you, but you have to swear to take this to your grave."

"You very well know if you ask me to, I will."

"Okay, here it goes. When I was in high school, I was a bit obsessive about Dr. Medina—or rather, his research."

"God, you were such a nerd," Sara teased.

"Anyway, Dad knew about it. I just want to tell him in person without anyone there to sway his thoughts about it."

"What? You mean, like mention that you actually combed your hair, *and* you wore something other than scrubs to meet him?"

I eyed her menacingly and pointed with one finger. "Yeah, something *exactly* like that."

"I doubt Mr. Ramirez remembers. And if he does, why would he care anyway?"

"You don't get it. I had three posters on my wall growing up. One was of *Industrial November*. One was a vintage cover of *Jane Eyre,* and the last was the abstract of Dr. Medina's published paper on his first clinical trial."

"You are such an enormous nerd that if it weren't for the *Industrial November* poster, I don't think we could be friends."

I introduced Sara to my favorite band during our freshman year in college when I met her. She hadn't listened to much music before that, so it would be a stretch to say she had any sort of musical taste, but after hearing Brenner's deep, raspy voice, she was a goner for heavy metal. "Yeah, *Industrial November* has saved me more times than I care to admit."

"Me too," Sara said with a broken voice. College was a dark time for her. Her family had been neglectful of her as a child— her parents were drug addicts—and she was just starting to break ties with them our freshman year. There was an anger in *Industrial November* lyrics that I think reflected what she was feeling, and she could finally let it out after bottling it up for so long.

"Fine, just tell Mr. Ramirez he owes me *chilaquiles* because of you."

"I will. Oh, and my shift ends at ten tomorrow. Want to grab drinks?"

"Woo, drinks on a Monday night. What a party girl."

Sara was standing now, and I threw my water bottle at her, which, of course, she caught before walking away with it.

Dad would take the news well. I had no doubt about that. He would actually be very proud Dr. Medina was so interested in my work. Most fathers wouldn't know the first thing to do about their daughter having an idol as strange as Dr. Medina, but Dad always understood and fostered my drive. I think he always realized how important Dr. Medina's work was to me. To a certain extent, his work was also important to Dad.

Still, I didn't want Sara or anyone there to suggest anything nefarious. It was strictly a professional relationship. One that I was getting very excited about. If Dr. Medina had been a woman, no one would have questioned my interest in her mentorship.

When I got home, I pulled my cell phone from my leggings pocket and texted Dad that I wanted to have breakfast with him.

Dad: *Claro, mija! I'll cook for us. Smile emoji, laugh-cry emoji, wide grin emoji.*

I shook my head with a laugh.

Me: *I'll be there in about an hour.*

Dad: *Besos.*

I drank a tall glass of water and picked out my clothes before heading into the shower.

It was unclear to me if it was the endorphin high from the run, the conversation I'd had with Sara about Dr. Medina, or the steam fogging up the glass shower door, but I couldn't tear my thoughts away from him. It would be hard for anyone with a pulse not to notice how handsome he was.

I lathered my body with soap as I thought of his gaze and those dark eyes roaming the conference room and landing on my face. He had rolled up his sleeves, revealing muscular, veiny forearms, and I bit my lip at the memory. I remembered his lips grazing his finger as he hinted at our secret—a secret we now shared.

Bringing my hands to my breasts, I circled my nipple gently. The hot water ran down my body, gliding the suds away from my skin. A flashback of his gaze with those dark eyes entered my brain, and my hand trailed away from my breast and down my soft stomach. I could nearly hear his voice in my head with that slight Spanish accent. The image of him taking off his tie and rolling up his sleeves would be etched on my brain forever —that handsome of a man starting to undress? I'd nearly reached my goal between my thighs when I snapped out of it.

What are you doing, Carolina? I slapped my own hand with a reprimand. I had just texted my *father* of all people with those very hands.

It had to be the suggestiveness of everyone around me. I had been a fangirl, and Valentina, Sara, even Keach, would all use that to insinuate something inappropriate. I didn't like him like that; I was only susceptible to those jerks placing ideas in my head.

But who was I kidding? I was lying to myself. I found Hector Medina very attractive. I needed to stop thinking of him that way.

I washed my hair much too vigorously and turned on the news to turn off my body as I got dressed in my standard jeans and white t-shirt. I didn't brush my hair. All that went on my face was sunscreen and lip balm before I grabbed my car keys.

The smell of *chilaquiles* hit my nostrils the second I entered Dad's tiny house. It was as if he could read Sara's mind. My mouth watered, and I felt only the slightest bit guilty about Sara not joining us for breakfast. This was probably the only time during our entire friendship that I had uninvited her from my family table.

Before me, Dad set a heaping plate of the reason I'll never

have a body like Sara's: *chilaquiles*, fried beans with a fried egg on top, and avocado slices. I loved this man so much I could cry.

"*Gracias, Papi*," I said.

"*Que gracias, ni que nada.* I'm not the one you need to thank." I rolled my eyes but took his hands in mine—his head already bowed. He said grace in Spanish and finished it off with a cross over his chest. "Amen."

"Amen," I echoed if only to appease him.

We ate, and we chatted about work, mostly.

My dad had owned *Tavo's Auto Repair* since before I was born, and though it was hard work, I knew he loved his job. "How's work?" I asked.

"It's doing great. I'm getting older though, and I have to tell you, I couldn't do it anymore without Ramiro's help running the business side of things. He's a great manager."

I ignored the comment about Ramiro; at this point, I was used to him mentioning Ramiro *casually* to me, always making sure not to leave out his many amazing qualities. As if I hadn't known Ramiro my entire life. I shook my head.

When we finally finished our breakfast, I refilled our coffees and sat back down to give him my news.

"*Papi*," I said. "Do you remember that doctor I used to look up to back when I was starting to think about going to med school?"

"Hector Medina," he said right away. "How could I forget?"

Well, he wasn't going to make this easy for me. "Yeah. Him."

"I remember you wouldn't shut up about him."

"That's the one. You see—"

"Said you were going to marry him when you grew up—"

"What?" I nearly spat the coffee over the dining table.

"Yeah. You were on the phone with your *Tía* Jacinta. You didn't know I heard—"

"Dad!"

"I wasn't eavesdropping, I swear!" His hands drew up defensively. "I was walking past your room, and your door was open. It's not my fault you have a big mouth sometimes."

"Oh my god, Dad." The truth was, I had zero recollection of ever having said that about Dr. Medina but knowing how big of a fangirl I had been, it did sound like something I might have said.

"A dad doesn't forget something like that," he said. "It broke my heart to think of you one day marrying someone and leaving me. I knew you wouldn't marry him, mind you, he was too old for you, but the mere thought of it drove me crazy."

"You don't make things easy for me," I admitted.

"What are you talking about?"

"I have a new boss." Better to rip off the Band-Aid, I figured.

"Don't tell me—"

"Yep." I swung my arms back and forth nervously. "Dr. Medina is the new attending at Heartland Metro and my new boss."

"Well, that'll teach me," he said.

"What?"

"When you said you wanted to marry him when you grew up, I comforted myself with the knowledge—or what I thought at the time was knowledge—that you'd never meet him."

"Please don't worry, Dad. He is married," I said, remembering the gold ring on his finger. "You know I would never—"

"I know, sweetie." My dad patted my hand with a reassuring smile spread wide on his face.

"There's more, though," I said. "He is here because of my research."

"*¿Cómo?*"

"I didn't know he was a grant reviewer at the FIHR. He read my proposal and came to Heartland to work on the trial. He wants to mentor me."

I'm not sure what I was expecting. Perhaps teasing like what

Sara had done, or if not that, congratulations on this exciting next direction in my career. *Pero no*. Dad could still surprise me.

"Of course he wants to work with you. I'm sure he is very grateful you are willing to work with him." He stood to take our coffee mugs to the sink, and I could only blink after the man I loved most in this world.

CHAPTER 4

THE LONG SHIFT

The first day of rounds with our new attending ran smoothly. Dr. Medina was mostly quiet; we all knew he was assessing us, making his mind up about our worth as doctors. The other residents were shifty and insecure with their answers, but not me.

Having a secret with him gave me armor. He felt human to me now, no longer the god he still was to my peers. My confidence must have shown through because he was receptive to all my treatment plans and encouraged me to keep speaking. In short, I was killing it. Poor choice of words for a doctor, but I didn't care. I was.

I would have been on cloud nine if it weren't for the dark cloud Dr. Keach kept sending my way. He stood next to me always, so I could clearly hear his heavy breathing and puffing. *I get it, Keach, I get it. You are pissed.*

But his fragile little ego wasn't my problem. If he wanted attention from his mentors, he'd have to work hard for it, just like anyone else. I pushed him out of my thoughts, so I could focus on what was important—caring for our patients.

Dr. Medina looked down at the list on his tablet. "Did we cover everyone for rounds who is not on Dr. Ramirez's clinical trial?" he asked.

"Yes," I said. "We have five potential trial participants left to assess and one participant already on the trial." I always called them participants. I hated the term 'subjects.' It made patients feel like lab rats, which they most definitely weren't. I had a hard enough time educating the public on what clinical trials were, persuading them that they would still get treatment even if it wasn't the experimental one, without making them feel like *things*.

"Great. I will join you. The rest of you—get to work. You have your marching orders," said Dr. Medina.

The circle broke, leaving me standing there awkwardly with him.

"Whenever you are ready," he said.

"Excuse me?" I asked.

"Lead the way, Dr. Ramirez," he said with obvious impatience in his voice. My first slip of the day.

"Yes, of course, Doctor. This way."

We saw my first three patients, and Dr. Medina introduced himself as a new member of their care team. He was confident and charismatic, so each of them instantly fell into a trust with him. I was most impressed when he lingered in Valentina's room and got her to warm up to him. She was so guarded, she hardly let anyone in.

I opened up the rounds, even though it was just the two of us in the room with Valentina.

"Valentina Almonte. Age twenty-four. Diagnosed two months ago. Accepted into the trial last month. Blinded standard treatment protocol for the last week." Valentina's arms danced like a symphony conductor's, and I paused speaking long enough to pin her hands down with my own. I arched an eyebrow as a warning.

"Okay, okay," she said. "I give." She squealed in her bed.

"Patient is responding well to chemoradiation." I let go but continued to pin her with my stare.

"You have a good team of doctors here, Miss Almonte," he said.

"Valentina, please."

Dr. Medina took his time in the room, reading her chart. He set it down on the counter in front of her bed, and Valentina took the opportunity to turn to me. She mouthed, *oh my gawd*, dropped her jaw, and fisted her hands to motion humping the air. My eyes widened with alarm, and I begged her to stop, waving her down as discreetly as I could. Dr. Medina didn't notice a thing.

"Valentina, I look forward to being on your care team."

"Thanks, Doctor," she said while batting her eyelashes. She was so obviously flirting with him, and I couldn't help but smile. I approved of anything that would bring her spirits up, and if that was Dr. Medina, then I would gladly throw him into the fire.

Dr. Medina caught me grinning like an idiot as we walked into the hallway. He rolled his eyes. "Stop," he said sternly.

"Stop what?"

"You know what."

"You must get that a lot, Doctor," I said, batting my eyelashes just as Valentina had. His eyes narrowed. I only stopped when I noticed the set of his jaw, and I wondered if he was too stiff and serious for a bit of joking banter. I checked myself and schooled my face back to its professional side.

"I apologize, Doctor. I forgot myself. If it makes you feel any better, that's the first time I've seen Valentina smile in weeks. Her spirits have been really low. With all due respect, if interacting with you will help her emotionally, I'm willing to sacrifice your dignity a bit to her whims. On the whole, she's harmless."

"I feel used, Dr. Ramirez," he said before turning to walk away from me. He shook his head all the way down the hallway, but I could swear, even by just looking at the back of his head, that he was snickering.

I didn't see him again until late that evening. I'd finished all the work I needed to with my patients, and now all that was left was to chart on my last three consults of the day. I grabbed my laptop, deciding to chart from the doctors' lounge where I could relax a bit. I hadn't gotten a chance to eat during my shift, so I grabbed a *Twix* bar from the vending machine and set it next to my laptop on the table. The details I was charting swallowed me for nearly an hour, which meant I forgot about the chocolate. That was incredibly slow charting, but I wasn't merely charting. I was analyzing every aspect of their disease: its presentation, treatment, and outcomes so far. I was scanning for clues. Anything that would help me beat this bastard called cancer.

The door swung open, and Dr. Medina walked in and settled in one of the sofa chairs. He didn't notice me at first.

"Hello," I said. "How's your first day going?"

He turned to me, startled to find me sitting in the corner. "It's technically my second day."

"Okay, how's your second day going?"

"All right. Nothing special." He walked over to the table and sat across from me.

For some reason, that comment stung a little. He smirked, and I realized he was teasing me.

"What is this?" He picked up the *Twix* bar.

"Dinner."

"*Dinner?* This isn't *food*, let alone dinner."

"Don't judge." I snatched the chocolate from his grip. I opened it and grabbed one of the two chocolate bars inside. As if to prove my point, I took a healthy bite. My eyes rolled back, and I moaned with pleasure. A thin strand of caramel fell to my lower lip, and I licked it off once I swallowed the bite. I opened my eyes to a stunned Dr. Medina. His mouth was parted, and he cleared his throat after a moment.

Then it hit me. I realized what he must have seen. He didn't know that was my standard response to chocolate. He probably thought I was still flirting with him and probably *not* in the joking way I had earlier after our visit with Valentina. I was about to apologize and further stick my foot in my mouth, but he beat me to it, breaking the awkward moment.

He reached for the other half of my chocolate. "I think I will try it after all—"

I snatched it away before he could. "You can't come in here judging my snack, insulting chocolate no less, and then ask for some."

"You *do* know I'm your boss, right?"

"And being my boss while forcing me to give up half my dinner is an abuse of power."

He opened his mouth to speak when the door burst open. Sara marched in with murder in her eyes. *Shit.* What had I done now?

"Carolina. Isabel. Ramirez. Fuentes," Sara huffed. She stood directly in front of me, both hands on her hips as she glared me down. She had long ago picked up Dad's trick of letting me know precisely how furious she was.

My full name. *Double shit.* "Chocolate?" I offered with a grin.

"Why didn't you tell me?" she whined.

Dr. Medina jumped in. "I'm sorry, this is the doctors' lounge, maybe you should—"

Sara brought her hand up to his face silencing him, and I cringed. "Do you enjoy changing your own patients' bedpans, Doctor?"

"Is she talking to me?" he asked, perplexed because Sara's glare never left me.

"Yep. I think so."

He gulped. "My apologies, Sara. Won't happen again."

It didn't escape me that he had learned her name.

"You are new here, so I'll let it slide. *This time.*"

"What's this about, Sara?" I asked.

"Your dad just texted me. You didn't invite me to the cookout."

"I'm not going to the cookout," I hissed.

"Yes, you are. I just paid off a resident to cover for you."

"Sara, you didn't!"

"I did. And you are going."

I slumped back in my chair, crossing my arms. This woman was giving me a headache. "I hate my birthday, Sara. You know that."

"It's not for you. It's for your dad and anyone else who loves you. Don't be so selfish."

"Selfish? It's *my* birthday."

"It's settled, missy. We have a bigger problem."

I groaned. By this point, I had wholly forgotten Dr. Medina was witness to this embarrassing exchange.

"It's Valentina," she said. I moved to stand, but Sara gestured me down to my chair. "She's okay. But it's time."

"Time?"

"I was brushing her hair tonight, and—"

"Oh," I said. My eyes watered. Valentina wasn't vain, but her hair was so beautiful. I was sure she would mourn the loss.

"She's having a bad night. I wouldn't go see her now. She wants to be alone. Let her cry. Tomorrow, we'll take care of it."

I nodded.

"How do you want to handle this?" Sara asked.

"Mary."

"You want to pull a Mary?"

"Yeah, I have the morning off. I'll do the shopping, and I'll meet you in her room at noon."

"I'll bring the equipment," Sara said. "And I *will* take the chocolate, thank you." She grabbed the wrapper on the table with half my dinner and walked away. She waved at us with the chocolate. "We're still having drinks at ten," were her final parting words.

"Sorry about her," I said. "She's a bit—"

"Shameless?" Hector asked.

I laughed, even as a tear escaped my eye. I wiped it away quickly as if nothing had happened. "Yeah, that's the best way to describe Sara. *Shameless.* You'll get used to it. The sooner you learn she runs this place—and we'd be lost without her—the easier your job will be," I said. "I'm sorry, I didn't mean to cry." I shifted in my chair.

"Never apologize for caring about your patients," he said softly.

"No, I know. I'm apologizing for crying. It's why so many people can't take women doctors seriously."

"No," he said, matter-of-factly. "Don't carry that weight on your shoulders. Any man who thinks that way is a piece of shit. I've cried for patients before. I'm not ashamed of it. I'm human. Some of them just get under our skin. It doesn't make us bad doctors. It makes us better ones."

He left then, understanding I needed a moment and giving me what I needed—my privacy. Even though what he said was true, the idea was so ingrained in me that I couldn't bear to cry in front of my boss.

CHAPTER 5

LA OFICINA

I was well on my way to becoming an alcoholic, and I had precisely zero shame about it. The job could be so rewarding, but it could also suck your soul straight out of your body and shred it to pieces. I downed a tequila shot, wondering how in the hell I was supposed to go into Valentina's room tomorrow. Yes, I was her doctor, and I was fighting for her life almost as hard as she was, but I just kept taking from her. I'd taken her autonomy, her pleasure, heck, her normal. Tomorrow, I would have to go in there and try to cheer her up as I took her hair.

She would not be the first one. I'd had many patients just like her, and many much worse. But Dr. Handsome's words swam in my head. *Some of them just get under our skin.* Yes, they did.

I tapped the tiny glass on the bar. "Barkeep! Another!"

Sofia walked over to me, shaking her head. "Slow it down there, Doctor," she said. "Sara isn't even here yet, and you don't want to outpace her. She'll never forgive you." Sofia grinned at me with those incredibly full lips of hers. If I swung that way, I would so dream about kissing her all day.

She wasn't just the friendly neighborhood bartender. Sofia was one of my closest friends. Sara and I drank for cheap, and sometimes free, ever since I stitched up Sofia's hand at no charge when she cut herself cleaning up a broken glass. We'd been friends ever since.

"You're probably right, but at this moment, I'm the one mad at *her*, so I don't give a rat's ass—"

"Okay, okay," said Sofia. "Who the hell am I?"

"And top shelf, darling. Something at the very least *reposado*," I said. Sofia never broke eye contact as she filled the shot glass to the rim. "Has anyone ever told you that you are like a dark angel? I envision your wings covered with raven-black feathers that match your hair."

"Are you already drunk? After your first drink?" Sofia asked only half-kidding.

"No. Bad day. I'm trying to distract myself. Just being silly."

The second shot, I savored. I'd never down good tequila without savoring it. I smiled as the silky liquid hit my stomach, sending the tiniest heat wave through my body.

"You know—"

I heard his voice, and I turned to face him.

"They say a woman who can drink tequila without making a face comes from hell."

Had he been there the entire time? And why was he everywhere? I laughed at his statement. "The person who said that never had good quality tequila. Also, they were sexist."

"Drinking all alone?"

"No. I have friends."

"The bartender doesn't count."

Sofia jumped to my defense. "Normally I'd agree with you, but this is one of those rare exceptions. Caro here is my girl."

I laughed because Sofia said it so motherly, so protective of me, and it warmed my insides almost as much as the tequila had.

"Stand down, love," I said to her. "We must be nice to him. He's my boss, don't you know?"

I brought up my glass and clinked it to his. "Cheers."

Sofia pursed her lips, then reached her hand out to him. "In that case, welcome to *La Oficina*. I'm Sofia."

He shook her hand. "Hector."

I snorted and nearly spat my drink. "Hector?"

"Yes. That's my name."

"I'm sorry. I just assumed you introduced yourself to everyone as Dr. Medina."

"Dr. Medina?" Sofia asked with interest. "Isn't he the one you —" She stopped herself when she saw the daggers I was shooting her with my eyes. "I have some inventory I have to do in the back. Help yourself if you need anything else, Caro."

Dr. Medina stared at me. "We are not at work. Why would I introduce myself by my professional title?"

I shrugged. "I guess I just assumed—"

"Has it ever occurred to you, Carolina, that you make a lot of assumptions about me?" He grabbed his drink and walked to another table, leaving me stunned. That was the first time I'd heard my given name on his lips, and I wasn't sure how I felt about it. I wanted to keep all my interactions with him professional. I wanted him to mentor me and work with me on my research, our research, but every time we were together, the universe played sick jokes on me, giving me foot-in-mouth disease.

I walked around the bar and poured two more shots of the most expensive tequila I could find. Sofia thankfully walked back out to chat with me, and in time, I completely forgot Dr. Medina was even in the room.

One hour into my drinks, I got a text from Sara.

Sara: *Please don't kill me. I can't make it tonight. I love you forever. Kiss emoji.*

"Let me guess," Sofia asked as she carried out a case of beer. "She can't make it?"

"Nope. One guess why."

"Don't go there, Caro. She's a grown woman."

"I know she is, but he is such a piece of shit. Why can't she see she deserves so much better?"

"Give her time. She needs to see for herself what a piece of shit he is. The more we tell her to dump his ass, the more she will withdraw from us. And when this blows up in her face, she will need her friends. We can't alienate her right now, no matter how much it kills us to not say anything."

I told her what I've told her a million times before. "You sure you aren't a clinical psychologist?"

Sofia laughed. "All bartenders are psychologists. Occupational hazard."

"I'm heading out. I have to get up early tomorrow."

I leaned over the bar and gave her a peck on the lips because I could never resist it. She smiled back at me. "Stay safe."

"I will."

I was grabbing my purse when I saw him again and remembered he was there. Dr. Medina was cleaning some of the drink that had spilled on his shirt, and I rolled my eyes. Poor guy couldn't handle a simple peck on the lips by two women. This, ladies and gentlemen, was the man I chose to follow blindly into my career. I shook my head in disbelief and walked out of the bar.

I searched for the car service app on my phone. I'd hit my self-imposed three-drink limit, so even though I felt mostly sober, three drinks were too many to drive. Sofia didn't even ask, because she knew me well enough, but given how quickly Hector, I mean, Dr. Medina, found himself outside with me, he clearly didn't trust that I wouldn't drive. He grabbed my arm above my elbow and started leading me away from the bar.

"I'm driving you home."

"No, you are not."

"Yes, I am. You've drunk too much."

"I know." I searched his eyes. "I'm not driving. See?" I showed him my phone and the app I was scrolling through when he found me. He sighed, and his features softened.

"Good. I'm glad you weren't going to drive. But I'd still like to drive you home."

"It's really not necessary."

"You would really rather pay for a car service than take a free ride?"

He had a point. I relented and let him lead me to his car. I was surprised to find he didn't drive a ridiculously expensive sports car like most doctors of his status. The newer model Honda sedan was discreet and unassuming.

We spent the first part of the ride to my apartment in silence, and oddly, it felt comfortable. Halfway there, he said, "I liked that bar."

"The bar or Sofia?"

"Why would you say that?"

I shrugged. "Every man who meets Sofia falls head-over-heels in love with her. I couldn't blame you if you did. It's almost inevitable. Hell, I'm completely straight, and I'm half in love with her."

He side-eyed me. "No. Not Sofia. She was nice, but I like the bar. The name is . . . interesting."

"*La Oficina?* Yeah. It was great when it first opened. We could always just say, 'hey, meet you at the office,' and anyone would think we meant we were working. The city smartened up, though, and now it has backfired."

"Backfired?" he asked.

"Yeah, now everyone knows about the bar named the office,

so you have to be careful. If you say you're meeting someone at the office, people can assume—"

"Got it. So, meet you at work is the accepted vernacular."

"Correct."

"This is a strange city."

"Your first time in Kansas City?"

He nodded. Even though I told him it wasn't necessary, he insisted on walking me to the door of my apartment building.

"Thank you. You really didn't have to—"

"Good night, Carolina."

THE TEMPTATION TO search for him online had never won me over. Not even when I was a teenager and a devout disciple of his work. It had always, always been about the work, about the magic of his brain, never about the man himself. To me, he had only been a brain—a disembodied organ innovating genius advancements in medicine, improving cancer treatments for all patients. Back then, I knew, just knew it in my gut, that he would have saved *her* if he had been her doctor.

But now I had met him. The man, not just the words he typed onto a keyboard hundreds of miles from where I stood. He was also now my boss, and knowledge about him could only serve to help me in my professional relationship with him. *Tell yourself whatever you need to do the deed, Carolina.*

I got ready for bed and curled up with my tablet.

Surprisingly, there was quite a bit of information about him, probably because of his wife. Andrea Medina. According to the search engine, she was the daughter of a prominent philanthropist. They attended many of his fundraiser events in Maryland, where they lived, and in New York and Washington.

I found a picture of them at a charity event for children's cancer research. She was leaning into him, her whole body pointing to him, and wearing a wide smile that spread to her eyes. He had his arm around her waist, and his head was bent as though she was whispering something in his ear. She was gorgeous. I had to admit it. She was a tall, slim, leggy, blonde with beautiful green eyes and delicate features.

He certainly had a type, so I didn't have to continue to feel awkward around him. I'd barely admit it to myself, but there was the tiniest bit of a barely-there crush somewhere in a dusty corner of my heart. But knowing it would never be reciprocated actually made me feel better about working with him and seeing him day in and day out.

Then I saw it, and my jaw dropped—a picture of them holding hands walking in New York City. He held one of her hands, and she grabbed her enormous pregnant belly under a beautiful blue sundress with the other. They both looked incandescently happy. I smiled at the picture of them, hoping my future held that kind of love.

He had to be a good man if his wife looked that happy. I scanned the screen for a date on the picture; by my math, his child would be about eight years old now. I usually find it in horrible taste to search for celebrity children. Even if he wasn't a true celebrity, I had the same feeling about looking up their child. But I wasn't looking for a tacky tabloid. It was purer than that. I wanted to see the human manifestation of the happy couple in those pictures.

In the search bar, I entered: *Andrea Medina and Dr. Hector Medina daughter*. I smiled, thinking about a little girl with his tanned skin and her bright green eyes popping in contrast, but nothing came up. Next, I entered: *Andrea Medina and Dr. Hector Medina son*.

There it was—the first hit—a headline from two years ago. Intense grief snaked into my bloodstream and latched on to my heart. I forgot how to breathe for several seconds as I read the headline: *Six-year-old grandson of prominent Maryland philanthropist dies in freak accident.* Two years ago.

My hand came up to my mouth, and I couldn't hold back the sickening feeling gripping me. I couldn't bring myself to click on the link. When I searched for his family, I wasn't expecting to see this kind of tragedy. I couldn't bring myself to pry into his private life any further than I already had. His loss wasn't for entertainment. I shut off my tablet and tried to fall asleep.

CHAPTER 6

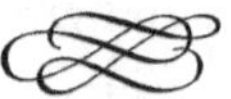

THE MARY

My hair was still dripping wet from my shower, clinging to my shoulders, when a knock at the door interrupted my morning routine. My brows furrowed. I wasn't expecting anyone. Once at the door, I bent to peek through the peephole. I couldn't make out his face, but I stared straight into a dress shirt over pecs I'd recognize anywhere. What the hell was Dr. Medina doing here?

Toothbrush still in my mouth, I opened the door.

"What are you doing here?" I tried to ask, but it sounded more like, "Wha a you dohee?" I gestured for him to come in then went back to the bathroom to get rid of the brush and rinse out.

"How did you get into my building? And more importantly, how did you know my apartment number?"

"I have my ways." He grinned.

I rolled my eyes and went to the kitchen to make a green smoothie. I had to offset Dad's cooking somehow.

"I'm surprised," he said as he walked over to the kitchen bar and sat on a stool.

"About what?"

"You look great."

I shot him my most insulted look, and he laughed.

"That's not what I meant. I just expected you to have a hangover."

"On three drinks? I'm not sure how you party, but three drinks won't get me there. And I also have *my* ways." I grinned back at him.

"Oh?"

"Yep. I stick to straight tequila, never switch drinks except sometimes maybe a beer, and I drink tons of water. The most I ever have in the morning is a slight headache."

"I've learned my lesson, then."

Horror struck, and I panicked at what I'd said. "I don't, uh—I don't actually drink very often. I just know my limits and what my body can take."

"Relax, Ramirez. I wasn't accusing you of anything."

I changed the subject. "So, what can I do for you?" I filled my blender with spinach, pineapple, carrots, and fresh ginger root.

"What do you mean?"

"Why are you at my house at eight in the morning, boss?"

He raised an eyebrow at 'boss' and took his glasses off to clean them.

He waited until I was done blending before speaking again. "Your car is at the hospital," he said.

"I have a car service app. Maybe you don't know this about me, but I'm a pretty independent woman. I've gotten around all on my own my entire adult life."

"I don't doubt that, but I was also curious about *the Mary,* and what that meant."

My eyes misted over at that. He'd heard Sara and me making plans for Valentina today. My heart ached as I thought about what we were about to do, but the point of the Mary was to be as freaking cheerful as possible.

"Then I guess you are taking me shopping."

"Okay, but drink that. There's no way I'm letting you take that green sludge into my car."

"You want one?" I asked and wiggled my eyebrows.

"Not for all the salsa in Mexico," he said.

He drove, and I respected his wishes not to bring my smoothie into his car.

When he parked, he groaned. "The mall?"

"Yep." I got out of the car and led him into a department store.

"What are we getting?" he asked.

"Oh, this and that. Follow me."

I picked out a beautiful silk scarf that was a deep ocean blue and got a gift box for it. Dr. Medina didn't say much while I browsed the store. We made our way to the makeup counter, and I got a coral-pink nail polish and a cream blush that complemented the nail color. It was only three items, but I had spent two hundred dollars, and it was worth every penny.

"Okay," I instructed. "When we get to the hospital, you can't be in the room. We will need privacy. But if you want to, in about half an hour, find yourself at the nurses' station by Valentina's room. You'll see what the Mary is." He nodded, parked his car in the parking garage, and we parted ways.

SARA MET me in the locker room. I changed into scrubs and followed her out, Valentina's gifts in my arms.

Sara walked into her room first, pushing a cart in front of her. The top of the cart was hidden from view with a towel draped over it. Valentina smiled at us weakly.

"Good morning," she said. I shot her a wicked smile.

"What?" she asked.

I didn't answer. I placed all the items on the counter and hooked up a speaker to the wall. I brought my phone out and played *Girls Like You* by Maroon 5/Cardi B because Cardi B was life and she could make any woman feel like a boss bitch. Valentina needed to feel that power.

I turned to Sara, who was already half dancing, half jumping around the room. I couldn't turn the volume too high, this was still a hospital, but I let the lyrics seep into the hallway just the tiniest bit.

I walked up to Sara and bounce-danced with my two left feet right next to her. It's a complete stereotype that all Mexican-American women know how to dance. I didn't care if I looked silly, though. Actually, if it cheered up Valentina, that was even better.

Valentina threw her head back with laughter that we hardly heard over the music. She was hooked up to an IV and too many wires to get up and join us, plus she wasn't strong enough, but she adjusted her bed so she could sit up. She bobbed her head and shoulders as Sara and I made complete fools of ourselves.

Our patient couldn't help but grin every time a nurse walked by the room, poked their head in, and belted a single line of the chorus before walking away again. I didn't miss when one of the residents popped his head in and sang the line as he locked his eyes with hers, and she blushed in response.

He wasn't *her* doctor, so I decided to look the other way and not say a thing about it. I wouldn't be the one to take any further happiness away from her. Some other doctor would have to say something if anything more came of that exchange.

Next on my power playlist was Cardi B's *I Like It*. Sara and I stopped dancing. She removed the towel covering the contents of the cart, and Valentina winced at the sight of the hair clippers but then nodded at her.

I grabbed the nail polish and sat at the end of her bed, cross-legged. I brought her feet up to my lap, and I started painting her toenails in the bright coral shade. She smiled at me, though her eyes glistened with tears as Sara began working on her scalp.

When Sara was done with the clippers, I handed her the nail polish, and she got to work on Valentina's manicure. I brought the volume down so we could talk over the music. I wrapped the beautiful scarf around Valentina's head with a bow at the back. I smudged a little bit of the blush on her cheeks, and even as thin and pale as she'd gotten, she was still absolutely beautiful. At least to me. She smiled up at me and squeezed my hand as if to say *thank you*. I squeezed back.

The next part of the Mary was to talk about boys in general.

Sara jumped in first. "Did you guys see that *Thor* movie?" She was still finishing up her manicure as she asked. "That Hemsworth kid. Mmm." She sounded like she was enjoying a juicy hamburger. Valentina and I eyed each other and busted out laughing.

"I don't know," said Valentina. "I kinda like my men nerdy." I gave a side-glance toward the door, trying to remember the resident who had made her blush. Sure enough, Dr. Dennis was a bit on the skinny side, had huge glasses, and bright red hair. I said nothing, though.

"Oh, *really*?" Sara said.

"Absolutely. I like me a big brain on a guy," said Valentina.

"*Just* a big brain?" Sara asked, and we all giggled like crazy at her suggestiveness.

Valentina asked Sara, "Do you have a boyfriend?"

"I do," she said without looking up from the hand she was working on.

"What was that?" Valentina asked me.

Uh-oh. "What was what?" I asked.

"That." With her free hand, she pointed back and forth between my eyes. "Your crazy expressive eyebrows almost did a back flip, you looked so angry when I asked Sara about her boyfriend."

Sara finally looked up and smiled at me but answered Valentina first, saving me from having to voice my honest opinion. "Oh, she doesn't like Brian."

"Brian?" Valentina asked.

"That's my boyfriend. Dr. Ramirez here doesn't approve."

"What's wrong with him?" Valentina asked.

"Oh," Sara saved me again, "she would never say. She's too good a friend."

When she refocused on finishing the manicure, I mouthed to Valentina: *piece of shit.* She nodded with a sad smile.

"How about you, Dr. Ramirez?"

I stiffened. I knew Dr. Medina was probably listening.

"I'm too busy concentrating on my career for that. I'm focused only on you."

"Uh-huh," Sara said. Done with her work, she sat back on the chair and crossed her arms. "What about Ramiro?"

Valentina perked up at that. "Who is *Ramiro?*" she asked, rolling the r's seductively.

"Lord, help me," I said, looking at the ceiling. "Ramiro is my oldest friend. He and I grew up together, and now he is a mechanic at my dad's garage. But I absolutely do not see him like that—"

"But *he* sees *you* like that," Sara said.

They were both staring at me now, expectantly.

"Guys, stop. I get enough of that from my dad."

"Oh yeah," said Sara. "He's already planning your wedding."

I rolled my eyes.

Neither Sara nor I asked Valentina if she had a romantic partner. She never talked about it, and we both intuitively knew it might be a touchy subject for her. Since I'd been her doctor, she'd never had anyone join her at any of her appointments, and no one came to visit when she was admitted overnight. This led me to believe she was alone in the world.

"Well," said Sara, "I have to get back to it. Let me know if you need anything, Valentina."

"Guys, thanks for this." We both nodded and left her room.

It was the absolute girliest thing to do. Neither Sara nor I were girly, and I knew Valentina wasn't either. Still, somehow, bonding over something as trivial as makeup was soothing to the soul. I knew we all felt lighter than we had yesterday.

I expected to find Dr. Medina at the nurses' station, watching our little show unfold and poking fun at us, but he wasn't there, and I sighed with relief. Thank goodness he was probably too busy to listen to us make fools of ourselves. He'd question if I was actually cut out to be a doctor.

CHAPTER 7

A GRILLING

I was hesitant to leave my shift on Friday. Valentina had been nauseous all morning, and now she lay in bed, tired, panting, and weak. We couldn't force anything into her body that she didn't bring back up. I sat next to her, watching helplessly. We'd been battling her cancer for weeks—battling it aggressively—and I knew it would get worse before the tide turned. Even though I was a doctor and knew better, there was that tiny voice in the back of my mind telling me this was not a battle to be won.

"Valentina, we need to explore—"

She raised a hand to silence me. "No," she said in a breathy voice that broke me.

"It's okay, honey. You don't have to stay on the trial. We can explore other options. Less aggressive treatment."

Valentina grabbed my wrist, and I could tell from her body shaking that she was trying to squeeze my arm fiercely, but the grasp was so gentle, my eyes softened.

"Okay. You are strong. So strong. I'm going to trust that you know your limits."

"I told you at the start, Doctor. I want to live. Put me through hell if you have to, but be as aggressive as you can. I can take it."

"I don't doubt it."

"I've gone up against ruthless fighters, bigger, stronger, more experienced. Sometimes they've beaten my body to a pulp, but I've still found a way to rise and keep fighting. Trust me, this right here," she swept her hand across her body as if it were on display, "this is nothing compared to some of the fights I've won. I'm a professional athlete—a *fighter*. This all you got, doc?"

I smiled at her confidence. This is what it took. *Sometimes.* Sometimes it took better doctors, but she already had the best. I didn't mean me. She had Dr. Medina now. It was at that moment that I knew deep in my gut that Valentina Almonte would live. She had what it took, and so did her care team.

Before I clocked out, I finished noting in her chart and met Sara in the doctors' lounge. The week had kicked my ass. Valentina's case was only the tip of the iceberg. I had many other demanding patients and a group of new interns who didn't know an esophagus from a rectum. I was exhausted and wanted nothing more than to sleep through my day off tomorrow. I was frowning when Sara spoke up.

"Don't even think about it."

"I didn't say anything."

"You are not bailing tomorrow. I won't let you break your dad's heart."

I groaned. "Fine. What time do I have to be there?"

"Six is good. And please do something about your face. I want pictures."

"I'm not doing my makeup for a cookout."

"Fine. But if you don't do your own makeup, I'll be doing it for you."

Sometimes I couldn't understand why I'd become best friends with such a bossy and intrusive woman. There was no way out of this, and I knew it. A voice we weren't expecting startled us.

"Am I invited?" It was Dr. Medina. We heard him but couldn't see him. Then, he sat up from where he had been lying down on the couch. He turned to face us.

"That's the second time you've mentioned a party in my presence. It would be rude not to invite me, don't you think?"

"Uh—" I'd never seen Sara at a loss for words, and this was amusing.

"I'm not sure it would be your thing, doctor," I said.

"Why not?"

"It's very casual. My Dad is hosting it, and the guest list does not include many, um . . ."

"Doctors," Sara finished for me, saving me from having to say, *dude, you'd stick out like a sore thumb in the barrio.*

"I don't only socialize with doctors." He looked from her to me. "And I don't know any people in this city. It will be nice to have a conversation with someone other than my cat."

I couldn't help the snort that escaped me. "You have a cat?"

"Is that funny?"

Who the hell was I to judge? "No, Doctor. Of course not. We'll see you at six." I rattled off Dad's address, and he asked for my phone number.

"In case I need help finding the place," he said lamely.

After he left, Sara studied me with a massive grin on her face.

"What?"

"He asked for your phone number." She wiggled her eyebrows up and down, or tried to, anyway.

I shook my head at her.

"Your children will have the eyebrows of gods."

"Shut up," I said.

"I don't think Ramiro will be very happy with you bringing home a date."

"It's not a—" but Sara had left the lounge with my soda in her hand before I could finish speaking.

OF COURSE, I didn't arrive at Dad's at six. I knew that man, and he would be working all day to get ready for the cookout. I wasn't even a little surprised when I showed up at ten in the morning, and Ramiro was already there helping.

I turned into the driveway, and the sight of his black pickup truck forced a sigh out of me. I loved Ramiro very much, but I'd never been in love with him. He was more like a brother to me, but he didn't see me as his sister. Not yet.

Both Mom and Dad had told me that after I was born, they had somewhat jokingly agreed with Ramiro's parents that I would marry their son one day. When we were little, and girls still had cooties, even Ramiro had recoiled at the idea. But as we grew up, his view changed, while mine remained the same.

When we were in high school, he told me he would wait for me forever, that I was his soul mate, but I knew deep down that I wasn't. I told him not to wait. He'd dated women over the years, but he always swore, even before starting anything with someone else, that he was only waiting for me to get back to him.

Ramiro kept waiting even when I insisted there was nothing to wait for. First, he waited for me to finish college. Then, he waited for me to finish medical school. Now, he claimed to be waiting for me to finish my residency, so I would be less busy. I'd assured him things wouldn't slow down after that. My career was not the reason I wasn't with him.

I couldn't deny part of the fault lay in me. I'd dated some, though no one seriously. Every man I'd ever given a chance to never went past a few dates. Either he hadn't understood the demands of being a physician, or he was a fellow physician who had a schedule as busy as mine, and we never saw each other. Each relationship was doomed before it had a chance to take off. But even though I'd dated plenty, and I was no virgin, I never had the heart to tell Ramiro; I swore to myself that the minute I got serious with anyone, I would tell him. Of course, I used to be sure there was someone out there for me, but these days, I wasn't so sure.

In middle school, I once tried to make true the future that seemed predestined. I caught Ramiro off-guard, and I kissed him. It could very well have been that kiss he held on to, even if I'd explained a million times that I'd been in a bad place when I'd done that. My mother had just died, and I'd honestly believed she wished for me to grow up and marry Ramiro one day. I knew now that she would much rather have seen me happy with someone else than unhappy with the boy she knew and had once chosen for me. I had long ago let go of that dream, but my poor *papi* still clung to it.

Dad was predictably in the kitchen, pouring spices and beer over trays of thinly sliced meat for the *carne asada*.

"*Buenos días, Papi.*" I kissed his cheek.

"*Pero,* what are you doing here? I told that *güera* you weren't supposed to be here until six. She never listens."

I laughed. "I wanted to help."

His shoulders slackened in resignation. "Fine. Go help Ramiro outside."

It was a herculean effort, but I resisted the urge to roll my eyes. I loved spending time with Ramiro, but more and more, I avoided it. I needed them both to understand that Ramiro and I were never going to happen.

What Dad clung to, I believed, was his inability to let go of his roots. Every immigrant parent's dream was for their child to become a doctor or a lawyer, but then I did. And he wasn't careful with what he wished for. Now, he was having a hard time letting go of the fact that I would never be the homemaker, traditionalist, child-bearer he'd envisioned his daughter being. He couldn't have it both ways, and the sooner he realized it, the better.

Because that is what it would be like. Ramiro wasn't the type who would be okay with my sixteen-hour shifts and overnight on-call rotations. He was the kind of man who wanted a home-body who would have his favorite meal ready on the table every Friday when he got home from work, tired from a long week at the garage. That woman could not—would not—ever be me. Whomever that woman ended up being would be very lucky to have him, but she wouldn't be me.

Ramiro balanced on a chair as he wrapped a string of twinkle lights around one branch of the tree in the backyard. He had earbuds in and didn't hear when I called to him. He wore dark denim jeans and a black ribbed tank. He was tall and barrel-chested. A heartbreaker in every sense of the word. If only I could have loved him back.

He turned, and his eyes lit up at the sight of me.

"Caro!" He jogged over, picked me up in his arms, and swung me around. "Happy birthday, *Corazón*."

"Put me down!" I smacked his giant shoulders. He was well built and hit the gym often.

"You weren't supposed to be here until six. We aren't ready."

"I came to help dad. Ramiro, you really don't need to be here helping him. That's what I'm here for."

His face fell for only one second before he shook it off. "You know better. You get treated like a queen on your birthday."

"You two spoil me almost every day, not just my birthday. How can I help?"

"You can tie the tablecloths down, so they don't blow away. That would be great."

With the three of us, everything was ready by four in the

afternoon, and all that was left was to fire up the grill when guests arrived. Ramiro left to get a bit of rest and change clothes. I went to my old room and took a quick shower.

I hadn't thought to bring clothes, of course, so I had to settle for whatever old items I had in my closet. Luckily, one of my favorite deep green dresses was there. I wore this dress on very rare occasions, but I loved the square neckline that showed off my collarbones without too much cleavage. I had more than plenty in that department, so I didn't need to be highlighting it more than necessary. The deep emerald looked beautiful on my dark, caramel-honey skin. It was also the perfect outfit for the hot, Kansan summer day.

Because it was so hot outside, I knew something was up when I laid eyes on Sara dressed in an outfit more suitable for fall. She walked in wearing a thin, long-sleeved blouse and didn't remove her sunglasses even when she was indoors. Not this shit again. I was going to kill him. Oath or not, I was going to kill him. I took a deep breath before leading her upstairs to my room—I couldn't take more control away from her.

Leading her to sit on my bed, I sat on the chair in front of her.

"Honey—" That's all it took. One word, and she broke into a sob.

"I'm sorry, Caro. I don't want to ruin your party, but I also couldn't miss it. I promised your dad . . ." She trailed off into her sobs and wiped at the tears on her cheeks.

"Oh, sweetie." I brushed her hair back. "You aren't ruining anything. You know I hate these things anyway." I smiled, and she laughed weakly. "Why don't you tell me what happened?"

Sara squared her shoulders and took her shades off. She'd done an expert job with the makeup, covering the blue and green bruises I knew were under that thin layer of pigment, but I couldn't be fooled because the swelling was clearly there. My fists clenched at my sides, and I couldn't help but bite the inside of my lip.

"Don't say it," Sara said. "I know he is slime. I know. I'm leaving him, okay?"

I'd heard this before, and there was not a shred of conviction in her voice, just like the last time. I wanted to shake her so badly, but just like the last time, I restrained myself. Even though it broke my heart, I couldn't help her out of this until she decided she was ready. So much power is taken from a domestic abuse victim, I couldn't bear to force her into anything she didn't want, even if it did everything short of killing me to hold my anger in check.

"When you're ready, I'm here for you. *We* are here for you; *Papi*, Ramiro, Sofia, and me. We got you. You got it?"

"I know."

"Why don't you stay up here and sleep it off? I'll tell Dad you're sick and resting here, and later I'll sneak you a plate of food."

Sara smiled up at me as I stood. "Did you make the salsa?" she asked.

"Yes. I made the salsa."

"The *molcajete* salsa—your mom's recipe?"

"Yes, with the secret ingredient."

"Bring extra?" she said as she curled into a ball under the blankets.

It was hard to get into the partying mood after that, but as tough as it was, we moved on. It was horrid to think it, but as often as that bastard Brian had beaten her up, Sofia and I had started getting used to it. And wasn't that just the shittiest bit of it all? We were the only two who knew because we were the only people in the world she couldn't hide her bruises from. We were too analytical.

Dad was happy, and we both knew this party was more for him. He'd invited all the neighbors—Ramiro's parents weren't present because they were vacationing in Florida—all of the mechanics from the garage, among whom were Ramiro's best friends, and Sara, but I kept her tucked away in her tower—my room.

The music came to a stop at six-thirty when we thought everyone had arrived. Dad said a few words, in Spanglish, of course.

"I want to thank you all for being here today to celebrate my *hijita.* It is a special day for me. She turns twenty-six today, and I'm the proudest dad in the world." As he spoke, out of the corner of my eye, I saw Dr. Medina enter our backyard. He carried a box wrapped in navy blue paper, finished with an orange bow. I smiled at him, and he waved back before placing the box carefully on the gift table.

Dad continued, and I returned my attention to him. "*Mija,* you are smart, strong, and beautiful. I don't know what I did in my past life to deserve a daughter like you, but I'm glad I did it."

"Don Gustavo." Ramiro jumped in, beer in his hand. "Mind if I say a few words too?"

I panicked. Oh, god, no. *Please, Papi, don't let him.*

"Of course, *mijo.*"

"Thank you," Ramiro started, and I sank into my chair. "I would like to propose a toast to Caro. *Todo el barrio* loves you. You treat patients for free at their homes when you can, and you are always helping your dad. You come from a hard worker, and I know you are a hard worker too. It's been a privilege to grow up with you, and I can't wait to start the next chapter of our lives. To Caro!" He raised his beer, and glass bottles clinked all around me.

Ramiro walked to the spot where I sat on my chair and offered me a hand. I grabbed it, smiling tightly, and stood to hug him. He went for a kiss, but I gave him my cheek instead of my lips. As I turned my head, I saw Hector still standing by the gifts, his eyes shadowed completely by his strong brow—his face unreadable.

I grabbed my drink before walking over to him.

"Dr. Medina. Hello."

"You look surprised I showed."

"To be honest, I am a little bit. I'm glad you came, though. You will be a novelty here tonight."

"I doubt that. They have you."

"I don't mean because you are a doctor." I laughed. "These people here, *my* people, are working-class people. The offspring of migrant workers, for the most part. I don't think you'll find many fancy Mexicans here tonight besides yourself."

"I'm a fancy Mexican?" he asked. At first, I thought he was joking but stifled my laugh when I sensed his earnestness.

I eyed him up and down, hand on my hip. "Yes. Definitely a fancy Mexican."

He stiffened when I laced my arm in his and led him to the opposite corner of the yard where Dad was grilling and talking to my uncle. I didn't miss when Hector used his free hand to straighten his tie.

"*Papi!*" I said. "I want you to meet someone."

Dad said a few more words I couldn't make out to my uncle and then handed him the apron and tongs. He came around the food table next to the grill. He smiled at me, but his lips thinned, seeing my arm was still linked with this strange man's.

"*Papi*, this is Dr. Hector Medina. My new boss."

Dad leaned back a bit and narrowed his eyes, studying him. Finally, after what seemed like years, he reached out his hand to shake Hector's, making him realize he had to let go of my hand.

"It's a pleasure," Dad said.

"Likewise. Thank you for inviting me to your home." I covered up my snort with a pretend cough. *Invited?* This fool invited himself.

Dad wanted to interrogate him further, but he heeded my

glare. This was my boss after all, and I owed him respect. He couldn't treat him like any other man I might bring home—not that I had brought anyone home for him to meet anyway.

"Can I get you something to drink?" I asked Dr. Medina, trying to break the awkwardness.

"Water would be great."

"Let's go into the kitchen, and I'll get you some ice."

He followed me back into my childhood home, and I suddenly felt very nervous about him seeing where I grew up.

"This is a nice house," he said, and I couldn't tell whether or not he was mocking me.

"I was happy growing up here."

Once the glass of water was in his hand, I suggested going outside for a plate of dinner, but he shook his head. "How about a tour instead?"

I almost choked on my beer. "A tour?"

"Yes. I'd love to see the rest of the house that was so happy for you growing up."

I cocked my head, unsure if I should give some excuse as to why that was a bad idea. I envisioned his childhood home in Mexico—probably a mansion—and I recoiled at the thought of showing him around. I couldn't come up with anything, so I led the way.

The living room was cozy, and I was glad I'd come early to help dust and tidy up a bit. I knew Dad abhorred dusting or any other household tasks besides cooking.

A row of picture frames lined the fireplace mantel. Dr. Medina's eyes zeroed in on them, and he walked over.

He picked one of me at the pool when I was six. "This is you?"

I nodded. "I'm an only child."

"That explains a lot."

"Excuse me?" I asked with mock-offense. "It's my birthday. I will not be put down on my birthday."

"My apologies, Dr. Ramirez. I meant nothing by it."

So, we were back to *Dr. Ramirez.* Okay. That was fine. "None taken, Dr. Medina," I said pointedly.

Next, he picked up a photo from my *quinceañera*, my coming-of-age party, when I turned fifteen. I winced, and my pride couldn't take it. I nearly snatched the photo from his hands, but it was too late. There I was, standing next to Dad, in the monster of a dress engulfing me in pink tulle.

Under different circumstances, I would have died before having the classical Mexican coming-of-age party. I would have opted for hell before agreeing to wear the Pepto-Bismol pink monstrosity, but as it was, I couldn't find it in my heart to say no to Dad.

"That's, um, a pretty dress—" my boss started to say. He tried to hold back a chortle but failed, and I couldn't help but smack his arm playfully.

"I did it for my father, okay?"

"No, really, really," he said between the laughter, "you were a very pretty cotton-candy."

"Where is your mother in the photo?"

And just like that, all the laughter went out of me. He sensed the clouds behind my eyes and started to apologize.

"It's okay," I said. I brought a hand up in a friendly gesture. "She had been gone a while by the time I turned fifteen. It's been my Dad and me ever since."

"I'm sorry, Carolina. That must have been very hard."

We were back to *Carolina,* and I offered him a weak smile. "It was, though it would have been much worse if my father had been anyone other than the one I got. He really is amazing."

"He must be," he said.

"What is that supposed to mean?"

"To have a daughter like you, he must be pretty amazing."

"Well, that's it. The house, as you can see, is pretty small. Not much else to see."

"Isn't there an upstairs?"

"Yes, but—" and just like that, he was off toward the stairwell.

I'd forgotten Sara was resting in my room but exhaled when I opened the door and she was gone. The sneaky little twat—she'd get it later. Instead, I found myself in my childhood bedroom with a very tall, very handsome man who was also my boss, barely fitting in the tiny space.

I froze when I realized what he was staring at on the wall next to my bed. It could only be one of three things. He was likely not a fan of *Jane Eyre,* so it wasn't that poster. He would certainly get points for being an *Industrial November* fan, so it could be the enlarged *Metal Red Day* album cover that drew him to the wall. Even if that were the case, that's not what he was staring at now. Sandwiched between the two was the first page of the abstract to his first published paper in a journal of medicine.

I forced my legs to move next to him. His mouth was parted slightly, and he swallowed. He was trying and failing to speak, and I couldn't find what to say in my defense.

If the earth could have swallowed me whole in that moment, I would have dived in head-first.

"Okay, please don't freak out. It really is not what it looks like."

He nodded but said nothing as he stared at his name printed on the page so carefully taped to my wall.

"Dr. Medina, I'm sure this must seem really inappropriate, but I swear, I'm not some stalker or anything like that." I cleared my throat. "I've known I wanted to do cancer research since I was ten. I was in high school when I first heard of your work, and at the time, I had no idea you would one day be my boss. I never thought I'd meet you."

The silence stretched as I allowed him a moment to answer, but he seemed incapable, so I, unfortunately, continued with the verbal diarrhea.

"I'm not in this room much, or I would have taken it down now that I know you." Everything I said after that sounded weak even to my own ears.

"It's okay, not a big deal," he said, finally putting me out of my misery. "Why don't we go back out, join the party? They must be missing you."

Once back outside, Ramiro's gaze latched on to us. I ignored it and introduced Dr. Medina to the neighbors. Merengue blared from a sound system that hadn't been in the yard before. Hector grabbed my hand. "May I have this dance?"

I laughed so hard, Hector frowned. "I'm sorry," I said. "It's just, I have two left feet. I don't dance. And this song," I kept talking between fits of laughter as I listened to Esa Muchacha by Los Hermanos Rosario, "is about a girl who can dance really well."

"Everyone can dance—"

"*Mija,* can you do me a favor?" my neighbor Mrs. Garcia called out to me.

"Sure, *señora.*"

I shrugged at Hector but was glad to be called away. It warmed me to my core when he took off his jacket and tie and rolled up his sleeves, so he could pass a soccer ball around with the two Garcia boys from next door. I sat with the boys' grandmother.

"I had a little accident in the kitchen. You mind taking a look?" She brought up an arm to display a burn on her inner forearm.

"*Hay, Mamá!*" Francisca, her daughter, and the mother of the boys now playing soccer with Dr. Medina, said. "I told you, she is not that kind of doctor anymore." She turned to me. "Sorry, Caro. I wanted to take her to the doctor, but she refused."

"Don't talk for me like I'm a child," Mrs. Garcia said as she glared at her with a fire I wouldn't like to be on the receiving end of. "Why would I go to a doctor," she continued, "when I know it's so minor and that Carolina would be happy to look at it?"

"I'm so sorry, Carolina," said Francisca, completely flustered.

"Don't worry, Francisca, I'm happy to help. Let me go inside and wash my hands. I'll be right back to take a look."

The burn was barely an inch in length, and only superficial.

"The good news is, you don't have to go to the doctor," I said to her with a smile.

"And the bad news?" Mrs. Garcia said, her brows furrowed.

I laughed. "No bad news. You just need to keep it clean and covered until it heals. If it's nice and pink, it's good. Once it scabs, it's good. But if it turns any other funny color, or gets any type of smell, we'll have to take a look at it again."

Mrs. Garcia stuck her tongue out at her daughter, and I couldn't help but laugh. "See?" she said. "I told you it would be nothing."

"Ramiro!" I called for my friend. "Do you mind grabbing my first aid kit from the upstairs bathroom? I also need a notepad and a pen."

He nodded and ran inside. I followed, leading Mrs. Garcia into the kitchen, where I washed her forearm with soap and water. Ramiro came back with the supplies, and I applied antibacterial ointment to her burn and bandaged it. I wrote down the name of a cream to use to treat it on a piece of paper and took it outside.

Ramiro and I walked Mrs. Garcia back to her chair. She wasn't too old or frail yet, but we knew she'd been dipping into the beers as usual. We sat her down, and I handed Francisca the piece of paper.

"It's really no trouble," I reassured her. "I'm always happy to help your mom. She *feeds* me when Dad is busy working."

It had been true once, though not so much since I'd moved out to my own apartment. But I still had a lot of love for the woman next door who had kept an eye out for us after Mom died. Like many at the party, she was more family than neighbor.

Not much longer after fixing up her mom, Francisca caught my attention as she chatted it up with Dr. Medina. And no, I was not jealous. Not one little bit. I loved Francisca almost as much as I loved her mom. Francisca was a single mom, sure, but she was a super-hot single mom. Not that I was jealous.

And because I wasn't jealous, I walked up to them to see what they were chatting about.

"It was great to see you," Dr. Medina said, "but I have to get going. Happy birthday." He said his goodbyes to Francisca then found Dad to do the same before parting.

"He is very handsome," Francisca said with a twinkle in her eye.

"Sure. If that's your type," I said dismissively.

"What? The tall, dark, and handsome type? Or is it the hot doctor type? Or the sexy Spanish accent type?"

I said nothing.

"So, you are not into him?"

"No! He is my boss." I was getting tired of having to tell everybody that.

"So you wouldn't mind if I gave him my number?"

My head snapped to her so quickly, she threw her head back with laughter and walked back to her mom, who was seated alone and happily kept company by a nice cold one.

Dad went to bed shortly after the last guests left at one in the morning, with promises he would pick up tomorrow. I remained to, at the very least, throw out the leftover food.

Grabbing my last beer of the night, I laid down on the hammock under the tree, looking up at the lights Ramiro had hung. The smell of the citronella candles had diminished now but was still detected by my strong sense of smell.

It had been a good night, as much as I had fought it. I liked seeing my dad so happy; he was in his element cooking for his friends. It still hurt that Sara couldn't be a part of it, but Dr. Medina showing up when I hadn't imagined he would made up for any shortfalls of the evening.

It was in this reverie that I found myself when the sound of a chair being dragged across the grass, and landing next to me, distracted me. I turned to meet Ramiro's handsome face.

He clinked my beer with his.

"*Salud,*" he said.

"*Salud.*"

"Was it a good birthday?"

"Yeah. Mostly."

"Mostly?"

I shrugged. "Just some drama with Sara. I'll talk with her about it tomorrow—err . . . today, I guess."

"I noticed she wasn't here. Was surprised."

Shrugging again, I took another swig of beer and placed my hand behind my head, looking up at the sky. I was definitely downplaying what had happened with Sara, but I wasn't sure how much she would want Ramiro to know.

"I was also surprised," Ramiro said, "that you brought someone else from work. That was a first." I glanced at him. We both knew what he was dancing around.

"You know Sara and her big mouth. She mentioned the party, and he heard. It was rude of her not to invite him, so she did. Trust me, I was just as surprised when he actually showed."

A small noise that sounded almost like an "uhuh," escaped him.

"You like him?" he asked.

"No," I said automatically. This was starting to sound rehearsed, it was asked so often.

"I saw the way you looked at him."

I sighed. "I looked at him the way you would look at David Beckham. He was my hero when I first started thinking about medicine. Now, I'm over the moon he will be my mentor." I didn't even notice when my tone turned. "And, quite frankly, I'm sick and tired of everyone assuming I'm in love with him or something. Maybe I'm in love with his work, but I want mentorship. That's all. If he were a woman, we wouldn't be having this discussion."

"Okay, okay. I give," he said with a gesture of surrender.

"I'm sorry. I shouldn't have snapped. I've just been getting a lot of that recently."

"I bet," he said.

I sat up on the hammock and dangled my legs off to the side so I could face him. I kicked off my sandals, and he tried to grab my foot and place it on his lap, but I bounced it back toward the ground.

"Ramiro—" I said before he cut me off.

"You know, if he had been a woman, and you were in love with her, I might've been into that," he said, trying to lighten the mood. This was the problem. We knew each other too well. It muddied the waters, and it had to come to an end.

I kicked him playfully, and we both laughed. "Ramiro, we need to talk—"

"Not this again, *corazón*. Please. Not tonight."

"It's never a good time. You never let me talk because you know me so well, you know exactly what I'm going to say."

His gaze dropped to the ground, and he buried the beer bottle in the grass. "On your birthday. That's when you want to do this?"

"It's one in the morning. It's not my birthday anymore."

Ramiro gulped a big breath and motioned with his hands for me to lay it on him.

"Ramiro, you need to move on. I've never seen you as

anything other than my brother. What do I have to do for you to believe that will never change?"

"It's because of him—"

"No. It's not because of anyone. This might hurt for you to hear, but I may never end up with anyone. I'm not someone who needs a relationship. I'm not saying it will never happen, but even if it does, there is one thing I am sure of. It will never be with you."

Because I loved him so much, the look of pain on his face crushed me. He winced as though I had stabbed him in the gut, but he wasn't surprised. He couldn't be. He'd known how I felt all along, but he wanted to pretend. I couldn't let this go on any longer. I wouldn't let a disease spread because the treatment might cause temporary pain, but somehow, I'd let it go unchecked in Ramiro.

"I want nothing more than for you to be happy," I continued. "You need to stop distracting yourself with women who aren't worthy of your love and find someone who is. You need someone who wants to care for you the way I know you will care for the woman you end up with. I wish—I wish with all my heart that woman could be me. It would make things so much easier—for both of us. And *I do* love you. More than you know, but I love you like a brother. It will kill me if what I'm saying takes you out of my life."

He didn't say anything as he let my words sink in. Instead, he stood and offered a hand as he had done earlier in the evening. I stood, and we were about an inch apart. He looked into my eyes, finding the same truth there that had come out of my mouth. He kissed my forehead, and I brought up my hand to his cheek so I could look at him again.

He was too manly to cry, but the glistening glare hurt as much as if he had shed tears.

"You will find someone, Carolina. You are too spectacular not to have a million men fall at your feet."

"Ramiro—"

"Maybe years from now I won't feel this way, but right now, the very thought of the man you choose in the end, well, I think it will kill me to watch. Though I have a feeling I just met him tonight."

"Don't do this, Ramiro. *Please.* We are family."

He shook his head. "No. I mean, yes. I will stay away. For a little while. Please do me a favor, huh?"

"Anything," I said, and I meant it.

"Don't reach out until I do? I'll be in withdrawals from you, and you know my ego can't take you seeing me as anything other than the virile man that I am."

We both laughed, but it was forced, and I punched him playfully.

"You'll come back to us?" I asked.

"You are my family, first and foremost," he said, reassuring me.

"You promise?"

"I promise."

ASSUMPTIONS

*W*here once there were two men in my life, now there were none. Three months had passed since the cookout, and I hadn't seen Ramiro at all, and I'd barely spoken to Dr. Medina.

Ramiro went to join his parents in Florida, Dad told me, but then stayed there when his parents came back. He asked Dad for extended leave from the garage, and considering it was his daughter who propelled him away—his words, not mine—he found himself obliged to consent to the request.

Dr. Medina, on the other hand, had pulled a one-eighty on me. He withdrew from the friendly banter we had started. I was given no attention at rounds, and it was almost as if he couldn't stand to look at me. I had no clue what was up his ass, but I refused to let it affect my work. Never meet your heroes—the best piece of advice I ever got that I stupidly ignored.

Focus on work, I told myself. It wasn't easy on this particular day. I'd drawn the short straw, though I suspected foul play from Dr. Keach, and had gotten stuck teaching a sensitivity training to our year-one residents.

"We've had four complaints this month," I said to the packed conference room, "of poor bedside manner." Some of the residents had the decency to feign some semblance of shame, and some shifted in their seats. "So," I said, "we are going to practice."

Groans skipped down the row of doctors like stones on water, so I lifted a hand to silence them. I pinched the bridge of my nose. "I don't want to be here any more than you do, but this is *your* fault, not mine, so take it up with the chief if you don't like it."

They shut it at that. Even among these baby doctors, I could tell which ones had issues with women doctors or women telling them what to do in general. It was the ones who took out their cellphones when I spoke or started hushed side conversations. I narrowed my eyes and called on that type first.

"One of the complaints was from a woman who said the doctor, and I quote, 'walked in the room, didn't so much as say hello, read my chart, and never even looked up at my face. Then, he took a thermometer and shoved it in my mouth. He didn't say what he was doing, and he didn't even ask me to open my mouth. He was very rude.'" I glanced up from the screen when a couple of the doctors cackled. They shut it immediately and straightened their postures.

One hour of hell later, I dismissed all but one of the residents.

"Dr. Dennis, why don't you join me? We have a patient who was admitted a bit late this morning, so we haven't been to round on her."

The redhead nodded. I purposefully selected Dr. Dennis because I remembered a distinct smile on Valentina's face when he was around. If she had to be back in her hellhole, at least she'd have a friendly face.

Valentina had been discharged, had been feeling a bit better, but then took a bit of a turn. Now, she was back, and I'd had to admit her for major surgery. I told her last time I discharged her that I hoped not to see her until her next round of chemo, but my wish was not granted.

We found Valentina standing at her bed, facing away from the door. She rummaged through a duffle bag, muttering something to herself. She was in her hospital gown, and the part down her spine provided just enough of a peek to see her light pink underwear. I cleared my throat to announce our presence. She whipped around and smiled at the sight of me.

"Doctor Ramirez!" Her grin broke mid-sentence when her eyes drifted over my shoulder, undoubtedly seeing Dr. Dennis. She drew her hand toward her backside to seal the mighty hospital gown gap. She turned chili-pepper red, but I couldn't bring myself to care. I was happy to see some color on her. "Rory—I mean, Dr. Dennis. Hi."

"Hello, Miss Almonte," he said.

"Valentina. Please."

"Of course. Valentina. Hello."

I let a moment pass between them before speaking again. "So, I thought I told you to stay away, young lady."

"I'm trying, Doc. I'm trying really hard."

"Are you ready for tomorrow?"

She nodded. "I remember the drill vividly."

"I know," I said. "But I still have to go over the procedure with you. Risks, all that."

Valentina rolled her eyes. "Yeah, I know that drill too."

In that second, I got paged to Dr. Medina's office. *What now?* It felt like I was being called to the principal's office. We had barely spoken since my birthday and at work, had only interacted when absolutely necessary.

"Well, missy, if you are that bored of my rambling, maybe I'll have the capable Dr. Dennis go over the paperwork with you. Do you mind, Dr. Dennis? I was paged."

"Sure," he said, taking the clipboard with the consent forms from me.

I TOOK a deep breath before knocking. Hector's mood lately had all of us in the oncology department avoiding him. I wasn't prepared to go into the lion's den.

"Come in," said Dr. Medina's gruff voice from the other side of the door.

"You paged?"

"Yes, please sit down." He smiled at me, but it wasn't the same smile as before. There was no playfulness in his eyes, and his lips were tight.

"What's this about?"

"You haven't seen your email today?"

"Not since two in the afternoon. I was in charge of a training with the residents today—"

"Yes, yes," he said, cutting me off. "Statistics got back to us. The preliminary data of the trial is in."

"It is?" My heart raced. This step of the trial wouldn't make or break it, but if it improved outcomes, it could mean . . . I couldn't go there. Not without the numbers to back it up. Dr. Medina simply nodded.

"Yes. A lot of it looks promising, but I have some questions, and I'd like to go over the data with you," he said.

"You looked at the data already?"

"Well, yes," he said, his brow furrowing.

"Why did they send it to you?"

"I asked the statistics department to cc me when the results came in—"

My pulse quickened with a rage I knew I wouldn't be able to tame. "You had no right. That is my data—"

"I thought you agreed we would work on this together?"

Dr. Medina looked aghast as if he couldn't understand where I was coming from. I counted to ten to suppress the anger building. He was overstepping on *my* trial. He wasn't used to people telling him 'no,' I could tell. But someone had to.

Taking a deep breath, I said, "Dr. Medina, from now on, I'd appreciate being the first one to see the results of *my* trial."

"A sensitivity training is not more important than this," he countered.

"No. But I won't set aside my other hospital duties. Research is one big part of the whole. I'm also expected to teach—"

"I don't see the problem here," he said.

Clearly, I thought. "You are overstepping on my trial, Dr. Medina."

He leaned back in his chair and scratched at the stubble on his jaw. "I'm not sure what to do here."

"Look, moving forward, I'd like to be in charge of the trial *I* wrote. I'm grateful for your mentorship, but that doesn't mean you can just take over—"

"I see—"

"I mean no disrespect, Dr. Medina."

"Well, what's done is done. I'd still kill to go over the preliminary data with you."

He offered no reassurances, but I was already on dicey ground with my boss, so I let the matter go. We could always revisit the conversation if he continued to overstep.

"Fine. I have time this evening," I said.

"No, I can't this evening. I'm on call tonight."

"Oh." I slumped back in my chair, thinking about my schedule.

"How about Friday night. You're off, right?" he asked.

"I am. But I can't Friday. I have plans."

He cocked his head to the side as his eyes narrowed. I could swear a storm was brewing there.

"*Cancel* your *plans*," he said between gritted teeth.

"I'm sorry. I can't. I can work with your assistant to find a time that works for both of us if you'd like—"

"No. I can do it this Friday. I want to get it over with as soon as possible."

Over with? I hadn't asked him to do this. He wanted to work on the trial. I never asked him to, and now he was trying to make it seem like some great inconvenience while at the same time overstepping on it?

"No," I said. I took a deep breath. "I'm afraid the plans I have on Friday can't be canceled."

My shift was over, so I stood to leave. "I'll find a time with your assistant."

"Dr. Ramirez, we are not done here," he said.

"I'm afraid we are, Doctor."

Putting distance between the hospital and me was the best thing I could do for my sanity. It had been a challenging day between the sensitivity training, Dr. Keach hovering over me, and now this. I speed-walked to the conference room where I'd left my tablet earlier.

"Caro?" I heard Sara's voice as I sped by her. "What's wrong?"

"I gotta go," I said.

I'd just grabbed the tablet when I heard steps behind me.

"Not now, Sara, we'll talk later."

"It's not Sara," he said. I turned to face Dr. Medina, who I hadn't realized had followed me out of his office.

"We weren't done talking."

"Yes, we were. I have to go now."

"No. I need you to cancel your plans Friday."

"And *I told you*, I can't do that. I don't know what else there is to talk about."

He shook his head and took off his glasses to wipe them with a cloth he produced from his pants pocket.

"Your plans can't be more important than this."

"Frankly, it is none of your business."

"You can drink another time," he hissed.

"Excuse me?" I reared back. Had I heard him right?

"I've seen you outside of work exactly two times, and both times you have been drinking."

"Dr. Medina, with all due respect, sir, you are out of line." How could I tell off my boss? I couldn't. Not without risking my job.

"I don't think I am, Dr. Ramirez. If I think that it's getting in the way of your job."

"*What*? Getting in the way of my job?" He was silent for a moment—the audacity. "Dr. Medina," I hissed right back at him, "you might have seen me drinking two times, but if you can, please use your brain. Was I drunk or even tipsy? I don't drink often; you happened to be around for one special occasion, and the other was a girls' night out. I would never drink and come to work. How could you imply I would endanger my patients like that?"

More silence.

"The bottom line is, I have plans on my day off that I can't cancel. If you have a real complaint about my work, take it up with HR." It was his turn to rear back. He hadn't expected me to hold my ground. To anyone else, he may be a god, but I could see him now for what he was. His ego had everyone fooled, and he wasn't used to not getting his way when it came to work.

I couldn't escape because Sara had also followed me and now stood between the door and me. Why was she everywhere? She placed one hand on my shoulder with force to keep me in place and firmly inside the room.

Dr. Medina glared at us, his eyes darting back and forth from her face to mine. He wanted to say something, but he'd come to think twice about messing with Sara, just like every other doctor on the oncology floor. If only she could stand up for herself the way she stood up for her patients and loved ones.

"Dr. Ramirez," Sara said as she shot daggers at our boss with her eyes, "volunteers at the free clinic on two of her days off a month. You know how many days off a resident has, yet she gives most of them up. She would *never* break her commitment." Sara loosened her grip on my shoulder when she was done talking.

Dr. Medina's mouth fell open, and he hung his head but said nothing.

"Forget it, Sara. It's no use," I said as I walked past her and out the door. I could just imagine the stare down that was taking place in the conference room. I had to get out of there.

I was nearly at the locker room when Dr. Keach caught up to me. *Not this. Not now.*

"Fallen from grace so soon, Carolina?" he asked. I glared at him, and he backed off, but not before saying, "What did I tell you?"

If he tripped, fell, and broke his nose, I would not be upset.

THE DRUNK DOCTOR

"Sofia? What is it?" I asked with my heart lodged in my throat.

I was used to getting calls at three in the morning, but they were usually from the hospital. Seeing the name of someone close was jarring. *Please don't let it be Sara,* I thought.

"He's, um—*here.*"

"Who? Where?"

"Your boss. I closed the bar a few minutes ago, but he is barely coherent. I wasn't sure if I should send him in a cab or not."

She was asking me. I pressed a hand to my heart, calming myself down. It wasn't Sara. I rubbed the sleep off my eyes. "No —uh, no. I'll drive him home."

"Mind letting yourself in?" Sofia asked. "Got someone upstairs waiting for me in bed," she said playfully, and I smiled, shaking my head. I didn't even bother asking who it was because it was usually a different person every time. It would take someone incredibly special to make it into her bed on a repeat night.

"Yeah, I got the key. And hey, Sofia? Thanks for calling me."

"No problem."

She hung up the phone, and I slipped into sweats and my white sneakers. I grabbed the first pullover I could find. At three in the morning, the air would be crisp.

Dr. Medina was twirling an empty shot glass on the bar with his index finger when I found him. All the lights were out except for one near him. He looked up when he heard the door open.

"Carolina!" he said with a huge grin that reminded me of his first week on the job. "Look! It's Carolina Doctor, I mean—Doctor Carolina."

I looked around, but there was no one else in the room but him. "Come on, hotshot. I'll take you home."

"But the drinks are here." He looked at the glass bottles of liquor on the shelf.

"I'm sure you have drinks at home."

He shook his head. "No alcohol in my home. Ever. It's a rule," he said, nodding like a child.

Oh my god. Was he an alcoholic? Is that why he was so angry when he believed I was partying on all my days off? That would explain a lot. It would certainly explain why he was murderous on the night he drove me home when he thought I'd be driving after drinking.

"I'll get you some more on the way home," I lied. He'd pass out as soon as he got there.

I stood next to him, letting him lean on me for balance.

"I have to pay," he said.

"It's okay—"

"No. The pretty bartender. Where'd she go?" He looked around the bar as if he just noticed Sofia had left.

"She knows you're good for it. Besides, she knows where you work. You can close out your tab tomorrow."

Leading him to my car proved difficult. He was more off-balance than I thought he'd be, and suddenly I regretted not asking Sofia to stay up and help me. Funny how the lives of doctors and lives of bartenders are so similar; we both get our sleep when we get our sleep. Or we don't.

Before I opened the passenger door, I grabbed his wallet from inside his jacket. I was no skilled pickpocket, but he was so far gone, he didn't notice. I pushed his head down with my free hand to protect him from banging his head on the roof of the car.

Once behind the wheel, I grabbed his driver's license and copied the address onto my navigation device. His home was less than fifteen minutes away.

We entered the security code to his front door incorrectly twice before getting it right. He kept mixing numbers at first. Once inside, I was surprised there was a security system at all. There was nothing anyone would want to steal. The house was spacious and luxurious, with its crown molding and marble kitchen island, but there was no furniture on the main floor. Not a single item decorated the walls. Maybe he had just moved in.

After asking where his room was, he led us there. Getting up the stairs was more challenging than getting him in my car, but we finally made it. I was relieved to see he had a bed, even if it was the solitary item in the room apart from a dresser.

It was beyond awkward standing in a bedroom with my drunk boss. I thanked my lucky stars Sofia was the only one aware of this debacle, and I knew she'd never tell a single soul. Not even Sara.

The thought of his wife sent a shiver through my body. Where was she? From the pictures I had seen online, I would have bet five dollars that woman would have this house filled with cozy beige and white furniture. *She* should have picked him up from the bar—certainly not me. Hector had been in Kansas City several months—long enough for furniture, and long enough for his wife to join him.

I needed to stop thinking of him in any capacity not related to work. His personal life was none of my business, even if I now found myself in the precarious situation of having to drag his drunk ass home. He groaned on the bed, looking up at the ceiling. I took his shoes off, which I reasoned with myself was not crossing a line. I wasn't taking them off to touch him. Not at all. I was being a civil servant. Serving my fellow man.

"Good night, Hector. I think the person who picks you up drunk at a bar at three in the morning gets to be on a first-name basis."

"You're leaving?"

"Yes. I have to go to work in a few hours."

"Don go," he said, his words slurred, missing consonants.

"I have to."

"I'm hungry. I can't sleep if I haven't food."

I groaned. This fool was going to slice a finger off if he tried making something.

"All right, let's see what we can find in your fridge. But then I *have* to go."

He sprang up, and it was only a little funny when he clung to the rail for balance as he descended the staircase.

There wasn't much in the fridge, but I managed to find enough to make a turkey and cheese sandwich. I started a pot of coffee to hopefully sober him up.

As I worked, Hector sat on the single stool at the kitchen island. He bent over, his arm on the counter, and his head rested on his shoulder.

"How is Ramiro?" he asked with the subtlety of a bulldozer.

I winced. I tried not to think about him but answered after

handing Hector his plate. "I haven't seen him since my birthday party."

He looked up from the sandwich after the first bite.

"You haven't?" he asked.

I shook my head.

"Why?"

"He's in Florida." There was no way of knowing whether the move was permanent or not, so I refrained from voicing any assumptions.

"I'm sorry," he said.

"For what?"

"I'm sorry that you broke up."

"Broke up? Ramiro and I have never been a couple."

I tried not to get angry when he smiled.

"You haven't?"

"No."

"At the party, I could have sworn—"

"He's like a brother to me," I cut him off, wanting to be done with this conversation.

A soft 'meow' distracted me momentarily. That's right. He'd mentioned a cat. "Come here, kitty, kitty." I smacked my lips as I searched for the source of that soft sound.

"Canica," said Hector.

"What?"

"Her name is Canica."

"Marble? You named her Marble?"

He shook his head. "No. I didn't name her."

I had to assume he meant it had been his wife who named her, though why would the cat be with Hector and not her if it was *her* cat was beyond me. *None of your business, Caro.* "Canica, come here, girl."

"She's shy with strangers," Hector said.

I would be lying if I said it didn't melt my heart that he knew his cat's personality. "Right." I searched the kitchen floor until I came upon her food and water bowls tucked away in the corner. Hector didn't have much in the pantry, but he did have several cans of cat food.

I filled Canica's water bowl first and emptied a can of food into the second bowl. Lingering by the food, I hoped she'd come out to my offering, but she didn't do so until I stood a couple of feet back.

When she did reveal herself, she walked carefully to her dinner. She had a beautiful silver coat and piercing, bright yellow eyes. Once she was done, she approached me tentatively and wrapped herself around my left leg before springing away toward Hector. He picked her up to land a kiss on the top of her head before putting her down again.

"I'm sorry I had it wrong about Ramiro," Hector said, bringing back the subject to where we'd left off our conversation. He took another bite, and I handed him the coffee, which he took black. "But I guess that leaves hope for Dr. Keach."

I dropped the package of cheese I was stowing in the fridge. *What in the hell?*

"Dr. Keach? What in the world are you talking about?"

"He likes you. I never thought he had a chance—you know, thinking you were with Ramiro, but now . . ." His left eyebrow lifted as he trailed off mid-sentence.

"Dr. Keach does not like me."

"Yes, he does."

"No, he doesn't."

"Does."

"*Hector.*"

"*Carolina.*"

Oh, brother. We sounded like little kids.

"Remind me to never pick your drunk ass up again."

"Why do you think he is always in your face?"

"He *hates* me."

"Nope. He can't stand to be away from you. Always finding

excuses to be around you, to get a rise out of you—provoke you."

It was that moment that I realized he'd been paying attention. He'd been watching me this entire time, not with the interest of an employer for his employee, but with interest in my personal life.

He scarfed down the sandwich and coffee in record time. Slowly, his words became more coherent, and he found his center of gravity again.

"Why do people say that?"

"What?"

"That when a guy is mean to a woman, it means he likes her. I used to hear it so much as a kid. *If a boy teases you, it means he likes you.* Mom used to say it. Dad said it. It's so wrong. It's so ingrained in us from the time we are little kids." I shook my head. "No wonder so many women grow up to confuse abuse with love." My mouth dried up at the thought of Sara.

"I'm sorry, Carolina." I found nothing but sincere repentance in his eyes. "I'm sobering up with the food and am starting to realize I've placed my foot in my mouth quite a bit tonight."

His words were indeed less slurred. I nodded in acceptance of his apology, and his muscles relaxed.

"Besides," I said dismissively, "if it happens to be true that Keach likes me—which I very much doubt—I would never accept affection from a man who chooses to show a woman he likes her by torturing her and messing with her. That wouldn't be my type at all. Too childish." I crinkled my nose.

Hector raised an eyebrow. "What *is* your type, Dr. Ramirez?"

I thought about it for a second, and he patiently waited. I had never been in a significant relationship, not that I'd tell Hector that. I'd dated, of course, but nothing had ever gotten serious. I finally settled on saying, "I'm trying to think of a throughline in the men I've dated, but they were all so different, I don't think they fit a particular type."

"Okay, but you must know what you like—traits you value."

"Yeah. Sure. Let's see. Smart. Smart is a must. Mature. I like a man who is self-assured, but still humble—not that you would know anything about humility. Balance, I guess. I'm so boring, aren't I?" I chuckled.

"No, Carolina. You are not boring. And I don't know what you are talking about. I'm the best at being humble."

"You realize that very statement proves otherwise?"

Hector threw his head back with laughter.

"I really have to get going. I won't even have a chance to sleep now, but I do have to get ready to go to the hospital."

"I'll walk you out."

I let him stand first to make sure his balance was sufficient for him to climb the stairs by himself. He was steady enough, at least for me to avoid being in his room again. That would be a mistake.

"Carolina." He stopped me before I could open the door. "Thank you for tonight. And I'm sorry for what I said. There is no excuse."

"It happens. I believe intent is important, and I know you weren't trying to be malicious."

He stepped closer to me, nearly pinning my back to the door. "No. It was not my intent to be malicious."

My breath caught in the back of my throat. He leaned in closer—the distance between us now nearly nonexistent. He bowed his head until our noses almost met. My heartbeat loudened until it was all I could hear. I looked at his eyes, but his gaze was frozen on my lips. My eyes dropped to his mouth —I couldn't help it—and his lips parted.

There was no confusing this moment. It was *want*. I wanted him, and his body made it clear he wanted me too. It was a beautiful fantasy, but it could never be more than that—*a fantasy.*

Hector's lips hovered over mine, and his gaze drifted back to my eyes, a question written in his. He was asking for my permission to seal the kiss that lingered like a ghost on our lips. I felt his movements as his arms went past me, and his hands landed on the door behind me. The muscles in his biceps tightened, and deep blue veins bulged to the surface. Restraint. He wouldn't deliver on the promise of contact—not until I accepted it.

I couldn't. My body almost gave in, but I was too practical. I knew if I let go, I would regret it. Not to mention he wasn't completely sober yet. My *good head on my shoulders* would be the ruin of me. I couldn't succumb to an affair that would undoubtedly hurt everyone involved.

Everyone.

"Andrea," I whispered her name, though the syllables tasted bitter on my tongue. His arms dropped from their iron grip on the door behind me, and he stepped back.

My hearing returned as my heart slowed. We both sobered and killed the lust we'd let escape to the surface for a moment. How could we have been so careless? I guess we were only human, after all—not the gods we played at on a daily basis at work.

"You are married," I said, more loudly now.

He nodded and looked down at the gold band around his ring finger. He twisted the band around a few times before laughing. "Right. My *wife*," he said, but there was something off about the laugh. "Good night, Carolina. Thanks again for everything."

"I think you mean *good morning*, Dr. Medina."

WORK AS A DISTRACTION

To my surprise, things were better after our near-miss. Hector remained respectful of me and all our interactions were nothing but professional, but his good mood was back. He stopped ignoring me, and it felt almost how it had when he'd first joined Heartland Metro.

Now that Dr. Keach had planted that seed of doubt, however, I was once again the main target for his jabbing. I hadn't pieced together why Dr. Keach had backed off, but my bliss had only lasted while Hector ignored me. Now that I featured back on Hector's radar, Dr. Keach gravitated back to pestering me, taking any opportunity to put me down in the presence of Dr. Medina.

He found me at the nurses' station going over my next patient's chart. "I see all is well in paradise again," he said.

My eyes narrowed. "Excuse me?" I didn't look up from the screen.

"You and Dr. Medina. You're back in his good graces, I see."

"You should be careful what you insinuate, Dr. Keach. Your daddy's name can only protect you from so much. You sure you want to antagonize someone like Dr. Medina?" I raised an eyebrow.

That's right, Dr. Keach, I thought. *The mom and baby wing may be named after your father, but even your last name plastered on the hospital's wall is laughable.*

There was simply no way he would have gotten matched to this hospital without some serious money being involved. His father was a physician here before his retirement and was a regular—and generous—donor to the hospital. But Dr. Keach was not worth more than the research funding Hector could bring in.

Dr. Keach's lips thinned and his nostrils flared. No one had ever called him out on his bullshit. I'd been tempted many times before, and I wasn't exactly sure why I'd finally done it after all this time. Probably because before, his attention only affected me, but now he was also soiling the name of a mentor I valued. I refused to acknowledge any other feelings for Hector—even to myself.

"You really are clueless, aren't you?" asked Dr. Keach.

"Please, enlighten me," I taunted.

"Dr. Medina will be selecting the recipient of the fellowship in two years. The chief wanted fresh eyes on the graduating residents next year."

I shifted in my seat. Of course Dr. Keach would have this information. The Chief of Oncology kissed his ass constantly. It came as no surprise that he would give him the advantage. It also stung a little that Hector hadn't offered me the same upper hand by telling me his role in selecting the winner.

Hector wasn't witness to any part of this exchange. Dr. Keach was tactical in his attacks on me, and I knew that taking it to HR would only result in his word against mine. It chafed knowing that at this moment, his word would be worth a heck of a lot more than mine.

I didn't see Hector until the next day when I had to work out his schedule with his assistant. We managed to free up the latter half of the day so we could go over the statistical report we had been neglecting.

Hector hadn't changed much in his office in the few months since he'd joined Heartland Metro. From what I could tell, the only change was the appearance of a solitary picture frame on his desk. Once I sat down, I turned the photograph over to see what could be the only thing in his life important enough to look at every day. The simple black frame contained a black and white photograph of Hector and an older, shorter woman standing next to him. "Who is this?" I asked.

"That is Marisela Medina." He smiled, and I put the frame back to its original spot on his desk.

"Your mom?"

He nodded. "Ready?"

We were going over the numbers together. We made a promise to open the email at the same time—he hadn't gotten that far before we'd fought about it. He read one line, and I read the next.

An excitement very close—though also very different—to what I had felt at his house two nights ago crept up. My heart began racing.

"Are you seeing this?" Hector asked.

I couldn't look up from my screen. My mouth dried up, rendering words inaccessible. I only nodded.

"What did I tell you?"

I looked up at him then, the question clear on my face. "Is this real?"

"Carolina, you are amazing. It's going in the right direction."

I nodded, too stunned to speak.

The results were what I was expecting—*eventually.*

Hector read out loud, letting the words wrap me in an embrace. "Thirteen percent difference in remission between the control and experimental groups at six months. Carolina, the experimental group treatment is thirteen percent more effective than the standard of care. I can't wait to see data from year three and year four. I bet you it could go up as much as fifty percent when it's all done . . . Carolina? Are you okay?"

I bolted out of my seat and ran out of his office. Luckily, the bathroom wasn't too far down the hallway from his office. I made it just in time to vomit. I rinsed my mouth, and when I exited the ladies' room, Hector was leaning against the wall across from the door, his brows knitted together.

"Are you okay?" he asked.

I nodded and walked back to his office. I sat and tried to listen to whatever he was saying, but I couldn't. My eyes prickled with tears. He said he thought this could be up to fifty percent better than the standard of care. That, plus all the advancements in medicine since I'd lost her, meant she could have beaten it if she had been diagnosed today instead of so many years ago. I tried to do the math in my head. *Yes.* I was confident she would have lived.

"Carolina." Hector stared at me.

Taking a deep breath, I met his gaze. "Sorry," I said. "I think I'm in shock."

"It's okay. Take a minute."

After a long silence during which I tried to compose myself, he finally spoke.

"Who was it?"

"Who was what?"

"The loss that drove you to this mad battle against cancer."

I pressed my lips together in thought, not sure I was ready for him to know so much. I didn't like talking about it in general, not even to Dad, with whom I shared everything.

"You don't have to tell me if you don't want to, but I very much want to know, Carolina."

His eyes were so soft, so full of empathy, I couldn't help myself.

"My mother."

He nodded but didn't ask any more questions.

"I'm sorry." His glasses came off as he searched for whatever he was going to say next. "Please don't get offended by what I'm about to say. It's hard to put my feelings into words."

"Okay . . ."

"I envy you. Not because you lost your mother, obviously that's not what I'm trying to say. I only mean many people who lose someone do nothing about it. You decided to go into the toughest profession and fight for a spot in a competitive residency so that you could save another little girl's mom."

"No offense taken," I said. "I think I understand what you are trying to say."

"I also envy that you have a reason, a strong one, for doing this."

"What? You don't?"

"No. Not really."

"So then, why did you decide to be a doctor and get into oncology?"

"See, this is where I find it tricky to explain myself. When I was younger, I was very concerned about my legacy. About what contributions I would make to the world before I died. I guess I still am, in a way."

"I think that's a great reason."

"There is nuance there if you look carefully. It sounds noble to aspire to do good in the world, but no one ever admits the selfishness of the sentiment. All of us dreamers and would-be philosophers have the same thing in common: our bloated egos. You'd think we'd want to do good in the world for the world's sake, but it's more selfish than that. We do it for the personal satisfaction." He grinned, pleased with his explanation. "See? Selfish."

"I don't think it's selfish at all."

"You don't?"

"No. Had you been my mother's doctor and been successful in saving her life, do you think I'd have given a rat's ass about what led you to that success? Dr. Medina, you've done so much good in this field. I expect you will continue to do good in the latter half of your career. The patients you save—and their *families*—don't care why you do it, so long as you fucking do it."

He chuckled. "God, Carolina. Sometimes I think you know me better than I know myself." He paused. "Could you be any more perfect?"

I adjusted in my seat. I refused to turn this moment into something uncomfortable. This was my first significant trial, and all signs were pointing to success. I'd also had a beautiful moment with my mentor. We couldn't turn this into something else and mar my memory of this day.

"Well, I'm getting hungry. Would you like to get a bite?"

"Dr. Ramirez," he scolded me, looking at me from above the line of his glasses, now back on his face. "We have a lot of work to do."

It was true. Now, we needed to adjust the treatment protocol and submit it to the internal review board (IRB). In phase two of the trial, all patients would receive the experimental treatment, but not before the IRB approved the protocol change. The process would take a few weeks, so the trial would be placed on hold until then. Suddenly, I had a few more days off.

"We don't have to go anywhere," I said. "I can have my RA order us some food and bring it back."

"You have a research assistant? How come I haven't met her?"

"She works at the information desk mostly, so she's not around much. Doesn't need to be. She schedules appointments, interviews prospective trial subjects, handles data entry—that kind of thing. She was only working the front desk part-time, and when my grant got funded, I offered her a part-time position as an RA. Now, she is employed full time by the hospital and eligible for health insurance benefits."

"That was nice of you."

"I'm lucky to have her. Amanda is pretty amazing. She's more than just an assistant. She's a great visual artist. I'll introduce you sometime. Do you like sushi? I'll have her bring it right over."

"Sure. Sushi sounds great."

I needed to go to my locker and grab a credit card to give to Mandy, but before I left, I turned to him once more. "Oh, and Dr. Medina?"

"Yes?"

"I'm far from perfect. I have my own demons and insecurities, just like anyone else."

CHAPTER 11

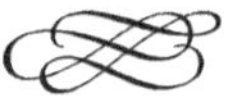

THE BROKEN GIRL

Valentina's test results from last week were back, and I called her in for a follow-up appointment.

She waited patiently in exam room five. My face fell when I saw her. She looked better physically. Her hair was growing back into a sort of a pixie cut, and some of her weight was back, though her muscles weren't yet. But what threw me off was her pale complexion, her tightened lips, and, most of all, her perfectly-shaped eyebrows, almost fully grown in to their previous length, pulled-in, a crinkle forming between them.

"What's wrong?" I asked her. "Are you not feeling well?"

"You tell me," she said.

"Nothing's wrong, Vale. But you look as though you've seen a ghost."

Her expression not changing, her gaze fell to the floor.

"I read on the forums," she said, "that if it's good news, I get it over the phone. If it's bad, they call me back in for a follow-up."

"Oh, Vale, honey—"

"It's back, isn't it?" Her breath hitched as she formed the question.

"No!" I hastened to answer. "Valentina, I wanted to give you the good news in person. That's all. Please stop reading about treatment or procedures online. It's not the first time it's gotten you in trouble." I arched an eyebrow at her.

"Good news?" She looked up, hope misting her eyes.

"Yes, Valentina. Good news." I grabbed her by the shoulders and squeezed them gently. "Six months remission. It's a great milestone."

"Really?" A tear spilled over and ran down all the way to her neck. Something inside me moved. Despite the hell and pain I put her through during her treatment, this was the first time I'd seen her cry.

"Really," I said. "I thought we should celebrate. I'm actually not working right now. Let's go across the street to the bar. Champagne. My treat."

WHEN SOFIA ASKED what we were celebrating, I looked at Valentina. It was her choice who she wanted to tell—if she wanted to tell anyone at all. Many of my patients who didn't want family around for the treatment didn't tell them unless the treatment failed. I was in awe of Valentina. Not a soul helped her or took care of her, not that I knew of. She had zero support system, but she made it through. It was incredible.

"Six months in remission," Valentina said fiercely. I imagined this was what she looked like after a fight.

"Wow. Congrats!" Sofia said.

"Thanks," Valentina said.

"On the house." Sofia placed two glasses of her best champagne in front of us. "All cancer ass-whipping is rewarded at *La Oficina.*" Then, she turned to attend to her other customers.

Valentina and I looked at each other, and we started giggling as we grabbed the glasses. I was about to raise my glass to make a toast when Dr. Dennis approached the table.

"Dr. Dennis," I said.

"Please, Dr. Ramirez, call me Rory outside of work."

"Okay, then, please call me Carolina." I smiled at him.

"What are we celebrating?" he asked.

I turned to Valentina who was trying to tame her pixie hair back into place. *She is self-conscious all of a sudden,* I thought.

"You want to tell him?" I asked her.

"I, um—" the fierceness with which she'd told Sofia was absent from her voice. "Remission. Six months."

"That's great!" he blurted a little too enthusiastically for my taste.

Dr. Dennis had never been part of her care team. He was present at one of her rounds, from what I remembered, and I asked him for help maybe one other time. I didn't think going over a consent form with her counted as being a part of her care team, but he was teetering on crossing a line. I was sure of it. He was still a doctor, and she was still a patient in the same department.

I couldn't say shit, though. I was in a grey-area myself. Drinking with one's patients wasn't precisely in the hospital's manual, but I couldn't imagine it being okay with the oncology department leadership.

I rarely broke rules. I was too practical. But fuck it. Valentina had no one. She'd hinted at being estranged from her family, and the fact that no one ever visited or accompanied her to any follow-ups made me think she was alone. This was an important milestone to celebrate, and if she had no one, well, damn it, I was going to celebrate with her. To hell with the rules.

"Rory," I said. "Why don't you join us?"

He turned to Valentina, ensuring it was okay with her too. I smiled approvingly at him. Valentina nodded, and he sat across from us.

"Sofia," I called out. "One more, please?" She tipped her chin, and soon after, a third glass of champagne joined the table.

I raised my glass, and they followed suit. "To kicking the shit out of cancer," I said.

"To kicking the shit out of cancer," they both sing-songed after me, and we all took a sip.

Rory had started asking Valentina about a fight she had won prior to getting sick when I heard the buzz of my phone coming from my purse.

"Excuse me," I said, and pulled out the phone.

There was one text waiting to be opened.

Sara: *Can you please come to the emergency room?*

Something wasn't right. I wasn't on call, and this wasn't an official hospital page. There was no reason Sara would be unofficially paging me to the ER. This wasn't for a patient.

I had every intention of standing up and running, but the stone in my stomach pulled my center of gravity down.

Valentina must have noticed because she nudged me. "Is everything okay?"

"I don't know," I said, with my eyes still glued to the text. "I, uh, have to go."

"Sure," Valentina said.

Rory nodded at me, and I felt perfectly comfortable leaving them together.

HER NOSE WAS BUSTED—A bandage covered it from cheek to cheek. I reached for the computer to look at her chart, but the ER doctor rolled the medical computer cart away from my grasp.

"It's okay," Sara said. "She can see my chart."

He nodded and rolled the small cart back toward me.

Sara grinned at me with her eyes closed.

"She's had quite a bit of pain meds," he said. "Someone will come shortly to take her up to X-ray."

"Thank you," I said.

Sara was drifting in and out. When her eyes opened, she would look up at me and grin. I schooled my face. I was too angry, and there was no point in arguing with someone that far gone into their morphine. She would likely not remember this anyway.

I scrolled through the chart to avoid looking at her and landed on the physician's intake note.

```
Patient presents to the emergency room
with blunt force trauma to the nose,
left arm, and ribs. Paramedic
administered morphine on-site due to
patient complaining of severe forearm
pain. X-rays of right forearm and ribs
have been ordered. Social work consult
recommended after patient is admitted.
Awaiting patient transfer to x-ray.
```

I ROLLED the computer cart away from me and sat in the only chair in the small exam room. Sara woke up when the x-ray technician walked in, ready to transport her. I followed them to x-ray and waited outside while they completed her scans. This was where Hector and Chief Stuart found me.

"Is it true?" asked the chief. "We just heard—"

I nodded.

"I'm sorry, Dr. Ramirez. I know she is a close friend," said the chief.

I nodded again. Other than the *thank you* I'd offered the ER doctor, I hadn't said a word to anyone since I saw her.

When I thought of the asshole's name, Brian, a sensation like a thousand tiny snakes slithering through my veins coursed through me. He was a revolting man who did a revolting thing. My fists balled. I wanted to punch something. I'd never punched anything in my life. I am too controlled, and I suddenly understood the allure of Valentina's profession. I never so much as punched a pillow in anger. Yet, here I was, the eternal pacifist, ready to punch something, if not someone.

"Do you know who it was?" Hector asked.

I nodded.

"That's good. I'll call the police," said the chief.

"No," I protested, finding my voice.

"Excuse me?" said the chief.

"You can't take that away from her. Let her be in control of *something*. When the medication wears off, I'll let her tell me what happened. It's up to her if she wants to press charges. Believe me, chief," I added at his expression of horror, "it *kills* me not to call the cops right this second."

"She's right," Hector said. "We can't be the ones to take more power away from her."

I stared at him, surprised he would agree with me. Most men in my life would go in search of the guilty party and serve their own justice. His cool head gave me comfort—a comfort that was a constant recurrence whenever Hector was around.

Think positively, I told myself. She's alive. She likely had some broken bones, but she would live. I hoped this was her rock bottom—the catalyst she needed to leave him once and for all.

"Can you do me a favor?" I asked the two men, and they both nodded.

"Don't be here when she comes out." Before they could protest, I provided the reason. "She will be embarrassed enough as it is. Oh, and Dr. Medina? Do you mind finding me a hospital computer? I want to see the X-rays when they are up."

Both men nodded and left me standing there. Not long after Hector brought me a laptop, Sara was rolled out in her wheelchair. An admitting nurse came to the exam room to process paperwork, and we were taken to a patient room while we awaited Sara's doctor.

It was bizarre entering the hospital via the path patients typically took. There was endless waiting. Empty moments of time in which we, the loved ones, could only worry and imagine the worst.

My work life in this hospital was always rushed. I pushed on from patient to patient and from chart to chart. There was never enough time, and the hours flew by.

Now, a single hour turned into a day. I drummed my fingers on the laptop and refreshed the page every five minutes or so. Finally, the X-rays were available. I looked at the images closely.

She had a *Monteggia* fracture. The ulnar bone was fractured, and the head of the radial bone was dislocated by the elbow joint. Her ribs were only bruised.

A different doctor walked into the room, and he introduced himself as Dr. Morgan. I'd seen him around the hospital and knew he was the chief of ortho, but I rarely interacted with the orthopedic surgeons—all except one. I shared my findings with him to get confirmation.

"You are oncology, right?"

"Yes," I said.

"And how long has it been since your radiology or ortho rotations?"

"A while."

He studied me. "You are spot-on about her fractures. If you ever want to change fields to ortho, we'd be happy to have you."

"Thanks, but I've found my calling." I smiled weakly at him. Any other day, I would have jumped with joy at being on his radar. Already, I was thinking of ways to include the ortho department on future grant proposals, but Sara groaned, and my attention drifted back to her.

"What about her nose?" I asked.

"We'll wait a few days until the swelling goes down, and I'll do another exam. It looks like a minor fracture with no major misalignment, but I'll reassess in three days."

"Thank you, Doctor," I said.

"I'll need consent for surgery to repair the forearm. I'll be back in an hour to chat about it with her when she is more awake."

"No need," I said. "I'm her emergency contact and have power of attorney. I can consent on her behalf."

"Great. I'll have someone bring the consent forms in a bit, and I can do the surgery tonight."

He smiled at me suggestively. I didn't care if he thought Sara and I were a couple. Right now, the only thing on my mind was getting her better and past this, so I didn't correct him.

The fact was that even though Dad and I had adopted Sara into our family as an adult, I still wanted to make it official. One year for my birthday, she gave me legal documents, including power of attorney. It would have seemed morbid to an outsider, but to us, it was a binding contract that made us family —officially.

Finding myself in this situation, I couldn't think of a better birthday gift that I had ever gotten.

SARA'S SURGERY WAS A SUCCESS, and I got to take her home the next day. They'd made two incisions, so she'd end up with two badass scars—the scars of a survivor.

I called Dad and told him what happened.

"*Pedaso de mierda*," said Dad—the man who never cursed. I didn't have the heart to comment about it. He was right. Brian was a piece of shit. But Dad agreed to get my room ready for her. I wanted her safe, and I knew Brian would never show his face at Dad's.

I was helping her out of the car when I heard a *thump* from the driveway next door. I turned, and Ramiro was jogging to us, several grocery bags abandoned on the pavement behind him.

"Is she okay? Let me help you."

"Here, take this." I handed him the duffle bag I had put together with clothes from her apartment. Brian was one lucky slime ball to not have been there when I showed up to get her things. They didn't live together, but Sara's apartment was nicer, so he spent a lot of time there.

Ramiro took the bag and was doing his best trying to help but was unable to grab Sara's arm in a splint. He helped me get her upstairs, and I asked him to leave so I could help her change into pajamas. I gave her two more pain pills and went back downstairs.

"You're back," I said to Ramiro who was pacing in the living room.

"Who was it?" he asked, nostrils flaring. A vein in his forehead made its way to the surface of his skin.

"Why'd you stay away so long?"

"Stop dodging!" he growled.

Ramiro had never grown as close to Sara as I had, but they were still friends, and he treasured her as part of my family. There was no way I was going to tell Ramiro, temperamental fool that he was, anything about the person who had hurt Sara. Not until he calmed down.

"I'm not dodging. I'll tell you, but not until you calm down."

"I'm calm," he said, but he was gritting his teeth, and his jaw was set.

I snorted.

"I am," he repeated.

"First, tell me why you stayed away so long. We missed you—"

"You know why," he said, interrupting me. "Now, *please*, tell me what happened."

"It's not my place, Ramiro. I'll give you the gist, but you'll have to talk with her yourself if you want to know more. Okay?"

"That's fair."

"She's been dating this guy—"

"How come she didn't tell us . . .?" He narrowed his eyes at me as he trailed off on his question. "Wait, *you* knew she was seeing someone?"

I nodded. "Yes. It's been just over six months."

"How come she never told your dad or me?"

"I think she was a bit embarrassed by him. As you can see, he's not a great guy."

He sat down on Dad's enormous recliner. He bowed down and rubbed both hands over his short, military-style buzz-cut.

"He did this to her," he said, but it wasn't a question.

"Yeah."

"His name."

"I can't do that."

"His name, Carolina."

"I can't. Ramiro, don't do anything stupid."

"You want us to all continue to be family . . . even after everything? Families talk, don't they? I want a name."

I sighed. He'd get it out of me, or he'd get it out of Sara, and I couldn't have him go upstairs and try to intimidate her right now.

"Fine. His name is Brian."

"Brian what?"

I shrugged. "I never knew his last name."

"Where does he work?"

"Ramiro—don't. Don't go there."

"Where?" he hissed.

I sighed. "I don't know that he has a real steady job. He sounds like a bit of a deadbeat, but I remember her saying something about him doing maintenance work at an apartment building near the hospital. That's all I know."

He sprang up from the chair and left before I could protest again.

THE NEXT DAY, I went to Dad's to check in on Sara. She was still in my old room, and I knocked softly on the door in case she was sleeping.

"Come in," she said.

She smiled up at me as I walked in. She had removed the bandage from her nose, so the wreckage of her body was exemplified by her face. My jaw clenched at the sight of the deep purple and green nebulas stretching over her nose from cheek to cheek.

"Hi. How are you doing?"

"I'm good," she said, though her words were garbled by something in her mouth. She swallowed the bite. "The splint is super itchy. It's *so* tempting to shove a pencil in there and scratch."

"You know that's a bad idea."

Sara sighed. "I know."

"What are you eating?"

She pulled a box from the other side of the bed and offered it to me like a platter. "You want one?"

I looked down at the box filled with artisan chocolates painted so beautifully it seemed a sin to eat them. "Those are gorgeous," I said.

"I know," said Sara. "I stopped myself from eating them as long as I could. But you know—*chocolate*."

"That was nice of Ramiro," I said.

Sara cocked her head to the side. "Ramiro didn't bring these."

"Oh. Dad, then?" I didn't think Dad would bring Sara something so decadent and fancy. If anything, he would bring her favorite Mexican candy: *Mazapánes*.

She shook her head. "No. Dr. Medina stopped by to check on me. You just missed him." She pointed with her chin to my dresser, where a vase contained a spectacular arrangement of yellow tulips, alien-like purple plants, and tiny little baby pineapples that could fit on the palm of my hand. Next to it sat an enormous card, flipped open to reveal signatures and well-wishes from nearly everyone on the oncology floor.

"Dr. Medina?" It made more sense to me that one of Sara's nurse friends would have dropped off a collective card and flowers. Though the signature chocolates and the extravagance of the selected flowers—*that* had 'Hector' written all over it.

"Yep," she said as she shoved another chocolate in her mouth.

"What did he say?"

"Oh, he asked how I was doing. If I was in any pain. And since your dad was at work, he offered to help if I needed to get up or go anywhere."

"Wow," was all I could say.

Sara eyed me with a glint in her eye. "Yeah," she said. "*Wow*."

There was something so incredibly sweet about him checking in on my friend and trying to cheer her up. He remembered when she had stolen my chocolate. He was observant even about my friends and always thoughtful about what he did.

I snapped out of it. "Well, that was nice of him," I clipped, and changed the subject. "Have you moved from the bed at all, missy?"

"I got up to open the door when he showed up." She shot me a toothy grin half-smeared with chocolate.

I laughed. "That doesn't count," I said.

Sara was wallowing, but two days of it was more than enough. I told her to go for a walk. She needed to get moving and get under the sun a bit. In the meantime, I could get some work done around the house for Dad.

I was mowing Dad's front yard when the familiar black pickup truck pulled into the driveway next door.

I took my earbuds out and stopped the music on my phone so I could say hi to Ramiro. I hadn't seen him since he'd left Dad's after seeing Sara a few days ago. My lips tightened when I heard him slam the door to his truck. He sped to his front door, but not fast enough for me to miss the slight glint of red rolling down one side of his face.

"Ramiro?" I said as I started walking toward him.

"Not now, Caro."

"What did you do?"

"Not now, Caro!" He slammed the front door of his house— like that would stop me.

He groaned when the door creaked open. He was lying on the couch when I walked in. I got close enough to him to see the line of blood starting at his forehead and dripping down to his jaw. It had started to congeal, and some of it was smudged, probably from his attempts to clean it up on the drive back home.

I ran to Dad's to pick up a clean towel and my first aid kit, then went back to Ramiro's house. He didn't protest the second time I entered. I wet the towel and set the supplies on the floor next to the couch where he was still lying, looking at the ceiling.

He didn't wince when I cleaned up the blood. His eyebrow was busted, but he wouldn't need stitches.

"You found him." I wasn't asking.

"I don't know what you are talking about."

It was no coincidence that on learning Sara's boyfriend's name, he'd disappeared for a day and came back home with blood on his face.

"But you should see the other guy," he said, one side of his mouth quirking upward.

"Thank you," I said. I knew he had executed the task I had so wanted to do myself. He wanted to give me plausible deniability in case the little shit pressed charges against him, so I didn't ask him any more questions. I knew he would always protect me—us: Sara and me.

Neither of us told Sara what Ramiro did, but I knew we both had the satisfaction of knowing that justice had been served, whatever happened next.

CHAPTER 12

FREE CLINIC

"What are you doing here?"

The last person I expected to see at the free clinic was Hector.

"I thought I'd volunteer a shift," he said. "Check it out."

"Right."

"I didn't realize the med students run it in conjunction with the hospital."

Hector sat at one of the desks in the shared office. The room was packed with students getting ready for the huddle at the start of the shift. We had an hour before we opened the clinic, and already the waiting room was packed.

I was the lead resident for today, so I called the huddle.

"We have six volunteers tonight, so let's work fast. For those of you who are here for the first time, you will call patients from the waiting room and take them to the conference room— no more than three in the conference room at a time. Refer any emergent patients to the emergency room and triage the rest into the clinic. Our maximum capacity tonight is thirty. Stop triaging once that quota is met and refer them to the emergency room, if necessary."

"So, what do I do?" Hector asked once the medical students had dispersed.

"Oh, Dr. Medina. Sorry. I forgot you were here."

"Thanks," he said dryly, looking hurt, but the corner of his mouth quirked up a bit.

"Sorry. That's not what I meant. I didn't really have time to get you up to speed. There's really not much to do." I clasped my hands together. "We have an assistant updating the board with patients and their room numbers. You and I are basically here to be a prescription pad if the med students need it, and if they have any questions."

"That's it?"

"Mostly. The students will start trickling in here soon. They will each give us a run-down of patient symptoms and their proposed treatment plan. We will have to approve or adjust the treatment and write any prescriptions necessary."

"I don't see the patient?"

"You don't have to unless you want to or would like to ask the patient more questions."

"Got it."

Hector fell into a quick rhythm. It didn't escape my notice that it was the female students who gravitated most toward his counsel instead of mine. They flirted, but he didn't flirt back. He remained professional and respectful the entire time.

Halfway through the shift, Hector and I were talking when one of the newer volunteers approached us.

"Excuse me," she said shyly. I turned to her.

"Yes?"

"I have a twenty-nine-year-old female patient. No complaints, but she needs a prescription for birth control."

"What? She came to the free clinic for birth control? Who triaged her into the clinic?"

The med student flushed red. "I did," she said.

"Okay, you are new, right? Routine preventive and ongoing care needs to be referred to a primary care—"

"I know," she said, interrupting me. "But please, let me explain."

"Go on," I said.

"She doesn't have a primary care physician, and I know the protocol is to refer her to one, but I think this is a special circumstance. The patient is a mother of five and struggling. She is Catholic, and she doesn't want her husband to find out she's taking birth control. She's been saving for a long time to pay out of pocket for an appointment so that it wouldn't show up as a claim on the insurance she shares with her husband."

I nodded at her, encouraging her to go on.

"She scheduled and paid for an appointment with Dr. Tyler Smith."

"No," I gasped. I counted to ten.

She nodded.

"What is it?" Dr. Medina asked, looking between the volunteer and me as we both seethed in silence.

The med student continued. "He said he wasn't comfortable prescribing birth control and sent her on her way. She is devastated and says her family is barely scraping by with the kids they already have. She used up all her savings for that appointment."

Hector stepped in and asked the student to go to her next patient; we would take care of this one.

"What's wrong?" he asked me when she was gone.

"What do you mean?"

"You have murder in your eyes. The only other time I've seen that look was when Sara was hurt."

"Dr. Tyler Smith's philosophy on birth-control is to keep

your legs crossed. He probably told her that too. I'm sure she feels guilty enough as it is without her doctor putting her down."

"Maybe I should speak with her. I don't want you to say something you will regret."

"I've been a doctor a while now, Hector," I said with irritation. "I'm perfectly capable of composing myself."

"Then, you won't mind if I join you. Just to observe."

I couldn't very well argue with my boss again, especially so soon after biting his head off about taking liberties with my trial data, so I let him shadow me during my consult with the patient.

After our introductions, I pulled out my prescription pad. I handed her the prescription and told her to take it to a pharmacy for it to be dispensed. She almost cried with gratitude, as though I was handing her a lifeline.

"Don't see Dr. Smith anymore, okay?"

"I definitely won't," she said, clutching the piece of paper to her chest.

I grabbed the prescription pad again and started writing on it.

"This is my assistant's phone number. Her name is Amanda. When you need a refill, call her. She will arrange a prescription to be sent to any pharmacy you want. No charge."

"Really?" Her eyes glistened with tears as she clutched the prescription.

"Really. I do need you to keep up with your pap smears, though. You think you can get those on schedule with your husband's insurance?"

"Yes. He would have no problem with that. It's cancer prevention, right?"

"That's right. You'll want to get a copy of your results, send them to Amanda, and I will get you prescriptions for as long as you want them. Okay?"

She left, showering Hector and me with words of gratitude, even though he'd not said a word; he was likely waiting for me to say something disparaging about one of our doctors. I didn't give him the satisfaction. Besides, I couldn't do that. There was no law against what that physician had done.

When the last patient left, most of the med students had gone. The new student stayed behind, helping me tidy up the office space. I looked at the badge hanging off her short white coat.

"Dr. Stuart," I said. "Good job today. Keep it up." She must be the chief's granddaughter. He'd mentioned she would be graduating from medical school soon.

She beamed at me and waved goodbye. "Good night."

"Good night."

"I like this place," Hector said.

"Really?" I said, and my brow arched.

"Why does that surprise you?"

"Doesn't seem like you would enjoy being around . . ." I trailed off, unsure of how to remain politically correct.

"Around *what*? Humble people? Poor people? Hardworking people?"

"Yeah . . ."

"Why do you think I'm some pretentious ass on my high horse? I get that I have a bit of an ego, but—"

"A *bit*?" I laughed, and my eyes widened to the size of dinner plates when I realized the sound had escaped against my will.

He shook his head.

"Sure, Dr. Ramirez. I was born with a silver spoon in my mouth and rubbing shoulders with peasants offends me." A tone of irritation laced his voice.

"I'm sorry. I don't know what I'm talking about. Just tired, I guess."

"Apology accepted. Want to make it up to me?" His grin reappeared.

My eyebrows raised all the way to my hairline.

"Get your mind out of the gutter, Carolina. I only meant I need help shopping."

"Shopping?"

"Yeah, shopping. I hate shopping, and my mother is coming to visit next weekend. I need—"

"Furniture?"

"Exactly."

"A table, chairs, linens, towels, pillows? Hell, a second set of dishes?"

He groaned. "I knew there was stuff I hadn't thought of. I need her to be comfortable, and I have no clue about any of that. I've never had to pick stuff out for a house before."

"All right. I'll help you if only because I've never seen a pathetic side to you, and I'm rather amused."

HECTOR WAS amazed when I told him we could order most of the things he needed online and have them delivered. I would still need to go over to his house again to take another look at the spaces and measure to make sure the furniture I selected would fit. He gave me a budget and told me to pick out everything.

"Thanks for agreeing to help," he said as soon as I stepped foot in his home.

"No problem. Consider my assistance your house-warming gift."

"I appreciate that."

I set my laptop on the kitchen island and scrolled through a few online furniture stores. Hector wasn't being much help and gave no indication as to his own personal taste.

"Look," he said. "I really don't care about any of this, but my Mom will. Just pick out what you like. I'm sure she'll love it."

"All right. Tell me a little bit about your Mom's home in Mexico. Anything you remember that might give me an idea as to what she likes?"

"I really don't know, Carolina. I don't pay attention to that kind of stuff."

I pinched the bridge of my nose. This was going to be more difficult than I'd imagined.

"What about your old house before you moved here? What was that like?"

"My wife decorated it. If it made her happy, I was fine with it. But it wasn't really my style—"

"Okay, see, you do have a style!" I said. I was not going to ask him why his wife wasn't decorating *this* house, not even with the opening he offered. *Don't get personal, Carolina. It's none of your business.*

"No. I don't have style, but I can rule out hers. It was very pristine, all white, clear crystal, that kind of thing. I was afraid to touch anything."

"Okay, so practical, durable, and easy to clean. That's a start."

I couldn't resist it any longer, and before I could stop myself, I blurted out, "Why isn't your wife helping you with this?" I clasped my hand to my mouth. "I'm so sorry, I didn't—"

"It's okay." Hector's smile was lopsided now. "I'll tell you about her, but not today. Today is a happy day. Okay?"

"Forget I asked. It's none of my business."

We turned our attention to our task and moved past a subject I could already tell was a sore one. I picked out a console cabinet for the living room, some vases to go on top, and a few framed landscape prints. When I showed them to him, he shrugged. "Do *you* like it?" he asked.

"I do," I said and smiled wide. I'd kill for that kind of furniture.

"Then it's perfect."

We repeated the process for every room in his house, from

his guest room and bathrooms to dining room and dinnerware. He had no opinion on anything, though he did, at one point, say he thought his mother would approve of my taste, and that fueled the rest of the shopping experience.

When we were done, I sat back, pleased with myself. His house was going to look amazing. I hoped his mother agreed when she arrived.

Without a task occupying our collective mental spaces, being alone in his home became awkward. Too intimate in the still, echoey space.

"So, that's everything. You'll have to be here for deliveries. I sent appointments to your calendar."

When I was ready to leave, Hector took my hand in his but kept it there for one second too long. "Thank you, Carolina," he said. "You are really saving me here."

CHAPTER 13

HUMBLE BEGINNINGS

*H*ector was surprised at how much we got done online without having to go to any stores. But I still promised to help him on Saturday morning, after the deliveries all came in, to arrange everything and stage any finishing touches. He didn't have to pick his mom up until six in the evening, so I showed up at ten in the morning to get started.

He was right: he had no idea what to do with any of it. He had given the delivery men completely wrong instructions, making me question if he had been sleepy or drunk while everything was set up.

"Have you no concept of *feng shui*?" I asked him.

"That's the manual on how to arrange furniture, right?"

My nose crinkled at his definition. "Sort of."

"Well, what's wrong?"

"Her bed is facing the door. We can't have that. We need the headboard side of the bed up against the wall with windows, so the feet point toward the solid wall."

Hector burst out laughing.

"Are you making fun of me, Dr. Medina?"

"I'm sorry, I don't understand why it matters, but sure. Let's move the bed. And please, outside of work, let's use our given names."

I nodded. "You didn't wash the new sheets?"

"I was supposed to?"

"Oh. My. God," I said, taking the sheets and asking for his washer and dryer, which, thankfully, he did possess.

Everything was nearly ready by two in the afternoon. We were both a mess, sweaty, disheveled, and out of breath from moving all the furniture.

"You owe me big time," I said.

"I definitely do."

Hector grabbed us two glasses of water, and we sat in the living room around the coffee table. I took the room in, pleased with what I had accomplished.

The results were cozy and understated but with a modern edge. The mahogany console now displaying art and fresh flowers was to die for. The coffee table was dressed with a candle, a tray with a stack of art books, and a sculptural design I thought Hector would like. Knowing little of his tastes, I'd done my best.

"So, what do you think?" I asked.

Hector shrugged. "Do *you* like it?"

"Not this again. It doesn't matter if I like it. I want to know if you do." I almost rolled my eyes at him.

He nodded. "If you like it, then I like it."

Stubborn man.

"By the way," Hector said, changing the subject. "I never got the chance to tell you—I thought what you did for your patient was really nice."

"What are you talking about?"

"I think you called it the Mary?"

I almost spat out the water from my mouth. This entire time, I thought he hadn't seen it. "You saw?"

Hector nodded. "Why do you call it that?"

"Um—Mary was kind of a legend. She was a patient during my first year of residency and Sara's favorite patient. She was an older woman—in her fifties—and she had been a beautician. Whenever she was admitted, and on the days she had the energy, she would go around the oncology floor and give little mini-makeovers to the other patients. It might have been as simple as putting lotion on a patient's hands and giving her a hand massage, all the way to full-blown makeovers.

"Eventually, she started adding music to her rounds. Mostly hip-hop and soul music, but usually the more upbeat variety. The staff really grew to love her."

"I bet," Hector said.

"Yeah. She could completely turn around the outlook of a patient having a rough day."

"She make it?" Hector asked.

My face turned. "No," I admitted. "Breast cancer."

"I'm sorry," Hector said.

"Me too. She was an amazing woman. It's a tribute to her that we keep the tradition going. If we have a patient who is really down, we have a girl's day. It's silly but—"

"Not silly at all. You know as well as I do that patient outlook is a big factor in resilience and is as important as chemotherapy or radiation."

"Yeah, I know. Thank you."

"I've also been meaning to ask you—"

"What?"

"Why do you volunteer at the clinic?" he asked.

"Hector, if I offended you, I'm sorry. I didn't mean to place doubts on your motives for volunteering."

"Relax. That's not why I was asking. It's just . . . you seem overwhelmed by everything you take on."

I pinched the bridge of my nose with joking exasperation. "Okay. Number one, never, and I mean *never,* tell a woman to relax. You will have the opposite outcome—"

"Noted."

"And number two, don't underestimate me. Besides, I only volunteer for a few shifts a month. I can't imagine not doing it."

"But why did you get into it in the first place?"

My gaze drifted away into space as my thoughts turned to many years back. I was starting to realize that as much as I hated talking about my mother, for some reason, Hector always got it out of me.

"My mom. She didn't have insurance before she was diagnosed, so she ignored the symptoms for too long."

"And if she'd had access to a free clinic, things might have been different," Hector finished for me.

I nodded, unsure of what else to say, but the doorbell literally saved me. "You expecting someone?" I asked.

"No. It's probably another shipment of something you ordered for the house."

"Nope. I had you pay out the wazoo for expedited shipping so everything could be here before your mom arrives."

"Thanks for that, by the way," he said wryly.

"Anytime." I grinned after him.

He shook his head as he opened the front door. "*Mami!*" he exclaimed.

I sprang up to my feet and walked over to them. Hector embraced a small woman, barely five-one in height. There was no way that tiny woman had birthed him. If she did, she could run the world one day.

She wore a pink jacket, and her hair was perfectly pinned back into a low bun. I smiled, realizing she wasn't coloring the gray out of her hair. This was a woman I could look up to.

Mother and son froze for the entirety of a minute. Eventually, they broke contact, and he let her inside.

"Hello, Mrs. Medina," I said. She looked at my outstretched hand and pushed it to the side. She caught me by surprise into a hug, and I couldn't help but hug her back. It was hard not to become emotional. I hadn't embraced a mother of any kind in a long time.

"Please," she said in broken English, "call me Marisela."

Once I could see her face, I realized she wore a little bit of makeup, and short, pearl, teardrop earrings. She gave off an air of elegance, but it was understated and subtle. I could only describe her in one word: *Grace*.

"We can switch to Spanish if you'd like," I said in Spanish. After that, all our conversations were in Spanish. It intimidated me a bit. Obviously, she and Hector would speak the proper Spain-derived Spanish of the Mexican elite, while mine would be Mexican *barrio* Spanish—'hood Spanish. I was relieved when neither of them commented on my linguistic shortcomings in our native tongue.

"Who is this?" she asked Hector but didn't move her mother's gaze away from me.

"This is Carolina Ramirez. She is a doctor at the hospital I work at now."

"Oh?" his mom asked as she studied me from shoes to face.

"Yes, Mrs.—I mean, Marisela. Your son is my boss. I helped him get the house ready for your arrival."

She looked back and forth between us, making me shift my weight from one foot to the other.

"*Mamá*," Hector whined. "*I* was going to pick you up from the airport."

"I'm perfectly capable of taking a car," she said.

"*And* you lied to me about what time your flight was coming in."

"Well, how else was I going to manage to get a car? You are too busy. I wasn't going to bother you." She playfully palmed his cheeks twice. "I'm starving," she said. "Let's go out to lunch."

"I'll be heading home," I said. "Marisela, it was so nice to meet you. I hope you enjoy your time in Kansas City."

She turned to me and pinned me with a look of warning. "No. You must join us."

"I can't . . ." I said as I looked down and pulled on the hem of the ratty old workout t-shirt I had worn in preparation for sweating and heavy lifting.

"Oh, you both can go as you are. We aren't going anywhere fancy."

"That's right," Hector said. "Mom loves going to American chain cafés when she's in the states."

"I do," she said. "Please join us."

There was no way out of this lunch. I wasn't supposed to meet his mother. My part of the deal was to help him get ready for her arrival, not to *meet* her. Still, I couldn't stop grinning.

We drove separately so I could make my escape after lunch and give them time to catch up. When we got to the café, Hector ordered our food at the counter. Marisela and I settled in at a corner table with a view of the patio.

"So," she said, "how long have you been working with my son?"

"A few months."

"Is he a good boss?"

"He's okay," I said, surprising myself.

She laughed. "I value honesty."

I smiled at her. Hector brought us our coffee after placing our order. "You two talking about me?" he asked.

"We wouldn't dare," his mom said.

"So," I said. "Where in Mexico do you live?"

"Oaxaca," she said.

I expected Hector to have grown up in Mexico City for some reason. "And do you like it there? I've never been," I said.

"Oh, it's beautiful. Beautiful people and beautiful food. Whenever you want, you have a home there," she said.

"Thank you."

"Do you have any suggestions on things to do while I'm here?" she asked.

"Let's see . . . if you are interested in art, I suggest the Nelson-Atkins Museum. You wouldn't think it of Kansas City, but we have a rather spectacular collection, including a Caravaggio." I didn't know where I pulled that suggestion from. I'd only been to the museum once and only knew about the Caravaggio in the collection because Mandy wouldn't shut up about it. I guess I was trying to impress her.

"I was thinking something more . . . *casual*?" she suggested.

That took me aback. I had always assumed Hector came from money. I expected his mother to be cultured and want to see the more elegant aspects of the city. I certainly didn't expect her to ask for *casual* ideas.

"Um—well, not far from that museum is a beautiful rose garden," I said, hoping she would be satisfied with that answer.

"I love roses," she said with a sparkle to her eye. "Maybe Hector can take me there tomorrow." She looked at her son expectantly.

"Of course, Mom. Whatever you like."

We had a pleasant and superficial conversation the rest of our lunch until Hector had to take a call from one of his residents about a patient. He stepped outside for privacy, leaving me alone with his mother. I didn't feel as uncomfortable as I thought I would.

"Okay, now that we have a minute alone, I'd like to talk with you about Hector," Marisela said, peering out the window to confirm that Hector wasn't yet coming back from his call.

"I'm not sure—"

"I like the way he looks at you," she said.

"What?"

"He hasn't smiled like this in years," she said. "I'd like to thank you for that."

"Oh. Please don't get the wrong impression—"

"Don't worry." She cut me off. "I know you aren't together. But when you haven't seen your son happy for many long years, believe me, you will grasp at anything that brightens his life."

Hadn't been happy for years? What was she talking about?

"You don't know anything about the state of his marriage, do you?" Her eyes narrowed.

I only shook my head. She turned once again to peek out the window, then returned her attention to me. "Hector is too stubborn to let go of the past. I'm sure he hasn't told you."

"Told me what?" I couldn't help asking.

"Oh, a great many things. For example, I don't think he has told you he has been separated from his wife for a couple of years now."

My hands got clammy, and I wiped them on my jeans, grasping at the cool fabric. I wasn't sure Hector would want me to know these profoundly personal details.

Why was Marisela telling me all this? The thought of Hector being available sent my head spinning, but separated or not, he was still married. To me, there wasn't much difference between being separated and being married. Nothing could come from Marisela's revelation.

"I can tell by your reaction that I was right. He hasn't mentioned anything."

"Marisela, I don't know if he'd want me to know—"

"*I* want you to know," she said. "Andrea is a good woman. She knows about you."

"What?" Blood pounded in my ears. How in the hell did his *wife* know about me? If I hadn't been sitting down, I would have lost my balance at Marisela's words. Suddenly, I was joining Marisela in her paranoid checks for Hector outside.

"Don't worry," she said. "She is glad Hector has found someone who makes him happy." Marisela studied me for a moment as I digested her words. "And," she added, "I think she also hopes that his finding someone else means he'll finally agree to the divorce."

I was dazed, and my head swam. Surely, this is what was meant by an out-of-body experience. Not only did his wife know about me, for some reason, but she was discussing me with his mother. This was all too weird.

"Few marriages can make it through the tragedy of losing a child. I'm sure you know what happened."

I nodded, still wordless. I didn't know the details, but I knew their son had died.

"Andrea became very depressed. The poor thing. It's understandable. She ended up drinking and having to go to a rehabilitation center. Don't worry. She's doing much better now. But even before his marriage, my son had led a tough life."

The revelations about Hector were coming in waves, and I was growing uncomfortable at knowing so many details about a life which he clearly wanted to keep private. I had never imagined he'd had a hard life prior to the tragedy of losing his son.

"We were very poor when he was growing up. I'm sure you can imagine, for a poor, brown kid from Mexico to make it as far as he has in life, it took a lot. He's always had to fight. I tell you this because I think it is important for you to understand his character. He doesn't know how to not fight, or how to stop once he's started."

I couldn't believe he had come from nothing. I had always assumed he was from an upper-class Mexican home. I'd convinced myself he'd grown up with a silver spoon in his mouth. Though his mother didn't give many details, I understood that being poor in Mexico was much more dire than being poor in the United States. My heart constricted at the thought of a little boy balancing grade school and work—selling things or stealing things. Did he go hungry? Had they even had basic utilities when he was little? I couldn't have been more wrong about him. He was what he was because he made himself from the ground up. No one handed anything to him. He had every right to be as proud as he was.

"Why are you telling me all this? It really seems very private to Hector."

She cocked her head to the side. "I tell you because he never would."

I nodded again, this time egging her on. She nervously glanced out the window to ensure Hector was still on his call. We had precious little time now.

"Still," Marisela said, "even though her mental health has improved, Andrea could only repair things with Hector at the expense of her sobriety. She is not willing to make that sacrifice, and so Hector has stayed away. At first, he held onto the hope that time would heal their relationship, but Andrea is moving on. Hector needs to also. You understand?"

"I'm not sure," I admitted.

"She's asked him for a divorce many times over the last two years, but he always refuses."

"He still loves her," I said.

"No." Her forehead scrunched up a bit. "He doesn't love her. He will always care about her, but the romantic love they shared is gone. For both of them."

"Then, why won't he give her the divorce she wants?"

"You've met my son, right?" She laughed. "He's got some ego in him. He believes himself to be perfect, and a perfect man wouldn't get a divorce. He won't admit defeat."

"So it's pride?"

She shrugged. "I don't know. I think it's pride but also something more. He took his vows very seriously, Carolina. Even now that he has met you, he is battling himself to let go of his past. The vows he has made to his first wife are still important to him, even if he isn't in love with her anymore. She is also the mother of his only child. He's having a hard time releasing his responsibility for her."

Hector joined us back at the table, and I couldn't ask her any of my million questions.

I had been so wrong about him and what I thought he cared about. I had misjudged him, and I had no right to. Marisela was obvious with her intent. I knew a Mexican mother matchmaker when I saw one. She took one look at me, like Ramiro's mom used to look at me, and decided I was meant for her son.

If Hector was indeed engaged in an internal battle to let go of the past, I couldn't be the one to nudge him in the opposite direction. While I wasn't too concerned about getting married, I knew if I ever did, it would be for life—no matter what. I understood Hector's demons now, and I couldn't stand between him and Andrea, despite what Marisela wanted. This was Hector's life, and he had to live with his own choices.

"I'm taking some time off," he said slowly as if he were trying to get my attention.

I focused on his words. "Okay," I said. "Going anywhere fun?" I sipped on my coffee.

"Yeah. I'll show mom around here for a few days, then I'm taking her to Colorado Springs before she heads back home. I've never been, and I think she would enjoy it."

"Colorado Springs is great," I managed to say.

As we said our goodbyes, Marisela drew me down to her level to embrace me. I returned the hug, and she whispered in my ear. "Give some thought to what I said."

CHAPTER 14

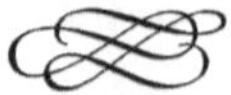

WARPATH

$\mathcal{H}$ector left town shortly after his mother arrived. They wanted to take a short trip, which left me with plenty of time to think about what his Mom had said. There was no doubt Marisela hoped for Hector and me to be something . . . more.

But I couldn't bring myself to cross that line. Separated or not, I couldn't push Hector to betray that golden band around his finger—especially if it still meant something to him.

I can't say I wasn't tempted. A door had been opened for us —Marisela made sure of it—but we couldn't very well step through and forget about the real world.

A married man was still a married man, and I couldn't be budged on that point. I decided then that I wouldn't follow Marisela's counsel. Maybe I'd see her again someday and explain why I continued to stay away.

My thoughts were more traitorous than my intent, however. I daydreamed about two signatures on divorce papers, a parting of ways, and a different sort of relationship between Hector and me. We would devise new research together, discuss patient cases before bed, offer treatment adjustment suggestions. It was a type of future I was willing to envision, unlike any I had ever considered with anyone else from my past.

When Hector finally returned, he went on a rampage. I briefly worried that his mother had told him what we had talked about, but I quickly dismissed the idea. He wasn't only being an ass to me; he was treating everyone at the hospital the same.

No one at work had seen his wrath before. He had been nothing but a cool-headed boss, and he was well-liked in general. He never belittled anyone he was teaching, and he always looked at ways to improve the skills of all the residents under him.

Which is why everyone was taken aback when, after returning from vacation, he was a changed man.

"Are you an idiot?" Hector asked Dr. Dennis.

"Excuse me?" Dr. Dennis asked, his cheeks becoming rosy.

My jaw dropped. *What the hell?*

Hector shoved the tablet into the young doctor's hands.

"Look at it very carefully."

With shaky hands, Dr. Dennis did as instructed.

"Now, read the chart carefully," Hector hissed. "What did you do wrong?"

Dr. Dennis shrugged. "I'm not sure what I should be looking for—"

"He doesn't know what he should be looking for," Hector said, this time mocking Dr. Dennis.

I glanced at the patient, who was luckily heavily medicated, and she didn't stir at the loud voices in her room.

Dr. Keach had been standing next to me, and I clearly heard him snicker, though he tried to cover it up by clearing his throat. I felt horrible for Dr. Dennis who looked like he had shrunk several inches in height. I'm sure he heard Dr. Keach's laugh as well.

"Either you're an idiot, or you're trying to kill her," Hector said.

"No—I, uh," Dr. Dennis started to say, but Hector shoved him to the side as he snatched the syringe from Dr. Dennis's hands before he could administer it into the IV line.

"The dose you ordered is twice as much as the patient needs."

Dr. Dennis reddened. "I was only following the dosing from the night physician."

"And if the night physician ate shit, would you eat shit too?"

"Dr. Medina," I snapped. "We are in a patient's room. Why don't we take this to a conference room or the lounge, perhaps?"

He turned to me with a storm brewing in his glare. The hairs at the back of my neck raised. Something was wrong. Something had happened when he went on that trip. Hector closed his eyes, nostrils flaring, and I knew he was counting to ten. He stormed out of the room.

Taking the resident's tablet, I scanned the patient's chart quickly and suggested the dosage Hector would have prescribed. I knew the way his mind worked that well. While the patient could do with half the ordered dose, what the night physician—and then Dr. Dennis—had ordered wasn't outside protocol restrictions. Neither of them had done anything wrong. "Don't worry, Dr. Dennis. I'm sure this isn't about you," I reassured him, and he nodded.

I ran out of the room, trying to catch up to Hector so I could find out what was going on before he abused any more residents and scared them away from the hospital for good. He entered the physician's lounge, and I followed.

It was lunchtime, and the room was packed. I took a deep breath before approaching him by the refrigerator.

"Who the hell took my lunch?" Hector roared and slammed

the refrigerator shut. All eyes in the lounge turned to him. Shit. This wasn't good.

"Dr. Medina," I said. "Can we please talk in your office?"

"It's not the time, Carolina," he said. "I'm in no mood to talk."

He'd said my first name at work, in front of my peers. My eyes closed for a moment as if I were trying to rewind the last few seconds. I felt the stares as all eyes turned to me.

"Dr. Medina, it's urgent." I pointed out of the room in a gesture for him to lead us outside.

He groaned, but then, as if suddenly becoming aware of all the eyes, he charged out of the room. On my way out, I noticed Dr. Keach. He had followed us and was lingering by the door. As I passed him, he said, "Lover's quarrel?" loud enough for anyone near us to hear.

Fuck off, I thought. "He is having a personal problem," I tried to explain.

"Oh, I'm sure it is *personal,*" he said suggestively.

"Dr. Keach, I don't have the time or the crayons to explain to you what *personal* means." I also spoke loudly enough for people to hear. I left him standing there, stunned, his mouth open.

Shit, I thought as I dashed to Hector's office. Dr. Keach wouldn't forget that public insult so easily—but that was a problem for another day.

I busted into Hector's office, and I was fuming.

He stood facing the window, arms crossed, as he looked onto a view of an autumn Kansas City turning yellow and orange and golden below us.

"What the hell, Hector?"

"I'm sorry," he hissed, but it didn't sound sincere. He didn't turn to face me, either.

"That little stunt you pulled," I said, "was so unprofessional."

"I know," he said, this time resigned. He turned and sat at his desk. He buried his head in his hands with shame. "I know. I'm sorry."

"What is happening?" I asked as I sat in front of him. He sat up and stared me in the eye.

"Carolina, I—I'm having a bad day."

"I was able to deduce that, thank you, Doctor. But you can't call me by my first name at work when you are angry. It looked like we were fighting, and you know the rumors will pick up—"

"Oh, fuck the rumors, Carolina."

Don't lose your temper. I schooled my face. "Dr. Medina, you are a well-established and well-respected physician. *I* am just starting out. I can't just say *fuck the rumors,* as you have so eloquently put it."

"I'm sorry. I know. I really meant it when I said it wasn't a good time to talk; I knew I'd be an ass. I have a temper."

"It's good to know you have flaws."

He smiled, but it was weak on his lips.

"Now, will you please tell me what's happening?"

Hector threw a sizable yellow envelope my way. "Go ahead. Open it. I don't mind."

I pulled the stack of papers out and scanned through the first page.

I took a deep breath. *Oh, no.* "Divorce papers?"

Hector nodded.

"I'm really sorry," I said.

"Yeah, me too. I had a great trip with my mom. I was looking forward to my first day home, ready to get back to work, but instead, my morning started with getting served divorce papers." Hector laughed bitterly.

"I am so sorry," I repeated, feeling stupid. But what else do you say to someone who is utterly devastated?

"Thank you . . . she's been asking me for a divorce for a while now. I've always said no, hoping we could get back to where we were, but it never happened. I guess she got tired of waiting for me to get on board with the separation—went ahead and pulled the trigger on our marriage."

"That sucks, Hector." Part of me meant it; another smaller, meaner part of me didn't.

"Yeah, it does."

"But it doesn't excuse the way you treated that resident."

"I know." He sighed.

"Nor the scene you made. Now, everyone thinks we are—"

"I'll fix it. I promise."

I wiped my clammy hands on my scrub pants. I shouldn't ask, it was none of my business, and yet I had to know. "Are you going to sign?"

His lips pressed together, but then he shook his head. "No. Not without one last-ditch effort to save things."

He was a good man, and he was doing the right thing. Why, then, did it feel like that one year Dad forgot my birthday?

"Well, I need you to do me a favor. Take the day off. Go home. Stop making an ass of yourself."

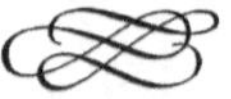

HOT MAN READING

"You have a minute?" I asked as I peeked into Hector's office.

"Sure, come in."

I dropped the thick stack of papers organized in manila folders onto his desk, where they landed with a heavy thud.

Hector blinked at me. "What's this?" he asked.

"The admission questionnaires for the trial. We have ten potential participants, and three are borderline. I'd like to discuss them with you."

He let out a long breath and was likely considering how to get out of this, but he knew he couldn't. This was the part of clinical trials no one liked: Deciding who got in.

"Fine," he said. "Close the door."

We went through the seven I was certain we would allow into the trial, and he agreed on each of them. Then, the hard part began.

"She is so young and has a baby—" I defended my position on one of the potential participants.

"Even if she weren't young or didn't have a baby," Hector argued, "it doesn't change the staging—"

"But it's barely outside the trial criteria—"

"Say that word again?"

I blinked at him. "What word?"

"What you used right after 'barely.'"

I rolled my eyes. "Outside. You want me to say it's outside the trial criteria. I know that Hector, but—"

"Look, I appreciate you wanting to save everyone. I do too. But if we bend the trial criteria, we are skewing the results. And you know in order to change the protocol, we'd have to go through the internal review board again anyway—"

"Yeah. Yeah. I get your point."

It was so frustrating to have someone I knew would benefit from the new treatment protocol but couldn't get it because the trial wasn't yet widely available.

"Hey, thanks for this," I said after I had a moment to process my disappointment. "The trial needs your sternness."

"You can be stern," Hector reassured me.

I scoffed.

"You can," he insisted. "I wasn't always like this. When I first started out, I was just like you. I wanted to put everyone in my trial."

"You did?"

Hector nodded. "I did. But I couldn't, and neither can you."

The second borderline participant we deemed eligible, and I stacked her file with the other seven. And the last one, like the new mom, was deemed ineligible. I shrank deeper and deeper into my doctor's coat as we made those life-altering calls.

Finally, I straightened my spine. We had to do what we had to do. Moping about it wouldn't change a damn thing.

"Can I ask you something?" Hector asked.

"Sure."

"When I first started working here, you were worried that I was mad about you ripping off my trial. Why did you think that?"

I shrugged. I didn't even want to think about Keach right now. "I guess it felt like a big coincidence you came here for this trial."

"Okay, stand up," he said as he stepped around his desk.

"What?"

"Stand up, Ramirez."

This man was acting strangely. "Okay."

We stood about three feet apart looking at each other.

"Research is a dance," Hector said.

What the hell? "A dance?" I asked with trepidation.

He nodded and stepped toward me. He took my hand in his and dropped his free hand to my waist. My shoulder blades tightened. "Hector," I said, "I wasn't kidding before. I don't know how to dance."

"Just humor me."

"Fine."

The hand on my waist pulled me toward him, and he stepped back on the same beat. "One researcher takes a step forward, and the next one takes the lead," he said, then pushed me back with the hand he had in mine. "That doctor spins the research into a twirl, pushing it further . . ." As he said this, Hector lifted our joined hands over our heads and pushed my waist forcefully until I spun around.

But I hadn't been lying when I'd told him I couldn't dance. I almost lost my balance when I landed the spin, and he expertly caught me. I peered at him through my hair—now a mess from the dancing. His eyes darkened as he took my face in, and we stood there, connected for two seconds too many. I wondered if he noticed that I shivered in his arms.

"Everyone can dance," he said, finally letting go of my hand

and waist. "With the right lead," he added, then threw me the cockiest grin I had ever seen.

THE NEXT DAY I called him at his office for a consult.

"What time are you off work?" he asked.

"In an hour. Why?"

"Why don't we go for coffee somewhere and discuss there? Unless the situation is urgent—"

"No. Not urgent. Sure. I know this great place on Westport Road."

I sent him the address, wrapped up everything I had left to do on my shift, and drove to my favorite family-owned café in town.

When I arrived, Hector was already waiting for me. He wore casual attire, and it worked for him. It worked for him really well. His t-shirt clung to his pectoral muscles in the most enticing way. His brow was furrowed as he turned a page on the book in his hands. Hot men reading was my kryptonite, but I shared that dirty little secret with no one. Not even Sara or Sofia knew that I frequently searched through #hotmenreading accounts on social media.

I needed to stop gawking at him, so I took a deep breath and settled on the seat across from his. "Hello," I said cheerily.

Hector grabbed a bookmark from the back of the book and held his place.

"What you reading?" He tilted the book to show me the cover.

"*East of Eden*," I said. "That's a great one. First time?"

"Yeah. I'm halfway through. It's fantastic."

"Since you haven't finished, I'll resist the urge to geek out about it. Don't want to spoil it."

"I appreciate that," Hector said. "Maybe when I'm done?"

"It's a deal."

The mood took a serious turn when I began to discuss a new patient I'd just seen for a second opinion. I knew deep down she was hospice-bound, but I also held out hope Hector would see something I was missing.

"I'm sorry, Carolina. You are right with your original prognosis."

"I knew you were going to say that," I said with less enthusiasm.

Hector's mouth curved into a half-smile. "Then, why'd you ask for the consult if you already knew?"

"I'm a masochist?"

He chuckled.

"Thanks for your input anyway," I said.

"Anytime."

Before leaving, I had to ask him about the fellowship. Since Dr. Keach had brought it up, I hadn't mentioned it to Hector. "Can I ask you something I'm fairly certain I shouldn't be asking?"

"I have a feeling you will no matter what I say."

"You are reviewing the fellowship applications next year, right?"

"That was supposed to be confidential. How did you . . ." Hector's eyes narrowed. "Let me guess. Keach?"

I nodded, a little surprised he guessed who had spilled the beans. Had *he* told Keach? My stomach churned at the idea of him selecting Dr. Keach over me for the fellowship. If he had, it would make sense for them to have already talked about it. "Um —" I cleared my throat. "How did you know it was Dr. Keach who told me?"

"The chief won't shut up about him. I can only assume he told Dr. Keach, who was so kind as to inform you," he said, his voice heavy with sarcasm.

I let out the breath I'd been holding. "Oh," I said. "Well?"

"Well, what?"

"Am I in the running?"

"You know I can't tell you that," said Hector, but he smiled from ear to ear and peeked at me over his glasses. That was all the reassurance I needed.

"Thanks again. I'll get out of your hair. Let you get back to your Steinbeck."

"You in a hurry?"

"Not really, no." I bit my lip. "But I don't want to impose."

"I enjoy the company, Carolina. It's nice to have someone to talk with outside of work."

"All right, then let me grab another coffee."

Instead, he offered to place the order himself and was back at our table with a smile I was glad to see again.

"Are you doing better—I mean since getting the divorce papers?" I asked him.

"It's sinking in. I'm feeling calmer, at least," he said and sipped his coffee.

"Good." I smiled in a way I hoped came across as encouraging.

"I appreciate you listening."

"Anytime. I'm glad you're giving it one last shot."

Hector's eyes narrowed. "You are?"

"Of course!" I said in a much-too-high pitch. I laughed, but it came out nervous. Could he see right through me? "I'd like to think, though we haven't known each other that long, we are friends—"

"We are friends, Carolina. You've taken my shoes off when I was too drunk—"

I laughed in earnest, remembering his drunken experience. "Well, I want my friends to be happy. And I hope you find your happiness too."

"Oh, I will," he said with a firmness that made my thighs clench under the table.

"So how are you gonna do it?" I asked.

"Do what?"

"Get her back?"

"Don't know. I'll think of something. Why? You have any suggestions?"

I swallowed hard. No. He couldn't ask me this. While it was true that I wanted him to be happy, I wanted no part in the creation of said happiness.

"Actually," he said, "this is perfect. I could use a woman's advice—"

"Hector," I whined, "I'm not sure that's such a good idea."

"I think it's a brilliant idea. Tell me, Carolina, if your husband was trying to get you back after a long time apart, how would you like him to do it?"

No, no, no. This couldn't be happening. The thought of him with another woman, even his wife, went down like cheap tequila; it burned to the core and left a bitter taste on the tongue. I'd rather have a catheter put in than talk about this. Didn't he have buddies he could talk with about this kind of thing?

"Come on." Hector nudged me. "I'm sure what you come up with will be a million times better than any of my ideas. *Please.*"

"You're being pathetic again," I said. "It makes it hard to say no to you."

He grinned again. "I know. You said."

I couldn't find a way to say no without also giving away that my feelings for him were growing. I'd have to play this cool. *You can do this, Caro.* "Fine. What did you have in mind?"

"Expensive roses?"

I shook my head. "Really? That's the best you can do?"

"Yes. That's why I'm consulting an expert."

"Ha-ha," I said in a mocking tone. "You have to think of something big. It's hard to advise because I didn't know you two as a couple. If it's personal, that's better."

"What do you mean?"

I took a deep breath and did my best to steady my voice. "One year when I was little, Mom and Dad had been fighting. I can't remember anymore what the fight was about. Let's just say Dad was in the doghouse for a week. Dad knew who mom's favorite author was, so he got our local bookstore to track down a signed copy.

"When Mom opened the gift, she started crying. I thought she would get mad all over again, but she just kept saying over and over how that author had touched the book she was holding, and now *she* was touching it."

Hector listened intently as I shared the little memory of my parents together. "That's sweet," he said. "But I don't think Andrea is much of a reader."

"You are missing the point. It's not about the gift itself. It was so effective because he knew something so personal about her. Something only he could have managed."

Hector scratched his head, thinking.

"Look, it doesn't even have to be a thing. It can be a place or an experience. Is there a place special to the both of you? Maybe take her there? Whisk her away. Women love being whisked away."

The minute I said it, I regretted every last syllable that had left my mouth. I placed the final nail on the coffin that was my jealousy. *Way to go, Carolina. You managed to make yourself jealous.*

"Maybe I'll do that," Hector said.

I cleared my throat. "Good." I smiled, but it was stiff.

No. Please don't go anywhere with any woman. I could picture them and their perfect bodies clad in swimwear in the Maldives. A romantic getaway for two, all because I couldn't keep my mouth shut.

"Are you okay?" Hector asked. "You look like you're going to be sick."

I smiled tightly at him again. "I'm fine."

CHAPTER 16

IN THE AIR

I called it. I called it and then some. It was hard not to pay any mind to the rumor mill. Sara was back at work, though only allowed to do paperwork until her arm healed. She kept me in the loop of rumors, whether I wanted her to or not.

It was bad. Really bad. I knew she wouldn't exaggerate or embellish. Luckily, Hector reverted to distancing himself from me and only approached me about work. It didn't dissuade the rumors, though. I really did my best to ignore them, but after a few months of nothing changing, I was ready to scream. Or leave.

I couldn't very well quit and leave my patients, but I could do the next best thing. I asked Mandy to clear my schedule for the next four days, and Dr. Stuart was more than happy to give me a few days off since I almost never used any of my vacation time.

The East Coast Oncology Research Annual Conference was

in two days. I hadn't initially planned on attending, but it was the perfect reason to get away. I needed distance from the hospital, from the rumors, and most importantly, from *him*.

I called my assistant.

She picked up on the second ring.

"Mandy?"

"What's up, Dr. Ramirez?"

"Please don't kill me," I said as I winced, even though she couldn't see me through the phone.

"What did you do now?"

"I want to go to the ECOR conference."

"I asked you about that months ago," Mandy whined. "And you said you didn't have the time."

"But you just cleared my schedule."

"I thought you were taking vacation time."

"Well, I need to get away. Can you *try*? I know it's a lot to ask."

I could hear her breath as she slowly let it out on the other end of the line. "Fine. I'll see what I can do, but I'm not making any promises."

"You are the most amazing assistant," I said.

"If you want to compliment me, say I'm the most amazing artist."

"That goes without saying," I said. "Thank you, Mandy."

Everything was booked last minute, but my amazing assistant managed to wrangle me late registration and did some sort of voodoo magic, I was sure, to get me a hotel room in the conference hotel that had been booked up for weeks.

I managed to get a window seat when I boarded the flight. I put my earbuds in, turned on soothing music, and leaned back. I wasn't nervous flying, and the flight would ordinarily put me to sleep. I closed my eyes and tried to relax.

The plane hadn't finished boarding when I felt a tap on my shoulder. "Not taken. Go ahead," I said, assuming they were asking about the seat next to me, but I didn't open my eyes. When the light tap repeated itself, I opened one eye.

"Mother f—," I started to say. I pulled my earbuds out. "What are you doing here?"

Hector blinked at me from the seat next to mine. "I'm going to the conference. What are *you* doing here?"

"I was trying to get away from you," I joked.

"Great minds?" he offered.

"More like fools seldom differ."

"Oh, I don't know. This could be fun."

"You realize I've been trying to get rid of the rumors. When everyone realizes we took the same days off, and if it gets back to anyone we were at the conference together—"

"I know, Carolina. I've been keeping my distance—"

"Yeah, I've noticed."

He looked at me, and his brows drew into a frown. "I thought it's what you wanted."

"It was—is, but now—"

"It wasn't intentional. I didn't know you were coming."

"I can't blame you for that. *I* didn't know I was coming until a few days ago."

"Let's make the best of it then, no?"

I nodded.

I could kill Mandy for putting us on the same flight to Boston, though I knew she hadn't done it on purpose. Or had she? If she had talked to Hector's assistant to coordinate flights, I was going to have to get a different research assistant.

And yet, as bad an idea as a trip together was, I found myself having to push down a small excitement that was building in my chest.

❧

THE FIRST PRESENTATION started at seven in the morning, so most attendees arrived the night before the conference officially kicked off. Hector and I took a taxi together and were at the hotel by six in the evening.

Once in the elevator, after checking in, Hector asked me to dinner.

"I'm not sure that's such a good idea."

"Just as colleagues. You once wanted me to be your mentor. You are supposed to mingle at these things. It's kind of the point."

"I don't know."

"There will be no better time. Away from the hospital—in another city."

He had a point. To a great extent, I had let the rumors rob me of the one thing I did want from Hector Medina: his brain. Everything went sideways, and the opportunity of a lifetime dangled in front of me like a carrot I knew I would never be able to reach. "All right," I agreed with reluctance.

We agreed to freshen up after our flight, and I met him at the hotel's restaurant an hour later.

I looked the menu over and was happy the prices weren't too outrageous.

"Would you like to hear the specials tonight?" our waiter asked as he approached our table.

"No, thank you," Hector said. He ordered a glass of red wine, and I didn't miss his glare over the rim of his glasses when I ordered only water.

After ordering—he steak and greens, and I shrimp pasta—we settled into the evening, more relaxed than I would have imagined.

He smiled at me, encouraging me to lead the conversation. "Why didn't you correct me whenever I assumed you grew up rich?" I asked.

"Ah. I was wondering when this would come up."

"Your mother—"

"She didn't say anything to me, by the way, about what you two spoke about. She wouldn't do that. That said, I know my mother. I can guess what she had to say to you."

"Hector, I wasn't trying to pry into your personal life. I—"

"I know. No need to apologize." He smiled, and there was nothing but truth in his eyes, so I relaxed a bit. "But to answer your question, I didn't think it was important."

"It's not, but I've said things, insensitive things—"

"Don't worry. I think intent is important." He grinned, throwing my words back at me.

"I'm afraid my intent wasn't very virtuous. I was trying to take a jab, and I'm sorry for that. The truth is, even if you *had* come from money, I shouldn't have acted that way, regardless."

"All is forgiven."

"Would you like to have lunch tomorrow?" I asked. I was enjoying our conversation tonight.

Hector cleared his throat. "I, um—can't . . . I, uh, have lunch plans."

I took a sip of my water, wishing it was wine. "Oh?"

"Andrea is in town for work. We agreed to meet over lunch."

"I see," I said, but my stomach twisted into knots. "That's good. Baby steps." I did my best to smile. Was this him whisking her away like I suggested? If it was, it was a sorry excuse for a romantic trip.

"Yeah. If I'm honest, I'm a little nervous," he said.

"Has it been that long?"

"I haven't seen her in over a year."

I blinked. Over a year? I thought it had been months, not an entire year. "I'm sure it'll be fine," I said and was desperate for the conversation to go anywhere else. I didn't need to hear any details about him and Andrea together. My poor heart couldn't take it.

Once our dinner arrived, the conversation relaxed into a

more leisurely pace, allowing me to take a breath after Hector's revelation.

"So tell me about home."

"What about it?"

"Growing up in Oaxaca. What was it like?"

He put his fork down and leaned back in his chair. He grabbed for his glass of wine, buying time.

"It's not something I like thinking about much. My only connection to the city is my mother, and she refuses to leave. It's a beautiful city, and she loves it. I understand her; her family and friends are all there. But for me—I have only bad memories."

"Forget I asked."

"No—it's okay. Let's see. My father left us when I was six. Wish he had done it sooner so I wouldn't have the vague memories I have of him. My mother struggled to support us. She had little help from my grandparents because they weren't much better off."

"What did she do?"

"What she knew how to do. She's a great cook, so she put a few pesos together and started a little food stand. She sold *memelas* because they were cheap to make. With that, she was able to provide for us. It was a humble start, but I'm glad for it."

"Why are you glad you grew up like that?"

"I don't think I'd be the person I am today if I hadn't. I know I can take myself too seriously at times, and Mom reminds me all the time that I fancy myself perfect."

"Yeah, she might have mentioned it," I said with a grin.

"I don't doubt it. That attitude of mine was probably what you were picking up on when you made those assumptions about me. But if you can imagine, think about what an arrogant bastard I am now. Then imagine how much worse that would be if I had started off in life as you assumed."

"The monstrosity," I gasped.

He threw his head back with laughter. "Indeed."

He was true to his word. The remainder of the meal was very polite, and no lines were crossed. I was pleased to see him not fighting me when I wanted to split the check with him. I wanted no room to interpret this dinner as anything other than a meal between colleagues.

I was taken aback when he exited the elevator on my floor.

"What are you doing? This isn't your floor."

"I'm walking you to your room."

"That's really not necessary."

"I don't mind," he said. Either he was oblivious to my discomfort or intentionally ignoring it.

I opened the door to my room and turned to stretch my hand out to shake his. He looked at my hand for one beat, then two. He grabbed it, finally, but didn't let go.

"Carolina—"

"Hector, don't."

"I'm trying not to." He stepped closer to me, my hand still in his.

"You're not doing a great job at it," I said, my voice breathy.

"Then you know how much I'm hating this. I hate not being in control." His voice deepened, and there was a hoarseness to it now.

I tried pulling my hand away from his grasp, but he was too strong. "Just one minute," he pleaded. "I lose all control with you. Why do you do this to me?"

"I'm not doing anything."

"You are doing it by existing."

"We really shouldn't—" I started to say, but I leaned into his personal space as much as he was invading mine.

"No, we shouldn't," he said. He closed the remaining distance between us. His hand came up to the side of my face. He pushed back a strand of my hair and carefully tucked it behind my ear. His hand then lingered on my cheek, his thumb hovering near the corner of my mouth. My chest heaved when he looked at my lips; a hunger burned in his dilated pupils.

This was a moment that could change my life if I let it. It felt very much like the night that I picked him up from the bar, but it couldn't be more different. He was sober, so there was no questioning what I found in his eyes, or what story his body told me, those muscles taut as he held himself back, his brows knitted together in pain—the pain of restraint.

We stood in the threshold of my hotel room, and he awaited the answer to the question his body was asking. He was charged like a wire, but ever the gentleman, wouldn't step a foot in my room if I didn't ask him to.

My body reacted to him too. How could it not? He let go of my hand and brought his second hand to the other side of my face. He was pleading now, and the skin on my arms broke into goosebumps at his touch.

I grabbed his hands and pulled them off my face. "I can't," I said panting.

Rejecting him wasn't what my heart wanted, but like always, my head won over. "I want to. I really want to," I reassured him as if the reaction in my body hadn't already told him that. "But I can't. There's work to think about. I can be fired if we start anything, but I wouldn't do that anyway. Not while you're married, even if you are separated. And then there's . . ."

"What?" he asked.

"Your wife, Hector. You're going to see her tomorrow."

"I know," he hissed then took a step back.

"You wanted to try with her again, remember?"

His jaw was set now, and a muscle clicked over one side of his jaw. "Damn it, Carolina, I hate myself. I feel like I'm failing."

"You aren't failing."

"I am. I'm failing myself, and I'm failing you. I promise I'll try harder."

I wanted to reach out to him, to touch him and reassure him

he wasn't failing. I wanted to ease the look of pain evident on his face, but I could only nod.

"I won't try to touch you again. I promise." It was the last thing he said before walking away from me. It was a vow that hurt more deeply than I could have imagined because now I knew.

Hector Medina was a man who kept his vows.

CHAPTER 17

UNDER FIRE

*A*fter the closing remarks of the conference, Hector and I left for the airport. Not surprisingly, he was returning on the same flight. It would be hard not to suspect this was intentional, but really, how many afternoon flights from Boston to Kansas City could there be? I let it go. There was no point in bringing it up now, not after our conversation that first night.

Hector never offered any information on the lunch with his wife or if anything came of it, and I'd be damned if I asked him, so I tried to concentrate on work. In the waiting area for our flight, I decided to check my email. I was excited to open the messages waiting in my inbox, ready to dive into work, and grateful for the distraction, but it all changed as I read them one by one.

"What's wrong?" Hector asked, no doubt seeing the concern plain on my face.

"This can't be right." I scrolled to the next email and the next, but they all said the same thing.

"What is it? You're starting to scare me."

I placed my phone in my pocket and looked up at him. "They all said no."

"Who? No to what?"

"My follow-up grant. The doctors at Heartland Metro, who I invited to sign on to the follow-up grant for the trial, all said no. I shared the preliminary data report to hook them in, and I pitched some ideas for what might be included in the proposal."

"Okay . . ."

"They all said no. Every doctor I invited to participate in the next trial." I let out a breath that shrank me like a deflated mylar balloon.

"What? All of them?"

I nodded. "Well, the physicians at the hospitals administering the current trial in California, Texas, and New York all said yes. But every doctor I contacted at Heartland Metro said no."

"How many?"

"Six. I re-invited the four on the trial now, plus two more. I wanted to add a psychological support component to the next trial, so I invited two of our top-rated psychologists as well."

Hector's jaw clenched. "Those sons of bitches."

"What could this be about, Hector? Doctors usually jump at a chance to be included in a project like this. I figured with you involved, it was an easy sell. I'd understand if one, or even two said no—especially if they were over-burdened with other projects. But *all six?* Something is off here."

"Don't worry. We'll figure it out when we get back."

We didn't have the opportunity to investigate, however, because, on our first day back, I was called into Chief Stuart's office. When I arrived, Hector was already in one of two chairs in front of the chief's desk.

"Dr. Ramirez, please take a seat."

"What is this about?" I asked.

"We'll get to that," Chief Stuart said.

"How was the conference?" he asked. "I wanted to go but couldn't make it work with my schedule."

He looked between Hector and me, and it wasn't clear to whom he had directed the question. *Shit,* I thought. He knew we had been there together. When we didn't respond, he smiled.

"Hector asked for the time off for the conference several months ago. When you asked, Carolina, I didn't put two and two together."

I nodded, and he continued. "We have a problem. I've been ignoring the rumors, but it's getting harder to—"

"Chief," Hector said, jumping in. "You have my word that the rumors are unfounded. We have done nothing that we would be ashamed of. Our relationship is purely professional."

Well, it was mostly true.

The chief turned to me, and I winced.

"Dr. Ramirez, do you have anything to add?"

"Yes, um—" Damn it, I felt like a kid in the principal's office, and all my confidence ran out the window. I cleared my throat. "I think the rumors stem from some professional jealousies. It hasn't always been easy since I got the trial funded. But I view Dr. Medina as nothing other than a mentor. I respect him, and I wouldn't dishonor his *wife* or their marriage by entering into any type of relationship that wasn't professional." And that was nothing but pure truth. I could see Hector from my peripheral vision as he turned to face me.

"Well," said the chief, "if it were all still rumors, eventually they would die down when everyone realized they were unfounded. But now, we have a bigger problem. We've received an official complaint through Human Resources."

"About me?" I asked.

"About Dr. Medina's preferential treatment of you due to an inappropriate relationship. This is why we have a hospital policy against superiors and subordinates dating."

"We are not dating. Who made the complaint?" I clipped.

"That is confidential," Chief Stuart said.

"It was Keach, wasn't it?"

"Complaints are anonymous." The chief leaned back in his chair. "But if it *was* Dr. Keach, I wouldn't be happy about it if I were you, Dr. Ramirez." He raised an eyebrow in warning. "This competition you two have going has got to stop. I realize the fellowship is prestigious and highly competitive, but that is no reason to act out. It will only ruin your chances."

"I am not competing with him. With all due respect, sir, all I'm trying to do is the best work I can, which I can do here or as an attending elsewhere."

Chief Stuart looked flustered, and he straightened up in his chair. "No one is going anywhere," he said.

Now that I was bringing in the big research dollars, Dr. Stuart couldn't afford to lose me. He would also be hesitant to let go of the Keachs' generous donations to the hospital. The chief had a choice to make, and I needed to make that clear.

"Things aren't getting easier for me, Chief. This will get back to you, so you better hear it from me. Physicians are taking sides. Every doctor I invited to participate in my follow-up trial said no. That has Dr. Keach's name written all over it. What do you have to say about that?"

"I'll talk with them," he said.

And I knew he would. He wouldn't lose out on the potential of millions of dollars in research funding for a petty little man who didn't have the chops to let his skills speak for him.

"You do that, Chief," I spat and stormed out of his office. I couldn't believe I had just spoken to the chief like that.

I ran to the stairwell; I needed a minute. I was great at keeping my shit together in front of the chief, but I was at a crossroads. How I handled this situation could make or break my career. It was such a delicate problem. One wrong word. One false accusation—and I could lose everything I'd worked for.

I sat in the stairwell, letting out the first tears I would ever shed on the clock during my professional career. They tasted bitter, and I resented them immediately. I wasn't that *girl*—one shaken up by a boy's club. This wasn't *me*—crying in a stairwell because of some rumors.

The rumors. The rumors that were this close to ending my career. My dreams. No. I wiped the tears away and straightened my light-blue scrub top. Even if it ended here, I would succeed elsewhere.

The door to the stairwell burst open, and Hector descended the stairs toward me. I was hoping there was no redness in my eyes or nose, but when his eyes softened, I knew the traitorous signs of tears were there.

"Carolina."

"No!" I hissed, and he stopped in his tracks. I looked up at him from several steps below. "From now on, it's *Dr. Ramirez* and *only* Dr. Ramirez. You will not address me directly. If you need to work out schedules, have your secretary talk with my RA. If you need to discuss a patient, reach out via email. The next grant proposal we can work on via email as well—"

"Carolina—" He closed his mouth when my glare snapped up to him at the sound of my name.

"No. You will not talk with me. You will pick a seat on the opposite side of the table in conference rooms, and as far away as possible at any presentations we may be attending at the same time."

My eyes stung when I saw him swallow hard, and his Adam's apple bobbed. But I had to continue. "If you get drunk, you will get a taxi; you will not call me. And if you see me in the hallway, do not say hello."

He looked like I had stabbed him in the gut.

"I'm sorry," I said. "I'm trying to fix this. I can't lose my career over something that isn't even happening."

He nodded.

And he followed my every order faithfully.
For two years.
The longest two years of my life.

TWO YEARS LATER

CHAPTER 18

"You know they're calling you 'Flash,' right?" Mandy said as she tried to catch up to me.

"What?"

"You need to slow down—"

"Can't. I've had a long shift, and I have to finish charting before I can catch a little shuteye—"

"Carolina!" Mandy snapped, and I halted at her tone.

"*What?*"

"Here." She pushed a tablet toward me. "You haven't checked your email today."

"I'll do it later—"

"No. Trust me. You'll do it now."

I took the tablet again, this time willingly. I let out a breath. I was so tired, and all I wanted to do was go home. But then I saw the email she had already opened for me. It was the statistical report to phase two of my trial that concluded year three. I read and reread the summary in the body of the email. I looked up at her.

"This can't be right."

"It is!" Mandy clasped her hands and bounced in front of me.

I shook my head. I must have read wrong. I read the email a third, then a fourth time. No. I hadn't read wrong. My breath was coming in shorter, more rapid bursts. My pulse quickened in excitement as I realized what these results could mean. When I met Mandy's gaze once more, she was smiling ear-to-ear, and her eyes were a little misty.

"Thanks, Mandy," I said in a near whisper, and I broke into a soft jog.

I had to tell him. He had to know.

Over the last two years, we never saw each other again outside the hospital. No more lunches together or meetings in his office. But now I didn't care. I had to share this excitement with him. Even if the rumors had mostly died down. Even if I had regained the trust of my colleagues and mentors. It didn't matter. This was a mutual success. He deserved his due credit.

I bumped into Sara on the way to Hector's office. Her brows furrowed at seeing me jog.

"Everything okay?" asked Sara.

I made sure she had regained her balance before I kept going. "Yeah! Great! I'll tell you later."

"Okay, Flash!" she called after me.

Huh. I guess they were calling me that.

I didn't care if he was with someone; I barged into his office anyway. He stood behind his chair, hunched over his desk, reading the laptop screen. Luckily, he was alone. At my entrance, he looked up, startled. Then he grinned when he realized it was me.

"Is this right?" he asked, hopeful.

I nodded. "I think so."

"I don't believe it." He looked back to his screen, aghast.

"Sixty-percent increased remission at year three over the standard of care national average. This is unreal." He looked up again and ran his hands through his hair. "Dr. Ramirez." His voice cracked a bit. "This is big. Really big. This will change how the world treats cervical cancer in this age group."

I nodded again. I was still stunned and breathy from my jog to his office.

"Congratulations, Dr. Ramirez!" He stood and spread his arms wide as he approached me. I didn't hesitate to embrace him back. Not even a little bit.

This was the first time we had touched since that time outside my hotel room, but it was entirely different. There was no electricity, no sensuality lacing our words, no hunger between us. It was a sweet hug of congratulations, and, dare I thought it, pride. It was a relief to be with him like this—and have it mean nothing more. He still wore that gold band on his left hand, so it couldn't be anything more.

"I couldn't have done it without you," I said once we parted.

"Sure you could have."

I shook my head. "No. You've helped so much since joining the trial team, but I actually mean your past work. If you hadn't made the strides you did, I wouldn't have thought of this. We wouldn't be here today."

I wasn't imagining that his eyes misted over, not unlike Mandy's only a few moments ago.

"This is all you, Carolina. And I'm sorry, I know I'm not supposed to call you that. Please forgive me this once. I am bursting with pride."

"Thank you."

"So what's next for you?" he asked.

"Well, cure cancer, of course," I said. Everyone always looked at me like I was crazy when I said that. I wasn't delusional; I knew I probably wouldn't be the one person who cured cancer. It would take a cooperative international effort to one day eradicate this disease from our planet, but I said those words like a promise: *I will do my part.*

Hector threw his head back with a laugh. "I don't doubt it. I feel bad for cancer. I think it has met its match."

"I have to go. I have to wrap up a few things and go tell Dad."

"Congratulations, Carolina."

DAD WASN'T at home when I got there. I turned on the television, but I couldn't concentrate on anything. I shut it off and paced the small living room. It was so quiet in the house that I easily heard the sound of tires coming up the driveway, signaling his arrival.

"*Mija*," he said as he entered the front door. "What's wrong?"

"Nothing's wrong."

"Then, why are you here?"

I knew he didn't mean it the way it sounded, but a pang of guilt radiated through my ribcage all the same. I had overworked the last two years, completely neglecting my family and friends. The clinical trial and my patients had consumed me. I had thought of little else. I worked to fill up the hours in such a way that I could not spend a single second of any day thinking about Hector and what we had almost been.

"I'm sorry, Dad," I said. "I know I've been busy, but I have good news."

When I told him the trial results and explained what that meant in non-medical terms, he wept.

My father was a proud man. He was a strong, hardworking, old-school, Mexican man. A man like that didn't cry, and still, he'd let me see him cry exactly twice. There was never any shame in it. The first time was at my mom's funeral, and the second time was at this very moment.

"Really?" He looked up at me with those glistening black

eyes. Wrinkles etched the outside corners of each eye—the echoes of constant smiling.

"Yes, Dad. Really."

He was sitting now, and I knelt before him. I placed my head on his lap like I had when I was a little girl, and he patted my head. I didn't care that his clothes were full of black stains from the garage, or that the smell of grease would end up in my hair.

"*Papi*," I croaked out. "I could have saved her."

It was a hard admission to make. I couldn't look at him. It was irrational—to feel shame at not being able to save her when I had only been a child. The scientific, rational part of my brain assured me it couldn't have been my fault. But my irrational side, the side that sometimes won out in internal battles, the side of my heart, *that side* didn't free me of the shame of failure.

He stroked my hair gently. We wept now, our sobs the only sound in the quiet house.

"I know, *mija*. I know."

"You think she would forgive me?" I asked, even fully understanding how irrational that line of thinking was.

"There is nothing to forgive," he said. "Look at me." He grabbed my chin and pulled my face up to force me into looking at him. I sat back on my heels. "Carolina Isabel Ramirez Fuentes, there is nothing you could have done. You hear me?"

"I know. But if it had been *now*, I could have—" I insisted.

"Yes. But time is stupid that way," he deadpanned. I let out a laugh, but it chortled and caught in all the snot from my ugly-crying. Us Ramirezes—there's a good reason we don't cry often. It's a fucking mess.

"This is what *I do* know," he said. "Your mother would be so incredibly proud of you. Almost as much as I am."

〜

THE ICE over my eyes helped. I pressed the frozen spoons to the skin that had turned into bags overnight. I'd gone home after speaking with Dad and cried myself to sleep. In the morning, I was paying the puffy-eye price. Nothing about crying is attractive.

The phone buzzed on the kitchen counter, and I had to set down one of the spoons to make out the name on the screen.

When Mandy called me, it was usually either really good or really bad.

"Hello?"

"Hey, can you come in?"

"No can do. It's my day off, and I haven't actually taken one in a long time."

"Let me rephrase. You *have to* come in."

I set the other spoon down. "What is it now, Mandy?"

"Dr. Stuart came to find me at the information desk and asked me to call you. He said he needs you in his office ASAP."

Had someone seen Hector hugging me? Were they trying to dig up those long-buried skeletons? It had been two years. This was unbelievable. I was beyond annoyed. I was pissed. I wouldn't let them do this again. I had more leverage, and I didn't have a single thing to lose anymore. Not more than I already lost: the best mentor I'd ever have in my career.

I actually saw the smoke coming out of my nose. "I swear to god, Mandy, if they are trying to bring up this old bullshit again, I'm taking my next trial to another hospital."

"Take me with you?" she asked.

"You got it. Please tell Chief Stuart's secretary I'll need an hour to get there."

Let him wait. I wasn't going to go in there, making demands and taking names, in my pajamas. I would look my best. I put on a pair of dark blue slacks and a crisp white shirt. My hair went up into a slick ponytail, and I put on the brightest red lipstick I could find. I wasn't one for makeup, but if I was quitting my job today, I was going to do it in style.

Three men waited for me—the chief, Hector, and a third I didn't recognize. They all stood when I entered the office.

"Dr. Ramirez, this is Dr. Drake."

"Hello, Dr. Drake." I shook his hand. "Have we met before?"

"No, we haven't, but you may recognize the name. I'm Chief of Oncology at Peak View Metro in California. We have two physicians administering your trial there."

"Is something wrong with the trial?" I asked, my heart lodged in my throat. Why would someone make the trip otherwise?

"Quite the contrary," said the chief. "Dr. Drake got on a flight as soon as his team got the report on phase two of the trial."

"Oh." I pressed my palm to my chest. This was good.

"I'm sorry if we scared you," Hector said, making his presence known once again.

"What can I do for you?" I asked.

"Dr. Drake would like to speak with you," said the chief. "He afforded me the respect of coming to me first before giving you an official offer."

I looked among the three men. They had been discussing me. Hector had a guilty expression on his face, and Dr. Stuart shifted his weight from one leg to the other.

"What's going on?" I asked.

"I wanted to talk with you about your plans when your contract is over here at Heartland Metro," said Dr. Drake.

"I was hoping to continue," I said. "I have something similar in mind for a breast cancer treatment trial. I was also thinking about adding a psychological component—"

"That's great!" Dr. Drake interrupted me. "I'm hoping we can compete with Heartland Metro. I trust you will find our offer more than generous."

The way Dr. Drake's long neck moved slightly when he

talked made me think of a snake. He was tall and slender, and his movements were precise but unnatural. My instincts were to step away from him, but I forced a smile. I'd never willingly work for a man who interrupted a woman mid-sentence simply because he could, but he was giving me leverage with Chief Stuart. The more the chief thought I was interested in going to a top-tier hospital in California, the better.

"Why don't you give Dr. Drake a tour of the hospital?" said the chief. "I'm sure you two have a lot to talk about. I'll submit Heartland's competing offer by the end of the week. Hector, mind staying behind for a bit?"

Dr. Drake and I were dismissed. By the time the tour was over, I had him convinced that I was sincerely interested in the offer. I imagined him slithering his way all the way back to California, thinking he had tempted me.

CHAPTER 19

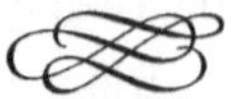

Back to Normal

"You are not seriously thinking about going to Peak View, are you?" Hector caught me between patients at the nurses' station. I blinked at him.

"I'm going to consider *all* offers."

Hector's eyes narrowed. "I'm sure the offers will start pouring in once we publish the first paper on the trial." His tone was frigid, but I could tell the smallest of smiles pulled at one corner of his mouth. It was almost as if he didn't care what hospital I ended up at, so long as it was my choice.

"That would be nice," I said. "But I'm not going to count my chickens. I'm just focused on my work right now."

"Very diplomatic of you," he said.

"That's me: diplomatic Dr. Ramirez."

Hector laughed, and I wondered how we could return to our old comfortable banter so quickly.

The rumors that had circulated about us a few years ago were all but snuffed out. Now, I had leverage with the chief for an attending position. And Hector was clearly still happily married, or he wouldn't be wearing that wedding ring.

So fuck it. I missed my mentor. I missed bouncing ideas off him and brainstorming for future trials. I wasn't going to keep pushing him away—not while he didn't want to remain at arm's length.

Much more quickly than I would have anticipated, everything returned to normal—the normal before we parted ways for the first time.

"This is nice," Hector said.

"What is?"

"Being able to talk with you. I've missed it."

I nodded. "I've missed you too."

His gaze fixed on mine like he couldn't believe I had said that.

"Does this mean we can go back to being friends? Work on the paper together?" he asked.

"I'd like that."

Hector smiled. "I'd also like to catch up. You free for lunch today?"

"Sure. I have a patient at one though, so it'll have to be the cafeteria."

"That's not really what I had in mind, but I'll take it."

We walked through the cafeteria line together, and I did my best to ignore the many eyes that followed us.

When Hector found his way to the hot food line, I pulled him away. "What are you doing?"

"Grabbing my lunch. The sign said it was turkey and mashed potatoes."

"Dr. Medina," I said, fighting back laughter, "have you *ever* eaten the cafeteria food here?"

He shook his head.

"Trust me; you don't ever want to go through the hot food line."

"What do you recommend then?" he asked.

"The cold sandwich station isn't bad, but if you ask me, there is only one thing here worth having."

"Please enlighten me, Dr. Ramirez." He chuckled, and I enjoyed the playfulness that was back.

"Pizza," I said.

We found a table in the cafeteria, and when Hector took a bite of his slice, I waited for his reaction.

"Not bad," he said.

"I told you."

"Yes. You did. So, how have you been, Carolina?"

"Busy," I said, taking a bite of my pizza.

"Yes. I know. I was worried you would burn out. I wanted to check in—"

"But I told you to stay away from me?"

He nodded grimly.

"I'm sorry about that. I'm not sure I handled it the best way I could have, but look on the bright side. It worked. I got my professional respect back, and I've had no issues with doctors joining my grant proposals since."

"I'm glad something good came of it. You aren't worried about being seen with me now?"

I shook my head and swallowed my bite of pizza. "No. I have options now, and it's time for Dr. Stuart to decide who is more valuable to the department."

"Good for you. I'm glad you are realizing your worth."

A flush swept over my face, so I decided to change the subject. "How about you? How have you been?"

Hector sighed. "Not quite as good as you. I was often tempted to ignore your commands and talk with you, so I took a lot of vacation time."

I blinked at him. "You did?"

"It hurts that you didn't notice."

"I was working too much," I admitted.

"I know."

"What did you do with all the time off?"

"I went to the FIHR to check on some projects I handed over before coming here. I also spent some time with my mom in Mexico."

"How is Marisela?" I asked.

"Good, though she can't forgive me for letting you go." He likely saw the shift in mood plain on my face. "I'm sorry. I shouldn't have said that. Won't happen again."

"Will you say hi to her for me?"

"Of course," he said. "I also wanted to ask you about Sara. I've seen her at work, and she seemed well, so I haven't checked in on her again."

"She's doing great. She will be finishing her graduate degree soon."

"And that mess back then. It's done?"

"That *mess* was a man who is not in her life anymore."

"Good," said Hector. It was still the sweetest thing that he worried about my friend. Sara was lucky to have so many people in her corner, even if she didn't realize quite the scope of it.

When we parted ways outside the cafeteria doors, I felt lighter. There was newfound excitement in the renewed possibility of picking the great Hector Medina's brain; with that assurance, nothing could possibly have the power to wipe the grin off my face.

I was wrong.

ALMOST AS IF evil could sense happiness, Dr. Keach got a whiff of our returned working relationship. Two days later, he sat next to me in the hospital auditorium during a grand rounds presentation.

I initially found a seat next to Dr. Bel, whom I liked and respected. Dr. Bel was an orthopedic surgeon, and though we didn't work together much, he had started residency the same year I had. Being a surgeon, though, he usually interacted with the cool kids—the jocks actually known as surgeons—of the hospital. Anyone who says cliques ended with high school is lying through their teeth. They were *everywhere.*

As we waited for the grand rounds presentation to start, I chatted easily with Dr. Bel until Dr. Keach's hot breath graced the side of my neck.

"Dr. Ramirez," Dr. Keach said.

"Dr. Keach." I nodded curtly.

"I hear paradise is back."

"If you mean Peak View was here just two days ago to offer me an attending position in their oncology department, then yes. I'm very happy about it."

Clearly taken aback, Dr. Keach stammered for only a second. His lips thinned, and he suddenly looked uncomfortable in his seat. "That's not what I meant," he clipped.

I shrugged. "No?"

"No. I meant all is well in paradise with you and Dr. Medina."

"If you mean, the results of our trial are more than we could ever have imagined, and the oncology department is still celebrating, then yes. All is well, Dr. Keach. Thanks for your concern."

His nostrils flared, and I thoroughly enjoyed the reaction I got out of him when he failed to get one out of me.

He turned to the doctor sitting on the other side of him and spoke loud enough for everyone in the vicinity to hear. "Not all of us can get into med school and get jobs because of affirmative action."

He went *there.* Dr. Keach freaking went there. When he failed at drumming up false rumors about Hector and me, he reverted to his previous favorite torture device. What he used long before Hector came to Heartland Metro. The line I thought he'd long ago forgotten, like a child with his old toys.

I froze. I didn't want to snap at him and give him the satisfaction he sought. The auditorium was nearly full, and even though everyone around us was engaged in conversation, a scene in the crowd would not go unnoticed.

Dr. Bel's hand drifted to my wrist, resting on the armrest between us, and he squeezed once. I blinked at him, but the motion was only a cause for me to be distracted.

"No, Dr. Keach," Dr. Bel nearly shouted. "Some of us get here on the coattails of our daddies." When Dr. Bel said *daddies* in such an infantilizing way, I almost lost it and couldn't suppress my snort. "And some of us keep our jobs because of the millions our families donate, not because of our talent. It's lucky, don't you think, Dr. Keach, that nepotism is still alive and well?"

Dr. Bel finished his little speech with a grin at me that said *I got you.* If I hadn't known he was happily married, I would have pounced him right then and there. Okay, maybe not right then and there, but soon. Why were all the wonderful men in the world taken?

Thank you, I mouthed to him, and he tipped his chin at me. Luckily, the presentation started soon after that, much too quickly for Dr. Keach to come up with a retort.

This was turning out to be the best week I'd had in a long time.

CHAPTER 20

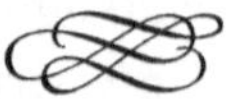

FOREVER CHILD

"I once had a friend who looked like you," said Sofia. "Her name was Sara."

"Ha-ha." Sara rolled her eyes.

I had forced Sara to go out with me to *La Oficina* for a drink. In the two years since that piece of shit had beaten her to a pulp, and she dumped him to the curb, Sara had become a recluse. Her way of putting herself back together was to start her master's program in the evenings while continuing to work full time. I understood that her need to work to a point of exhaustion meant there was no energy left to think and dwell—I'd done the same thing.

It also meant we'd hardly seen each other except for fleeting moments at work. I wasn't serious about leaving Heartland, but if I got the right offer, I might consider it. Now was the time to reconnect with my friends, just in case.

BUT THE UNIVERSE wasn't on my side. Almost as soon as I sat down, my phone dinged with a text from Hector.

Hector: *Do you have a minute? Can you call?*

Me: *I'm actually out with friends.*

Hector: *It's important.*

Me: *One sec. Let me step outside.*

He sounded off when he answered the call.

"Hi," I said.

"Can you come over?"

"Yeah, I'm just across the street at—"

"No. Not the office. My house," he corrected.

"I'm not sure that's the best idea."

"I promise no one will know."

"Is everything okay?"

"No. I need stitches."

His voice was calm. Too calm. "Hector, why do you need stitches?"

"I cut myself picking up some broken glass."

"Go to the emergency room, you big oaf."

He chuckled. "Don't want them to see me like this. I, um, had a few drinks earlier. And it's really not that bad. I'd do it myself if I didn't have to stitch left-handed."

I let out a sigh. "Fine. Put pressure on it until I get there."

"Yes, Doctor," he teased.

WHEN HECTOR OPENED THE DOOR, I couldn't stop the gasp that escaped me. His grey shirt was stained with—something. He wore grey sweatpants, which I'd never, not once, seen him wearing, and he had dark circles under his eyes.

"Thanks for coming," he said and led me to his kitchen. He held a towel firmly around his right hand.

He had been right. The cut was minor and only needed three stitches on the outer hand under his pinky finger line. He was a fool to refuse topical anesthetic, and while I could smell the alcohol on him from earlier in the night, he seemed sober now and would feel every stitch. Not to mention the hand is very sensitive to pain.

We didn't speak as I worked, and I was done quickly. He barely winced. His gaze was far off, miles away and in another time.

When I stood to clean up the supplies and throw out the used cotton balls, I took in the room. Two of the dining room chairs I had helped him pick out were on their backs. The coffee table, too, was upturned, and on the other side of the kitchen island, by the sink, shards of glass glittered on the floor.

"Why don't I clean this up?" I offered.

"Thanks."

Hector went to the living room and laid on the couch while I worked. I tidied up the place and went over to sit on the chair next to him.

He looked at his bandaged hand. "Glad I'm not a surgeon," he said.

"You still need it for other important doctorly things," I teased.

"Yeah . . ."

"What's going on, Hector?"

He looked at me with glassy eyes. "This is a bad day for me. I'm sorry. I'm not at my best."

"Nothing to be sorry about. We all have our bad days."

He nodded. We sat in silence for a while, and it suddenly dawned on me that this was about the same time of year when I had to pick him up drunk from the bar a few years back.

I couldn't remember the exact date, but it was definitely the same week. I'd bet my medical license it was the exact same day.

"What's today, Hector?"

He sat up, pressing his elbows to his thighs. He buried his head in his hands for a few breaths before looking up at me. "It's the worst goddamn day of the year, Carolina. I'm sorry you have to see me like this."

I nodded. Something inside me moved. I wanted to leach this pain from his body and absorb it into my own so he wouldn't feel it—whatever it was.

I moved next to him on the couch now that he was sitting. I placed a reassuring hand on his shoulder.

It was probably the worst thing I could have done to ask him for details, but I had to know. I repeated my question. "What's today, Hector?"

His eyes met mine, and he could no longer contain the sob. "It's my son's birthday," he said. I nodded, swallowing hard as I tried to push down the lump that had formed in my throat.

"He's gone," I said, but it wasn't a question.

"He'd be ten today," he said. "Jake. He was the best thing I have ever done, and he is gone."

My chin quivered at the sight of his pain. "I'm so sorry, Hector," I said, but they felt like the weakest words in the English language.

He patted my hand still on his shoulder. "Me too. Oh, Carolina, you would have loved him."

"I'm sure I would have. Do you want to tell me about him?"

"He was perfect," Hector said. "He didn't care about science or what I did. He said he was going to be a soccer player and play for *Real Madrid* someday. He was a good player too, for a six-year-old."

"I bet he was. What did he look like?"

"Like me. And like Andrea. He had my black, wavy hair and my deep, tanned skin, but he had her body type. All legs and arms—tall and gangly. If you can imagine, the brightest green eyes on that dark skin . . . he was beautiful."

"Perfect," I repeated.

"Perfect."

A long moment of silence followed before he pulled out his phone and handed it to me. On the screen was a school picture of a little boy precisely as he had described him. He was smiling wide—a gap in the center of his mouth from the missing two front teeth.

I smiled. "He was beautiful," I said. He took the phone back and put it in his pocket.

"When he died, Andrea and I . . . well, we couldn't cope. She blamed me, and part of me wants to blame myself too . . ."

"What do you mean?" My brows drew together with concern.

"He wanted to climb a tree. It was so stupid. Kids climb trees all the time."

"They do," I said.

"He wanted to go higher. His mom said no, but I'd always thought she was too over-protective."

My eyes widened with the horror and anticipation of what I knew followed next.

"I grew up with cousins. We were rough. We did dangerous things all the time. We climbed trees. We were boys. So I told him to go ahead. I didn't want him to grow up scared of things."

"Oh, Hector . . ."

"He kept climbing . . . a branch snapped, and when he fell, his neck broke on impact. By the time I got to him, it was too late. In an instant, he was gone."

"I'm so sorry." My tears were down to my chin by the time his story was over.

"I'm a doctor, Carolina. Do you know what that feels like? To be a *doctor* and not be able to help the person you love most in the world? How helpless that is?"

I did know. But this was *his* story. I only nodded.

"I don't blame her for blaming me. Part of me knows it

wasn't my fault, but there is a warring part that blames me as much as she does."

"Hector, it wasn't your fault," I said. "Kids play. There are hundreds of things that could happen to anyone at any time. You can't stop them all."

He smiled weakly at me. "That's why this day is so damn hard on me."

"You are allowed to not be perfect," I whispered. "This may sound weird, but can we try something?"

His eyebrow arched, but he nodded. I moved to the edge of the sofa and patted my lap. "Lay down," I said.

"What?"

"Lay down. Put your head on my lap."

He hesitated.

"We've crossed enough professional lines tonight. What's one more?"

He did as I said, and I stroked his hair. This was the most comforting feeling in the world, what Dad did for me when I was upset.

"That feels nice," he said with a moan.

"Good. Now, why don't you try to get a little shut-eye?"

I startled when Canica jumped on the couch and curled up next to Hector. I remembered Hector saying he hadn't named her. I smiled, thinking of a six-year-old Jake naming his new pet. Hector's eyes drifted closed, and I kept petting his head, sliding my fingers through his salt-and-pepper hair. He was a beautiful specimen sleeping. His features softened the deeper into sleep he went.

When the slightest of snores escaped him, I waited a few minutes then wiggled my way out from under him. Neither he nor Canica stirred. I went upstairs to his room and grabbed a blanket. Bringing it back downstairs, I covered him with it.

A sharp pain lanced through the center of my ribcage, and I

knew it was because he was hurting. I stared for longer than I should have. His pain was breaking me.

I loved him.

I couldn't lie to myself any longer. I was *in* love with him. If I wasn't, his pain wouldn't hurt me this much.

CHAPTER 21

THE BREAKING POINT

*H*ector took the week off both to give his hand time to heal and to get mentally back in the game. Officially, he called the laceration on his hand a 'cooking accident' and I was the only one who knew the truth.

I thought it would feel dirty, to have a secret with him again, but it didn't. It felt natural, as if that were the order of the universe.

We didn't see each other outside of work, either. We worked on writing and revising the paper we were submitting to the medical journal via email, and we texted constantly. At first, it was so I could check up on him, but it turned into a playful and welcome distraction.

Hector: *Just sent you the first revision. Please check.*

Me: *I'm about to see a patient.*

Hector: *This is more important.*

Me: *Nothing is more important than my patients.*

Hector: *Please clear your schedule. We have to publish this before it gets out.*

Me: *I'll get to it.*

Hector: *I'm not above going to the hospital and carrying you over my shoulder to my office.*

Me: *Please don't. Keach will have a field day. I promise before you wake up tomorrow, you will have a second draft.*

Even if I knew it would bring the rumors back, I would be lying if I said I wasn't tempted. The vision of Hector storming into the hospital and picking me up in those strong arms was a welcome one.

A fantasy followed, of me in his office, taken there by force, and thrown on top of his desk—*concentrate, Carolina.* I shook it off and reread my next patient's chart before going into the exam room.

I WAS NEARLY KEELING over with exhaustion, but I managed to address all of Hector's comments on the first draft. I almost cried when I saw all of his edits and comments. I swear, there were more red corrections than my original text. But I got it done.

He didn't receive the email until three in the morning, so I wasn't expecting the texts I got starting an hour later.

Hector: *This is good, Carolina.*

Hector: *Wait, am I allowed to call you Carolina outside of work again? You never said.*

Hector: *Just sent you the second draft.*

Hector: *I'm sorry. I just realized you are probably sleeping.*

Hector: *What are you dreaming about? Tell me when you wake up.*

Hector: *I hated not seeing you this week. Even when we weren't speaking, I at least got to see you from afar.*

I woke up at eight in the morning, ready to meet Sara for the run I promised her. A smile drew on the corner of my lips at the sight of the flurry of messages from Hector.

This was going down a dangerous road. I felt deceptive, somehow, not having told him how I felt about him.

Me: *I dreamt about medicine.*

Hector: *Really?*

Me: *No. You are not privy to my dreams.*

Hector: *Noted.*

Hector: *What am I privy to?*

Me: *Whatever I decide.*

Hector: *I can live with that.*

Hector: *When this is published in a few months, may I take you to dinner to celebrate?*

Blinking, I wiped the sleep from my eyes, not certain I was reading right. This was why I hated texting. There was no additional information provided by his facial expressions or his body language.

Was he being a boss? A mentor? Or was he hinting at a date?

More importantly, did it matter?

No. I decided it didn't. He needed to know how I felt as much as I needed to know why he still wore the wedding ring. Clearly, his wife hadn't returned to his life. Nothing had changed in his house, and there was no way he would have called me over to give him stitches if Andrea was back in his life.

He was in limbo. I wouldn't enter into any sort of romantic relationship with him while he was married, but he deserved to know that I would wait for him until it was indeed over. If he ever did get divorced, something could come of our relationship. I had to find out if he felt the same way.

Us—I was already thinking of *us*. At that moment, I decided the truth had to come out. The paper wouldn't publish for a couple of months. We could use that time to reestablish the friendship I ruined when the rumors started.

Me: *I'd love to go to dinner with you when the paper gets published.*

Hector: *Really?*

Me: *Yes.*

Hector: *What about the rumors?*

Me: *Fuck the rumors.*

IT WAS LIKE CHRISTMAS MORNING. I decided to stay at Dad's house so we could look at the website together. Sara, too, came over to spend the night with me. She startled awake when I sprang up from the bed.

"It's too early." Sara moaned next to me.

"Consider it payback for all the runs you make me do."

"Are we running after?" she asked as she rubbed the sleep from her eyes.

"No. It's my day. Now, get up."

I hurried to get my slippers on and tumbled down the stairs. Dad was already in the kitchen, making coffee. He had placed my laptop on the table, and it was hard-wired to the internet. No Wi-Fi mishaps this morning. He was nothing if not practical, and today practical was precisely what I needed.

"Good morning, *Papi.*"

"*Buenos días.*" He kissed me on the cheek, and I sat in front of the laptop.

"It's not up yet," I said.

"What?" Sara asked. Her eyes half-closed, she extended her arm until Dad placed a coffee mug in her hand.

"The article isn't loaded yet."

I ordered about twenty hard copies of the journal, which would arrive in a few days. Dad requested copies so he could give them out to our extended family. He didn't care if most of them wouldn't know what any of it meant, or the significance of it. He didn't care about any of it. All he wanted to do was brag.

Refreshing the button every ten seconds only increased my anxiety. As if sensing it, Sara stilled my hand.

"Why don't you give it a few minutes?" she said. "Maybe Ramiro would like to be here too."

At her suggestion, I ran to the door, but when I opened it, there he was, groggy and in pajama bottoms and a ribbed tank, but with a smile etched on his lips.

"Morning," Ramiro said.

"Good morning." I kissed him on the cheek. "Dad's got coffee going."

"Great," he grunted.

All three of us sat in front of the monitor. My leg shook under the table.

"Why don't you refresh it again?" Ramiro asked.

"She's done that already," Sara clipped, and Ramiro shot her a stink-eye.

I tried again anyway. The loading icon spun for a few beats longer than last time, and there it was—the article.

"Yes!" Dad yelled with a level of excitement I'd only seen from him during soccer games.

No. Something was wrong. I'd let Hector submit the final draft after his final approval, and surely he had made a mistake.

"What is this?" Sara asked.

There, on the screen before us, the article read: *Changes in Chemoradiation Treatment Protocols for Cervical Cancer in Women Under Thirty.* And listed as Primary Investigator: *Hector Medina, M.D.*

I scanned the list of contributors next. Listed were the physicians from the other hospitals, including Pike View and Heartland Metro. Listed in alphabetical order toward the end of the list: *Carolina Ramirez, M.D.*

It was a mistake. It had to be. Hector wouldn't do this intentionally.

"That piece of shit," Sara said through gritted teeth.

"What's going on?" Dad asked.

"He took credit for the trial," Sara said.

"What?" Dad asked.

"He listed himself as the primary investigator, and Carolina only as a contributor. He is saying it was all his idea," Sara explained to Dad.

"I'm going to kill that piece of shit," Ramiro hissed.

"No. No one is doing anything. I'm sure it was a mistake, and it can be fixed. We should be able to send a correction request to the journal."

"You are defending him?" Ramiro asked. He looked like I had slapped him.

"I don't believe he would do this," I said, pointing at the laptop.

"I hope you're right," said Ramiro. "But I don't think you are." He left after that, likely too angry to look at me again.

Take deep breaths, Carolina. "Okay. Here's what we are going to do. We are not going to panic. Dad, stay put. Please don't say anything about this to *anyone* until I find out what's going on. Sara, drive me to the hospital?"

My friend nodded. She didn't ask why she needed to drive. I was starting to panic despite having only seconds ago advised my family against doing exactly that. If this was on purpose, then I would be furious. My head swam, and there was no way I was going to be able to keep my attention on the road.

We both ran upstairs to change. I grabbed my dirty clothes from the day before, not caring one bit about the state of my appearance.

I found Hector's office empty—as in, he wasn't there, and neither were any of his few personal belongings. The solitary framed photograph of him and his mother was gone, and there wasn't another trace of him. Panic began to swell in my chest.

Next, I tried Chief Stuart's office. His secretary didn't let me inside his office. He was in a meeting, or so she led me to believe.

"That's fine. I'll wait." I sat in a chair in front of her desk, but after twenty minutes, I had to stand. I paced the small hallway in front of his office.

"What time is the meeting supposed to be over?"

She shrugged. "Could run long."

Meeting my ass. I would give him ten more minutes, and then I was going in there. If there was indeed a meeting going on, I would apologize for the interruption. If there wasn't, well, that would only throw more embers into the fire.

When the ten minutes were up, I ran in before the secretary could object.

"Chief," I said, looking around. No one was in the room with him, and he didn't seem to be on a video conference call either.

"Dr. Ramirez?" He looked up from his computer, but he didn't look surprised.

My stomach churned. "I'm sorry for interrupting, Chief, but it's urgent."

He motioned for me to sit in front of him, and I grabbed the chair across from his. "I don't have much time right now, but I can give you a few minutes."

"There has been a mistake with the article I submitted to the journal of medicine."

"Oh?"

I nodded. "Yes. It was uploaded to the website this morning, listing Dr. Medina as the primary investigator."

"I see." Chief Stuart clasped his hands over his belly.

"I was only listed as a contributor, but I was the PI, *not* Dr. Medina."

"Dr. Ramirez, I'm failing to see a problem here."

Was this man kidding me? This was *my* trial. Why would I let another person claim credit for it? I wouldn't. I would never.

"Chief," I said, disbelief etched in my tone, "the way the article published the paper gives Dr. Medina *my* credit. I'm sure it's a mistake. I couldn't find Dr. Medina in his office. I wanted to ask him about it before coming to you." I took a deep breath calming myself down. There had to be a rational explanation for this. "I'm sorry, Chief. I shouldn't have bothered you with this. I guess I just panicked. I'll write to the journal and request a correction—"

"Dr. Ramirez, I'm not sure how to tell you this, but Dr. Medina is gone."

"What?" My glare slashed through the chief.

"His contract was only for the duration of the trial. Now that phase two is done, he's gone back to the FIHR."

I blinked and shook my head. I couldn't have heard right. "Gone?"

He nodded.

As I stood to walk away in a daze, the chief stopped me. "And about that correction," he said. "You won't be submitting that."

I sat back down firmly on the chair. "Excuse me?"

"The more I think about it, the more realize it's better this way."

"With all due respect, Chief, I've spent the last three years of my life on this. It's the trial of a lifetime—"

"We have to think about what's best for the hospital."

"I've conducted research that will save so many lives. How is that not what's best for the hospital?" I hissed, hysterics starting to set in.

"It is great for the hospital. I agree. But you are still unknown in the medical community. Dr. Medina is a household name. The news of a follow-up trial at *our* hospital by *Hector Medina*, well, that would be great publicity for us."

If I could have taken a step back and looked at the bigger picture, I would have seen that it didn't really matter in the grand scheme of things. What mattered was that after publication, treatment protocols across the world would start to change, and lives would be saved.

What didn't square well with me was that something was being stolen from me, and it was something that would've had the potential to open many doors for my career.

It wasn't ambition for money. My ambition was one for knowledge and growth. After this trial, I was thinking of world-renowned oncology centers, hoping to do research there. Those thoughts would now be down the toilet if I were to follow the chief's orders.

"This isn't right. It's *my* trial." I felt like a child whining.

"Being chief isn't easy. I have to think beyond what's best for *one* doctor and think about the department and the hospital. I need to put them first."

"I won't let this happen—" I was going to say I was quitting and making the correction before he cut me off.

"Think carefully about what you are about to say. It will be your word against Dr. Medina's. The hospital will back up Dr. Medina's authorship of the paper. It's no secret he was your mentor and heavily involved in the trial. No one will question his authorship."

It felt like I was walking in slow motion getting back to Sara's car. She was waiting for me at the entrance, where she'd dropped me off earlier.

"Carolina?" she said when I got in the car. "Are you okay?"

I shook my head.

"What's wrong?"

"Hector's gone."

"Gone?"

I nodded. "Yeah. His contract is over. He left. And the chief won't let me correct the paper. Hector gets to keep authorship."

"That can't be right." Sara's nose scrunched up. "Did you talk with Hector?"

"No."

Pulling out my phone from my jeans pocket, I dialed his number. He had to explain himself.

"The number you have dialed is no longer in service. If you feel you have reached—" I hung up and threw my phone into the back seat, not caring if it cracked.

The sounds around me were far off and muffled like I was underwater. "He took my trial, Sara," I said.

When we got back to Dad's house, Sara opened the car door for me and helped me out—a complete reversal from when she had come home from the hospital two years ago. I leaned on her both for balance and for emotional support. Bile started to rise from my empty stomach, but I forced it down.

"What happened?" Dad asked, greeting us eagerly at the door.

"He took it," I said, still in disbelief.

"What did he take?" asked Dad.

"Everything."

PRESENT DAY

SEVEN YEARS AFTER HECTOR'S
DEPARTURE

CHAPTER 22

HOME

On the flight back home from the lecture in California, I didn't sleep as I usually did whenever I was in the air. I couldn't find a comfortable position, and I was left with all that time to think about the encounter with Hector—to think about our past.

I thought about that last week before he left seven years ago. Over the years, I had replayed over and over in my head every last thing he'd said. I pieced together conversations from memory, parsing them for clues as to why he had betrayed me. I did that for years, always coming up empty.

It didn't make sense. The self he presented to me seemed so genuine, it had been inconceivable to believe it was all an act. But as the weeks passed, then the months, and finally the years, without a word from him—I had to admit he had been simply *that* good. A master snake in the grass, and a fucking fantastic actor who had me believing that he actually gave a shit.

What followed in the wake of my destruction was devastating, and he didn't have to deal with it—I did. The humiliation had been somewhat internal. The majority of the hospital wasn't that involved, but those in the oncology department, as well as any of the physicians who knew me personally, all knew what happened.

It wasn't long before the vipers got to work with the gossip. As far as the oncology department was concerned, I was a slut trying to sleep myself to the top. Dr. Medina came out great in that version of the story. He wasn't having any of it and decided to leave after publishing *his* trial in order to get as far away from me as possible.

The worst part of it all was that I was credited with the reason for Heartland Metro losing a rockstar physician. It was a long time, many years, before I regained the trust of my colleagues.

I was lucky that I had enough people in my corner, people who knew my character well. If it weren't for them, I'm not sure I could have stayed at Heartland.

Then, there was Keach and his small group of friends who rarely let me forget what had happened.

It was a pleasure when, four years after the trial was published, Dr. Keach lost a hefty malpractice suit that resulted in the loss of his medical license. The only thing that could have made that moment better was if the demise of his career hadn't come at the cost of his patients' care.

The hospital was forced to take a side publicly. Not wanting negative publicity, Heartland Metro distanced itself from the Keach name and declined ongoing lucrative support from the family. The day the maternity ward took down the Keach name from its front door sign was one of the best days of my life. Dr. Keach was gone, and he wasn't leaving his last name behind to haunt me in the hospital hallways.

I HAD BEEN GONE a week on a small book tour prior to my lecture, so I wasn't surprised that Sara was over for dinner to welcome my return. On any other day, I would have been happy to see her, but now that I had grim news to share, I wasn't so sure I wanted her to be there to witness Dad blow a gasket.

How could I go into my father's home and tell him the ghost of one of the darkest periods in my life was back? He would find out sooner or later. I kept nothing from him.

The house smelled like heaven, but I didn't recognize the aroma as one from Dad's repertoire of recipes.

"Mmm," I moaned. "What did you make, *Papi?*"

"*Mija!*" He turned to me, apron still wrapped around his waist, and hugged me. "*Mole,*" he said. "Are you hungry? I tried to make Sara wait for you, but I couldn't stop the *comelona* of your friend from digging in." Dad pointed at her with the tongs in his hand.

"Hi, Caro," Sara said between bites of what I was sure was her second helping.

"You know how to make *mole?*" I asked Dad.

"I wish," Dad said. "*Mole* is a full-day affair unless you buy the pre-made stuff, which is really just sad. I got this from one of Sofia's friends."

"Who?" I asked. I thought I knew all of her friends, but I didn't think she knew anyone who knew how to make this.

"Ileana. She works at the bar a few days a month."

I thought back and remembered seeing her a few times over the years. Ileana was warm and friendly, and her smile radiated like the sun. It was hard not to feel lighter when you were around her—and this coming from someone who hardly knew her.

"How'd you get *mole* from her?" I asked.

"She doesn't work full time, and mainly works odd jobs. I went to *La Oficina* last Tuesday, and I got to talking to her." Leave it to Dad to make friends with a bartender. "When she mentioned she likes to cook, and I realized she lives pretty close by, I offered to pay her to share a few of her meals with me every week. She agreed to make extra for tonight, for your welcome home dinner. I didn't think she'd make *mole* when I told her it was a special occasion."

It warmed me to think of this woman I hardly knew spending two days making *mole* for my homecoming. I had only been gone a week, so I felt more than special to this stranger. I'd have to thank her when I saw her next.

It wouldn't have been polite to ruin such a perfect dinner with bad news. It could wait until we had finished our meal. My mouth watered when Dad lifted the lid to the pot of chicken smothered in brown sauce. I hadn't had a good *mole* in years. I served myself rice and a healthy helping of the chicken. Dad followed suit, and we both joined Sara at the table, though she was nearly done with her current helping.

"What even is *mole*?" Sara asked as she licked her fingers.

"It's a special dish. I think Puebla is the place to go for *mole*."

"But what's in it? This sauce is delicious."

"Dad, you wanna take this one?"

"Let's see," Dad said and started checking off fingers. "It has four different kinds of dried chilies that are lightly fried, and tomatoes." Sara nodded, and he continued listing ingredients. "Fried peanuts. Fried raisins. Toasted bread crumbs, Toasted sesame seeds—"

"Raisins? *Bread?* In a sauce?" Sara asked as she placed a hand on her stomach. Her face twisted a little, and I urged Dad to go on.

"Yes. It also has lard, cinnamon, sugar, a bunch of spices," when he said *lard* and *cinnamon*, Sara's hand went to cover her mouth. "What else am I missing? Oh, if the cook is really good and it's traditional *mole,* they always burn a tortilla and put the blackened tortilla in the sauce. It's what gives it its color. They also use chicken broth."

"Dad," I said with my eyes on Sara, "you are missing the most important ingredient."

"What?" He looked up at me and scratched his head, thinking. "Oh. Yes! How did I forget the main ingredient? Chocolate!"

Dad's smile was triumphant, and Sara's cheeks filled with air like a blowfish. She ran to the bathroom, and we clearly heard her yell through the door. "*Chocolate?*"

I burst into laughter, and Dad glared at me. "You did that on purpose," he said.

"I couldn't help it. Most people who don't know what *mole* is love it when they try it but can't handle knowing it's chicken in chocolate sauce."

"That wasn't very nice."

"Consider it payback for when I wasn't warned baked beans were sweet, and I spat them out in the school cafeteria."

Sara glared at me when she joined us back at the table. "You didn't have to ruin it for me," she hissed.

"I'm sorry. It was too tempting."

We all burst out laughing then, and I hated to bring down the levity of our dinner. We were all so busy, it was hard to get together like this, but I knew they wouldn't forgive me if I met Hector the next day and didn't tell them about it.

"What's wrong?" asked my perceptive father.

"I have something to tell you."

Both Sara and Dad grew quiet and focused on me. I swallowed. "I saw Hector in California."

Sara's jaw dropped.

"How could you do this?" Dad asked. "After everything he did to you—"

"Dad, I didn't do anything. He showed up at my lecture. I had no idea he was there until the end when he asked a question."

He seemed to relax a little when I said that. I winced as I went on. "He wants to see me tomorrow."

"No, Carolina," he said. "I forbid it."

"I think I'm going to go home now," Sara said. She never liked upsetting my dad. "I'll talk with you later, Caro."

"Yeah. Talk later."

Chicken, I thought.

I started loading the dishwasher as I listened to Dad go on.

"You can't seriously be considering seeing him."

"I am, Dad. I need some answers—"

"After everything—how could you? You broke my heart. It was so bad, Carolina, it's like you weren't there, but *I* was. You were devastated."

I swallowed hard. I knew I'd put Dad through a lot when Hector first departed. The chief had granted me a week off work until things settled down a bit at the hospital. I hadn't cried. It was like I had no feelings, a complete void of any emotion, a perpetual state of being in darkness.

After that, it didn't get much better. I finally snapped out of it enough to get back to work, but then I threw myself into work in an unhealthy way. I became a robot. I'd been hellbent on recuperating my reputation and outdoing my first trial.

In all that, I left Dad to worry. He must have felt so helpless, seeing me go through a depression like that, and then been completely shut out from my life so quickly after.

"I know it was hard, Dad. But it's different now."

"How is it different?"

"*I'm* different now. More experienced. And I have the advantage of knowing what he really is now. I'm not starstruck. I'm the star now."

He smiled weakly. "You are, *pero mija,* I don't understand why you would even entertain the idea of talking to him."

"To be honest, I don't really understand it myself. He said he had a lot to say to me. I guess part of me still wants an explanation, or at the very least an apology, for what he did."

The dishes loaded and the kitchen clean, I turned to look at him. He cocked his head to the side, and his eyes narrowed. "Are you sure that's all it is?" he asked. "Curiosity and a desire for vindication?"

"Yes, Dad. I promise I'll be really careful."

"Tell *him* to be careful. I better not lay eyes on him."

I chuckled. "I'll warn him, Dad."

IN THE MORNING, I was awakened by a call from Sara.

"Does your husband know you are calling me at all hours of the morning?" I groaned into the phone.

"*My husband* is sound asleep upstairs. Don't worry about it."

"Okay," I said.

"So I know your dad already laid it on thick, which is why I decided to leave, but, Caro, you can't be serious."

"You too?"

"Yes, me too."

The truth was, I wasn't sure what I was feeling. Something about Hector made me want to trust him all over again. I couldn't quite put a finger on it. I knew I couldn't be so stupid as to fall for the same trick twice, but there had been something in his eyes. It didn't seem like threat.

"Look," Sara said when I didn't answer again. "I think, when you saw him, you probably stopped thinking straight. I wanted to talk with you before you saw him."

"Okay," I said, sitting up in my bed to fully wake up for this conversation. "Shoot."

"Think clearly, Carolina. Do you remember everything he did?"

"Of course I remember. It was seven years ago, but it is definitely fresh in my mind. I didn't get over it quickly."

"Good. But just in case, let me remind you. First, he tried to seduce you when he was *married*. Next, he let the entire hospital speak about you without defending you *once*. And for his grand *pièce de résistance*, he stole your trial. A trial you had been working on for years. As if *that* weren't enough, he took the credit for *your* trial. He left town, leaving you to deal with the fallout, and Carolina, *the rumors*, they almost destroyed your career."

While she finished her rant, I rubbed my temple. She was giving me a headache. "Trust me," I said. "I haven't forgotten any of it. Dad already covered this last night but thank you for worrying about me."

"You are still seeing him, aren't you?"

"I have to. I can't explain it, but I have to. I need answers."

Sara let out a sigh of resignation. "Fine, but *please* be careful."

"I will. Promise."

"Love you."

"Love you too."

I had to give it to my family. They had really reminded me of my hatred for Hector Medina. My blood was nearly scorching by the time I started to get ready to go see him. He was going to have to hear me out too.

THE TRUTH

Deciding what to wear to a meeting with my nemesis was no easy task. I didn't want to give him the wrong impression by trying too hard, but I also needed to feel confident. In the end, I selected dark denim jeans, a burnt-orange chunky sweater, and topped the outfit off with knee-high brown boots. I left my long waves loose around my shoulders and took a deep breath in front of the mirror. *You got this, Carolina.*

Fall had barely begun to turn the city umber, but the chill was already prominent. Hector had coffee waiting on the table by the time I arrived at the café. He wore a thin, grey sweater that clung to every muscle of his torso—not that I noticed—with jeans and white sneakers.

"Carolina," he said. "Thank you for coming."

"Dr. Medina," I said curtly.

"I can get you a different coffee if you'd like. This one is probably cold."

I'd intentionally shown up twenty minutes late for our meeting. He needed to know who had the upper hand here. I held the cards, and that had to be clear.

"This is fine," I said, without tasting the coffee.

"You are never late," he noted.

"I'm never late when it's something *important*." I took a sip and tried to ignore the smile playing at the corner of his lips. "Dr. Medina, I'm a busy woman. You said you have a lot to say to me, so I suggest you get started." I glared at him.

"Can we start by using first names?"

"No."

He drew his hands up in defense. "Okay. This will do for now."

"What do you want? Why are you here?" I shot each question at him rapid-fire.

"I'm here for you."

I scoffed. Was he trying to pull this same old shit again? He couldn't be *that* stupid.

"I am," he repeated. "I stayed away as long as I could, but I figured it had been long enough."

"Speak clearly. I don't have time for games."

"I'm not trying to play any games. I swear."

"Then, *please,* tell me why you are here."

"I think it's time you heard my side of the story."

"Are you talking about what happened when you were last at Heartland Metro?"

He nodded.

"The right to tell your side of the story passed you by nearly seven years ago, Doctor."

He closed his eyes at my cool tone. "Just as well," he said. "I'd very much like to tell you what happened from my point of view. I owe you that much."

"You have no idea exactly how much you owe me."

Hector leaned back in his chair. He cleaned his glasses once before putting them back on his face and started speaking again.

"I'll get to it then. I submitted the paper *we* worked on after the last edits you sent me. At the time, I didn't realize Chief Stuart had a *personal* relationship with someone from the editorial staff at the medical journal."

"That son of a bitch," I hissed.

Hector nodded again.

"He knew we were submitting the paper soon. He alerted his contact at the journal, and the request to change authorship to me was made without my knowledge."

"Is that supposed to make me feel better, Hector? That you didn't want your name listed as PI? Because it doesn't. You should have requested a correction."

"I couldn't. My hands were tied."

"That's convenient—"

"Please, Carolina. Hear me out. I think you'll be glad you did."

I tried to relax my muscles a bit, but the tense situation made it difficult. "Go on."

"The night before the article would be uploaded to the journal website, I was paged to the hospital. When I got there, they told me to report to the chief's office, and he told me what he had done.

"I told him I would request the correction, but he ordered me not to. He had leverage over me at the time, and my hands were tied. Believe me, Carolina. If I could have fought it, I would have. We had a heated conversation, and I gave him an ultimatum. Either the authorship would be corrected, or I would end my contract at Heartland Metro."

"He told me your contract was over at the conclusion of my trial," I said.

"It wasn't. I had an ongoing contract, but I had the prerogative to end it whenever I wanted. It was one of the perks of being in that position." His ego reared its head.

"Don't get so cocky, Doctor. Don't forget that he chose to keep the authorship in your name instead of keeping you."

"Touché," he said.

"What I don't understand is why did he do it?"

"I have my theories, but it's probably better that you talk with him directly."

"Chief Stuart is no longer at Heartland. He retired a couple of years back."

"Yes, I know. Once he retired, I requested the correction in the journal of medicine."

"That was you?" I asked, my heart quickening in pace. He had fixed it. All this time, I had no idea why, years later, the journal had reached out to me with the correction. Did Hector think I was going to thank him for doing the very least he could have done?

I shrugged. "But I'd still like to hear your theories about why Dr. Stuart did it."

"All right. Do you remember when the results first came in? A doctor from Peak View in California was interested in you?"

"Yes. I remember. I turned their offer down."

"They didn't pull it?"

"No, why?"

"The chief wasn't too happy about the attention you were getting. When Peak View expressed interest, the chief perked up. He couldn't afford to lose you, but he couldn't afford a hefty competing offer while at the same time offering Dr. Keach the fellowship and an attending position."

"He was always going to have to make that choice."

"Yes. But was Heartland's offer even close to Peak View's?"

"Initially, it was, but it was conditional on the retirement of an attending who would leave the spot open."

"Did it change after the article was published?"

"Yes. It went quite a bit down."

"And I bet you had already turned down all other offers, thinking you had the luxury of staying in your hometown."

"He was running out the clock," I said.

"It's all speculation on my part, but I have a feeling that version of events is pretty close to the truth. The only other thing I could come up with was that his relationship with the Keaches was deeper and more twisted than we knew. He clearly wanted to sabotage your chances."

"He sabotaged more than just my chances," I said dryly.

"I'm sure it must have been tough. Carolina, what happened after I left?"

I cupped the mug between my hands, seeking warmth, and narrowed my eyes at him. Here went nothing. "You took my reputation with you," I said. "It took me a long time to gain back the trust of my colleagues, and it was two years before I could get a doctor to sign on to a grant proposal of mine again."

"I'm so sorry. I can't begin to tell you how sorry I am."

"I'm not sure I believe you," I said.

"You are smart. You shouldn't believe me. I wouldn't take my word for it if the situation were reversed."

He let a long silence pass before he spoke again. "Despite all the damage I did, your second trial was another success. I have to admit, I was surprised by the numbers. It's rare to see two back-to-back trials both so highly successful."

"Yeah, well, I had something to prove at that point. You know what the shittiest part of it all is?" I asked him.

"What's that?"

"You remember that supplemental grant proposal we submitted, to keep following up on the patients from the first trial?"

"Yeah, vaguely."

"The grant got funded."

"It did? That's great! Why is that the shittiest part?"

"Because to the world, it was *your* trial, but in reality, I had to deal with all the work involved."

Hector chuckled. "I'm sorry about that. Maybe you'll let me make it up to you one day."

I found myself smiling despite myself. That supplemental grant had actually been a lifesaver—a flotation device in a vast and empty ocean. It had kept me occupied, and I got to stay in touch with my patients. The money awarded with the grant kept my foot inside the door at Heartland when all signs pointed to my termination.

"Can you give me time, Carolina?" he asked.

"Time for what?"

"To show you that I'm telling you the truth. That I've never lied to you, and I never would."

I nodded, without permission from my brain.

"You look the same," he said, changing the subject.

It was a lot to digest, so I didn't halt the change in the conversation's direction.

"Wish I could say the same. You look older," I clipped.

Hector chuckled. "Yeah. I'm an old man. You must forgive me. We old men are stuck in our ways."

I knew he was eleven years my senior. It was a gap that hadn't bothered me back when I was hoping for more from him. Dad had been nine years older than my mother when they met, and they were the happiest couple I'd ever known.

"I'm not sure what you are expecting from me, exactly."

"I expect nothing," he said. "I only hope for time."

I was still suspicious, but my walls began to crumble the more he spoke. Everything he said made sense. I'd come into the café ready to tell him off, and yet here I was, doubting everything I believed I knew about him, and what had happened all those years ago.

"Listen, I have some things to get ready and some errands to run."

"Sure. I don't know how I feel about everything you've said, but I promise to think on it. There are still holes in this story."

"There are," he said. "Would you please have dinner with me on Friday? I'd like to fill in those gaps—start earning your trust back."

"I don't know, Hector. Don't you think it's better to let bygones be bygones?"

"No," he said. "Not when you don't have all the information. Just think about it. Here's my card."

I looked at the simple white card with his name, email, and phone number. The anger flooded back at the memory of that day when I had called him for an explanation, and his phone had been disconnected.

"I wouldn't hold my breath," I said.

"I'll keep trying."

CHAPTER 24

MENTORSHIP

I was picking up my mail when my phone dinged with a message.

Unkown: *Have you given any thought to dinner?*

Hector. Of course he still had my number. I'd never changed it.

Me: *I haven't decided yet.*

Hector: *Tell me nothing of what I said brought up more questions. Please let me complete the story.*

Me: *We'll see.*

He stopped messaging after that. When I got back to my apartment, I scanned through my mail and was surprised to find a hand-written personal letter. My pulse quickened when I saw the name on the upper left corner of the envelope: Andrea Carter.

With trembling hands, I tore open the letter and read, and then read it a second time:

Dear Carolina,

I'm sure you can guess the Andrea writing this letter is also the Andrea who was once married to Hector. I've taken my second husband's last name. I wanted to explain the change.

I know it's strange to receive a letter from me—I can hardly believe I'm writing it at this very moment, but I'm forcing myself to put this in the mailbox because while I may no longer be in love with Hector Medina, I will always cherish him as the father of our child. I still want his happiness.

Marisela has informed me that he is headed back to Kansas City and we can only assume he is trying to get you back. Please don't be mad at Marisela. We only want Hector's happiness, and she has convinced me you are the key.

Can you believe I am trying to wing-man my own ex-husband? I'll have my head examined about it soon.

Hector and I check in on each other on tough dates. Jake's birthday, holidays—that kind of thing. We remember our son together and keep the memory of him alive in our hearts. It's also a time to make sure the other is doing well. The last few times I've spoken with Hector on the phone have left me worried about him. He isn't happy, and now I know that unhappiness has everything to do with the distance and years he's placed between the two of you.

I know seven years is a long time, and I so hope you haven't moved on, because Hector hasn't. If you love him even a fraction of the way he loves you, then please, give him a chance.

If you do end up together like I'm hoping, I promise to never meddle again. And I sincerely hope you'll be okay with our check-ins with each other. Please trust they are all about Jake.

From a new friend,

Andrea Carter.

WHEN ONE DOOR CLOSES, a window opens—somewhere. It may sound contrived and even useless in dire circumstances, but it is also true. I wasn't lying to that university student at my lecture when I told her that there are great female mentors in the field of medicine, even if they are rare. *Extremely* rare.

In my case, I had found a unicorn during Hector's time away.

Dr. Monica Lopez joined Heartland Metro Hospital as the Chief of Cardiothoracic Surgery a year after Hector's departure. She was a female chief, which was rare, and Latina, which was even rarer. I had thanked the gods for sending me another mentor even if she was in another department.

Dr. Lopez understood many of the difficulties all women, and women of color especially, face when trying to enter any male-dominated field. She had been instrumental in helping me get back on track when everything had seemed lost.

She was also a no-bullshit kind of gal, so I knew she would have an unbiased opinion. I had always been grateful to her for also advising me on personal matters.

She agreed to chat between surgeries, but only if I brought food to her office, so I stole some of Dad's leftover chicken mole and rice for lunch.

"Carolina." Dr. Lopez greeted me from behind her desk as I entered her office. She wore light blue hospital scrubs and still had her scrub cap on. In her mid-fifties, Dr. Lopez was a stunning woman. She was short and curvy in all the right places. Her long, rectangular face was perfectly framed by thick, black curls when they weren't pinned back under a scrub cap. I only hoped that I aged half as well as she had. "How was your book tour?" she asked.

"It was good—mostly."

"Uh-oh. I know that look. What happened?"

"No, really, the book tour was great. All the talks went smoothly; I was able to manage my stage fright."

"No, missy, I know you. Something's off."

I handed her the lunch, and her eyes closed when she smelled the opened container. "You didn't cook this."

"No," I admitted.

"I wasn't asking. I *know* you didn't cook this."

I smirked. "No. Dad's friend did. You are safe, Dr. Lopez."

She took a bite and moaned. "You are a lifesaver, Carolina. My last surgery was ten hours long, and I have to go back in with my next patient in two hours."

"I'll keep this short then. I'm sure you'll want to sleep."

"Out with it, then."

"I would like some personal advice."

"Sure," she said between bites.

"Dr. Medina is back in Kansas City," I said.

The fork in her hand stopped mid-air on the way to her mouth. "What?"

I nodded, and she put the fork down so she could study me.

Dr. Lopez knew everything Hector had done—from my perspective. She'd caught some of the rumors when she first came to Heartland and advised me on how to handle them. She was so experienced, and she often made my head spin. I relayed all the information Hector had given me at the café.

"It's plausible," she said and reclaimed the fork to keep eating. "From what I hear, Dr. Stuart's *priorities* left the oncology department in a bit of a disarray. But your new Chief of Oncology should have more insight. Why are you talking to me and not her?"

"I respect her and value her opinion," I said. "But she is my boss; I don't really talk with her about personal stuff."

"I see you still keep up unnecessary walls."

"I'm working on it."

"Fine, so what's the problem now?"

"Hector wants to have dinner tonight. Says he has more to say. I was so angry at him then, I don't know what to do."

"And you don't want to have dinner with him?"

"I didn't, at first, but I still have questions. "

Dr. Lopez chewed as she mulled over everything I had said, so I continued. "Then, there's the fact that his wife sent me a letter."

"What?" She almost spat out the bite she was working on.

"Yeah. It was so strange, Monica. I swear I don't know what to make of it."

"What did it say?"

"She wants me to give Hector a chance."

"That is super weird," she said, but there was a twinkle in her eye, and the corners of her mouth turned upward into a smirk. "But I *like* this woman. She has *cojones*."

I threw my head back with laughter. "Yeah. I guess she does."

"Honestly, Carolina, I don't know why you are here. If you could stop listening to your head for even a second, you'd know what your heart wants."

I sighed and rubbed my temple but said nothing to that, because what could I say? She was right.

"Or are you too proud?" she asked.

"Too proud?"

"Yes. *Too proud.* Don't let an opportunity pass you by due to pride. I'll say it plainly: that would be stupid. Are you too proud to forgive him now that you know he didn't really intend to steal your trial?"

"It's not just that. I didn't have answers for seven years; that's a lot of time to forgive."

"Yes. I see it now. The pride—"

"Oh my god, it's not that—"

"It is, and we both know it. You've always had a chip on your shoulder, trying to prove yourself. I recognize it because it's the very same chip I carried on my shoulder for the first two decades of my career—only I didn't have an amazing mentor to point it out to me and help me shake it off."

"What on earth are you talking about?" I asked. "I don't have a chip."

"Yes, you do. Or are you going to tell me that proving to every man in this hospital that you belong here hasn't been the driving force of your career? Are you going to tell me that anytime someone made a comment about affirmative action being the only possible way you could have become a physician, it didn't bother you because you knew better?"

"I don't see what that has to do with Hector," I said.

"Everything, *amiga*. I saw how hard you worked to regain the respect your name once carried. You had to prove to the world, and more importantly, to yourself, that you could thrive without him. You did such a good job, now you are convincing yourself you don't need him—and before you say anything, no, you don't *need* him for your career to continue to flourish. But what if you *do* need him in your life, even when you don't need him in your career?"

"What are you dancing around, Dr. Lopez?" I asked.

"What if you love him?"

"I did once," I admitted.

"And are you so sure it's gone? Because just you, sitting here, in that chair, agonizing about whether you can believe him again or not, tells me there are still feelings there. If you are so done with him, as you seem to be convincing yourself you are, then it would be easy to dismiss him and move on without a glance backward."

Sometimes I hated this woman and all the sense she made. I narrowed my eyes at her.

"I know you, darling," she said. "And you wouldn't be here if you didn't already know what to do."

"You talk about me like I'm a petulant child throwing a tantrum."

Dr. Lopez placed the lid on the now empty container and handed it to me. "Aren't you?" she asked as she stood and pushed her chair to the side. "Feel free to stay here and think for a while if you'd like. I'm going to an on-call room to get a couple of hours of sleep before my next surgery." Before she closed the door behind her, she spoke once more. "Oh, and Carolina, when you come to your senses, I'd love to meet him."

She shut the door, and I sat there looking out the window. She was right, damn it, and it was so annoying. I knew I wanted to give him another chance to complete the story, but it would be the absolute last chance.

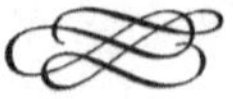

CHAPTER 25

RECOUNTING OF THE DAMAGE

"Fine. I'll go to dinner," I said, holding the phone to my ear. It was Friday afternoon, and I had waited until the last possible moment to agree to see him. We were on my timeline now.

"You won't regret it. I promise," Hector said.

"Where should I meet you?"

"I'll pick you up."

"Okay. Fine."

"Will you be at your apartment, or your dad's?"

"My place, but I live in a different apartment now."

I sent him the new address, and all that was left was to wait for him. It might have been safer to wait for him at Dad's, but I hadn't exactly told Dad about my dinner with Hector yet.

Mainly, he would have to tell me what leverage the chief had had on him then. It didn't escape me that he'd left that part of the conversation out. I hadn't asked him about it, thinking it might be personal, but I had to know—and he'd have to tell me.

"You look great," Hector said as he got out of his car to open the door for me. I hadn't wanted to give him my apartment number—there was still some distrust there—so I told him I'd wait outside.

I may have overdressed in a body-hugging little black dress because he wouldn't tell me where we were going. I decided to err on the side of caution in case we went someplace nice.

"Thank you," I said, purposefully not commenting on his appearance, though he looked handsome as ever in slacks and a button-down burgundy shirt.

My jaw clenched when he parked in front of his house. I was surprised he still lived at the same place he had when he worked at Heartland. Had he kept the house the entire time, or was he merely lucky to rent or re-purchase the same home?

I'd have to ask him later because I was doing everything in my power not to shout at him. I didn't wait for him to open my door; I got out of the car and started walking away from the house as I pulled out my cell to find my car service app. He was insane if he thought I was going to have dinner in *there.*

"Carolina!" he shouted. I heard the rapid footfalls of his jogging behind me. He grabbed my arm. "Where are you going?"

"I'm going home, Hector."

"Why? What's wrong?"

"You can't be *that* stupid," I said. "What made you think I'd have dinner with you at *your house?*"

"Please, just listen. This isn't something nefarious. I brought you here because some of what I have to say, it may make you a bit mad."

My eyes narrowed, but I didn't press the key to call the car yet. "Mad?" I asked.

Hector nodded. "I figured you might enjoy shouting at me or perhaps throwing something. I wanted you to feel comfortable doing that if you wanted to."

"You are not making me feel better about this dinner," I said.

"I'm sorry. I knew you wouldn't like a public scene. Listen, I've cooked, and I have nothing but dinner and your wrath planned for tonight. I promise."

"What did you cook?" I asked, only mildly curious.

"Shrimp *paella*," he said.

"I like *paella*."

"I know." He smiled, and it melted me.

I reluctantly followed him to his place because I was weak, but I kept the car app open should I change my mind.

"I made it earlier today. I'm just going to pop it in the oven for a few minutes to warm up."

I nodded and took a glass of white wine from him. I guessed the no alcohol rule had been abolished—not that he had heavily enforced it before.

When he handed me the glass, I realized for the first time since he'd come back into my life that his wedding ring was gone. I took a sip of the wine, and it was heavenly. It was a *vino verde* with a mineral tone that made me think of the sea.

I took the room in. Nothing had changed in the house since I'd helped him decorate it. So he *had* kept the house. For a brief moment, I wondered if he had somehow remained in Kansas City under the radar but then shook it off. There was no way. He had returned to the FIHR.

"You haven't changed anything," I said.

"No," he called from the kitchen. "I wouldn't. Not unless you wanted to change something."

I cocked my head to the side and studied him as he walked back into the living room. That was a strange thing for him to say. We both sat on the couch and set our wine glasses on the coffee table.

"Okay, Hector. I'm not getting any younger."

"Why don't we have dinner first? It would be a waste if you were too angry to eat, and I worked all day to make this dinner." There was a playfulness in his eyes as he spoke, and I was finding it more and more difficult to school my face into sternness.

Hector set the dinner at the table and played Carla Morrison in the background. The soothing sound of her voice was relaxing, and the mood lifted as we ate and killed the bottle of wine. He plated the *paella* expertly, so it was almost a sin to devour it, but devour it, I did.

"No!" Hector said in disbelief when I briefed him on Dr. Keach's fate.

"Yes. It was one of the best days of my life. Okay, I won't give him that much importance, but easily one of the top twenty."

"I wish I could have been there."

"Me too. I tried to stay away from him, so I didn't actually know what was happening until it was over."

"Still, that must have been a relief."

"It was, though, by the end of his tenure at the hospital, things were already a lot better for me. The new chief is a woman, and I think she recognized his misogyny for what it was."

"I wouldn't be surprised if Dr. Stuart also knew about his misbehavior but looked the other way. Your new chief must not have been willing to put up with it for money."

"You know, I'm a little surprised at all these accusations you're making against Dr. Stuart."

"How so?"

"He wasn't the best boss, sure, but back then, before he screwed me over, I really thought he was a good man. A good doctor. I respected him for many years."

"And even after he did what he did to you, you feel this way?"

I shifted in my seat. "No. I guess it's easier to believe after that."

"Some people are really good at acting, Carolina."

"Like you?" My eyes narrowed.

"No, baby. I'd never put up a false front with you."

My guard came down, and I blinked at him. Had I heard him right? Had he just called me *baby*? I must have heard him wrong. I shook my head, but his eyes held mine. "All right, Hector. We've had dinner. Will you please stop wasting my time? Tell me whatever it is you have to say."

"Would you at least tell me if you liked dinner?" he asked.

"It was okay." I crossed my arms over my chest and smirked.

Hector chuckled. "Oh, I think it was more than okay."

"No. That's your ego talking."

He chuckled again. "Okay." He stood and started picking up the dishes. I recognized he was trying to keep his hands busy to have this difficult conversation. I did the same thing when I was nervous. I stood and started clearing the table with him, but not before kicking off my heels.

"I know my mother might have mentioned Andrea when she was here."

I tried not to show any anger on my face. Did he not know Andrea had written to me? "Your wife? What does she have to do with anything?"

"Everything," Hector said. "When I joined Heartland Metro, we had been separated for several years already. That entire time, I had refused to give her a divorce. I knew it was over, and that we'd never get what we had back, but I was stubborn."

"I believe it," I said, fully recognizing his stubbornness. So far, everything Andrea had written was matching up with Hector's account of events.

"What you need to understand is that I came to Heartland only for you. At first, it was for your work. I was excited about medicine for the first in a long time when I heard about this young doctor who was inspired by my work, pushing the envelope of what was possible."

I smiled at the sight of his excitement, but I wasn't connecting the dots yet. He continued.

"Then I met you, and Carolina, *everything* changed. You have to believe that. I was suddenly less concerned about the perfect life and the perfect marriage I had drawn up for myself. Suddenly, giving Andrea a divorce didn't seem like the worst defeat of my life."

"But you didn't go through with it," I said.

"Actually, I did," he said, wincing a little at the words.

"*What?*" I asked through gritted teeth.

"I signed that first year I was at Heartland Metro. Within a year, it was finalized."

"What?" I hissed again. I couldn't form full sentences at that moment.

"I was divorced soon after I met you, Carolina. I was hoping we could have—"

"But you never said anything," I interrupted him. "You always wore the wedding ring."

"The divorce was finalized in that two-year period when you wouldn't talk with me."

"And after that, when things were better between us?"

"I couldn't bear to do it. The rumors had taken their toll and had just started to dissipate. I would have been damned before I let them affect your career any further than they already had. So I kept it to myself and kept wearing the ring, letting everyone believe I was still married."

"Hector, you should have told me," I said forlornly. "Back then, I wanted . . . *more,*" I said.

"I know, baby. You weren't very good at hiding your feelings. Neither was I. Why do you think the rumors caught fire like that?"

"I always blamed Keach."

"Sure. He ignited the rumors, but the blaze was all us. Even when it was clear we weren't on speaking terms, some still wondered if we'd actually had an affair that had ended badly."

"Don't remind me," I said.

"I wouldn't have believed us either."

"You give yourself a lot of credit."

"Come on. We've wanted each other for almost a decade. Since that first day in the conference room, I needed to know who you were. I couldn't imagine you were the doctor I had come here for. I can't tell you what it felt like, knowing it was you."

"Speak for yourself. I haven't said I've wanted you for years."

Hector chuckled. "Tell yourself what you want, baby. I know what I see in your eyes—what I've seen since the first day we met."

"What's that?"

Hector moved toward me, his chest puffed like a predator. I took a step back until I couldn't move any further against the kitchen island behind me. He caged me in with both his hands on either side of me, pressed firmly to the countertop.

"Desire, Carolina." Letting his grip off the countertop, he cupped my face in his hands, lifting my face to meet his. "I see it right there, in your eyes right now."

I dropped my gaze from him and let out a breath. He wasn't wrong, but damn him for knowing. The slight buzz from the wine electrified the sensation of his hands on my skin, and I had zero willpower to break free.

Hector grabbed me by the waist and lifted me to sit on the countertop. My eyes widened with the surprise of the movement, but then my legs parted, making room for him to press his body against mine. The air crackled around us.

He ran his fingers through my hair and cupped the back of my head, holding me in place. "Hector," I moaned his name. My breath was coming in choppy, and I didn't have the power in my limbs to push him away. I wasn't even sure I wanted to anymore.

"Tell me. Tell me you didn't want me then, and tell me you

don't want me now. Set me straight, Carolina. This is your chance. Tell me I imagined it all."

My eyes met his because I was no chicken-shit. I could see from behind the light stubble that his jaw was clenched as he waited for my answer. "I can't," I said with a challenging gaze. "It wouldn't be true." His eyes roamed my face looking for sincerity in it, finding an invitation instead.

His other arm was now around my waist, pulling me flush against him. He let go of my body and brought his hand back up, this time finding my lips. With his thumb, he rubbed my bottom lip, swiping from one side to the other, while my hands pressed against his hard chest.

"I've wanted to touch you like this for so long." His voice was deeper and now suddenly raspy. When he spoke, my skin broke into goosebumps, and my legs wrapped around his waist without my command, pulling him closer.

When his lips finally made contact with mine, the last nine years fell away. Every reason we had for not being together was gone. My hatred, even, had mellowed to a low flicker in the distance.

It was a gentle kiss—at first. He explored my mouth with restraint and grazed my teeth tentatively with the tip of his tongue. The smell of his musk mingled with the crisp taste of the wine still on our lips, and a moan escaped me. The hand he had cupping the back of my head bunched into a fist in response to the sound, sending a prickling sensation through my scalp. But the pain mixed with pleasure, and I could not voice a protest. I didn't want to.

My eyes flew open when I felt the length of him hardening through the layers of clothing. His slacks, my pantyhose, and underwear separated me from what my body *needed.*

I tightened the muscles of my legs to grip him even closer to me if that were possible. I needed to feel *all* of him. He pulled me away by the hair still in his fist, and he chuckled. The void I felt at his mouth no longer on mine was unbearable. The need for him was unmatched by anything I had felt for anyone, ever —by a longshot.

"My eager little Carolina," he said in a breathy voice. "We have plenty of time. Let me enjoy this."

Hector's grip pulled my hair, forcing my head back and exposing my neck to him. I grabbed on to his broad shoulders for balance. He kissed my jaw, then trailed kisses down my neck.

"I love you," he whispered, and my every muscle turned to stone. My hands dropped away from him and found the counter. My legs unraveled from him, retreating from his body and finding their way back to mine.

"What did you say?"

"I love you. I've loved for a long time."

My face twisted at his words, and I pushed him away. He let go of my hair so he could look at my face, which was now serious. He groaned with frustration, but he stepped back and away from me.

"You were talking about *desire*, Hector. Desire and love are two very different things."

"You must have known," he countered, now looking angry.

"No. You didn't love me. Someone who loves someone doesn't put them through what you have put me through."

"Someone who loves someone," he said, his teeth gritted, "will do anything, even if it means staying away for nearly a decade, before hurting them."

"What are you talking about?" I jumped off the counter and straightened my dress.

"Carolina, do you think I could have kept you, knowing that either way things played out, I would be hurting you?"

"Hurting me?" I shook my head. None of his words were making sense. "What are you talking about?"

"I was in a classic no-win situation. If we had been weak at the conference hotel that night, the rumors would have been true, and they would have ruined your career."

"But we weren't. We didn't do anything wrong."

"Like that mattered? Look at what happened anyway."

"Hector, that wasn't your fault."

"Yes, it was!" His voice raised a little. "And what if we had done things right? What if after my divorce came through, we had gotten together? What then? The hospital would have had a problem with it because I was your boss. But maybe I tried to solve the problem for you and left Heartland. Maybe I found another hospital so we could stay together—"

That was a beautiful possibility lost. "What would have been wrong with *that*?"

"Let's play this out. Do you think you would have the career you have now if everyone believed you slept your way to the top?"

I wanted to slap him. I wanted to slap him so much my palm tickled with the anticipation of contact, but I forced it to remain at my side. "I wouldn't have done that," I hissed.

"No. But that's what they would have all believed. But if we had gone further?"

"What do you mean?"

"What if I had proposed, because I wanted to Carolina, I wanted to propose to you back then. I was going to at our celebration dinner, but it never happened."

"You were going to *propose*?" I spoke gently, eerily gently, because the anger was swelling up in waves, and my breath kept getting caught in them.

"Yes. I was. But then I talked to the chief, and he opened my eyes. And he wasn't wrong, Carolina. What do you think would have happened if I had gotten my stupid happily-ever-after?"

"Well, I guess we will never know, will we?" I started to look for my shoes. I had to get out of there but couldn't remember where I'd kicked them off. Hector followed me around as I looked for them.

"Don't be obtuse. Dr. Stuart didn't point out anything I didn't already know, but I wanted to pretend I didn't. And you knew it too."

"I don't know what you are talking about, but this conversation is over."

"No, it isn't. Listen to me. If you had done me that honor and said yes, the honeymoon period would have ended so soon."

"Great to know you had so little confidence in the possibility of us—"

"That's not what I mean, and you know it. Carolina, would you be happy right now, if all your career you wondered if you achieved what you have achieved because you earned it, or because your husband was Hector Medina?"

I turned to face him again. "That's what stopped you?"

"Mostly." He cupped the back of his neck. He seemed calmer now, but sadder too. "The other part of it was Stuart's leverage."

"Yes, Hector, please tell me, what did he have over your head that was so important?"

"You."

"Me?"

"Yes. He was ready to sink your career if I didn't keep my name on the paper—and he could have done it too. That's why I had to wait to correct the authorship on our paper. I had to wait for him to be gone. I couldn't do that to you. And I couldn't stay and continue to have him use you like a pawn. I just couldn't, Carolina. I had to remove myself from the picture. I needed you to know that anything you achieved was because of you—and in spite of me. I didn't want anyone to ever think it was *because* of me."

"So, *you* decided."

"Don't you see? Everything I have done has been for you. I went to Heartland Metro for you, and I had to leave to protect you. I've stayed away for the same reason. Everything is always for you. You are my life, baby." He moved closer to me, his eyes softer, trying to appease me.

"No." I shook my head. "You chose. We lost nine years we could've had—"

"Let's not lose any more—"

"No. Not when *you* decide. You will never call the shots for me again, do you hear me?" I was shouting at him now, and I did my best to keep the tears pricking my eyes from escaping down my cheeks.

He looked at me like I had slapped him, even though I had the grace to resist. "You stole nine years from me and didn't have the decency to tell me. How could you do it?"

"I did it *for* you."

I found my shoes and put them on then made my way toward the door. Hector hadn't noticed when I had called the car, and I got the notification that it was waiting outside.

"Don't walk out on me, Carolina. We aren't over—not like this."

"Everything has been up to you, Hector. It's time to realize you are not my keeper," I said and walked out of his house.

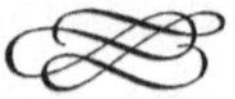

CHAPTER 26

FIGHT OF FIGHTS

My driver witnessed my breakdown on the car ride home. The tears I was so hell-bent on keeping from Hector spilled over with gusto. The driver looked in his rear-view mirror several times and asked if I was okay. I could only nod.

When I arrived at my apartment, I didn't even try to get to bed. I knew I wouldn't sleep. My entire body was the nucleus of a bomb amassing energy before it detonated.

I'd loved him, and he had loved me back, but he took our chance away. I had no say in the outcome. I'd never felt so powerless.

It was like mourning, but I went straight to the second stage of grief: Anger. I left his house because I wanted to hit him and didn't like the violence that was building in me. A violence fueled by the passion of the moments leading up to the argument.

I rummaged through the storage bin under my bed and

pulled out a gift box almost nine years old. It was wrapped in navy blue paper and tied off with an orange ribbon.

Opening the gift in front of everyone hadn't seemed appropriate, but then I'd forgotten about it after the party. It was placed in a box when I moved into a larger apartment. By the time I came across it again, the fallout had already taken place, and I couldn't bring myself to open it.

I'd come close a few times but never committed. Over the years, I would think about him and wonder what was in the box, but then the anger would wash over me, and I'd always put it away again.

I undid the frayed ribbon. Hopefully, it wasn't chocolate or something edible that had long ago turned rancid. I felt the heavy weight of it in my hands as I had so many times before. Breaking through the paper, I realized it was a book. I ran my fingers over the soft leather-bound tome. I turned it over to read the front cover and found the title of *Jane Eyre.*

When he went to my house on my birthday that day so long ago, I had found him in my room, frozen in place as he stared at the wall. I'd always assumed it was the copy of his paper that had glued him to his spot. I had thought he believed me to be a stalker but realizing now what he had brought as a gift, I had to believe he was in awe that he'd unknowingly selected my favorite book.

My eyes stung with tears. Anger and empathy battled within my body for a place in my heart. I wanted to forgive him, and I wanted to scratch his eyes out, all in the same breath.

It was reckless to drive back to his place with the rage still blinding me, but I was drawn to him even in my anger. We'd almost slept together, and I was too restless to go to sleep.

I gave myself several hours to calm down and returned to his house at four in the morning.

"Carolina?" Hector asked sleepily as he opened his front

door. His bedhead waves fell over his forehead, and he wore a white t-shirt with light-blue pajama bottoms.

Not waiting for an invitation, I let myself in. As I closed the door, I leaned on it, needing the balance for strength.

"How could you do it?" I asked, and a tear rolled down my cheek.

"How could I not? Tell me you wouldn't have done the same thing had the situation been reversed and it had been *you* threatening *my* career. You wouldn't have stayed away too?"

"I don't know. But I would have talked to you about it."

"I couldn't." He swallowed hard, and his Adam's apple bobbed. "I knew you would convince me that we could work it out, and I would have been weak. I couldn't chance it. I'm so, *so*, sorry."

He stepped forward and wiped away my tear with his thumb. "Please believe it was one of the hardest things I've ever had to do."

I nodded but took his hand away from my cheek. He kept his hand in mine and led me to the couch to sit next to him. The entire house was dark; he hadn't turned on a single light when he opened the door.

"I'm glad you came back."

"I'm not sure why I did. I mean, I had to cool off. Your instincts were right. I did want to hit you earlier."

He chuckled. "My instincts are always right." His white teeth almost glowed in the dark through his grin.

"I can think of at least one time when they weren't," I said, and I knew it was like a dagger to him.

"What's it going to take for you to forgive me?"

"Forgiving has never come hard to me, Hector. It's not about forgiveness. I'm not sure I can *trust* you." And that was the truth of it. I wasn't one to hold a grudge, with scarce exception. It was incredibly easy to forgive the people I loved, but this was so different. A grudge I didn't know I'd been holding, for perhaps the first time in my life, had been brewing for years.

"That hurts," he admitted.

"I'm sorry. I'm not trying to be hurtful—just honest."

"I know." A strand of hair fell over my eyes, and Hector swept it back, tucking it behind my ear. "But I'm still glad you are back. Even if it's to wound me," he said.

"I um—" I cleared my throat. "I opened your gift," I said.

Hector's brows drew together. "My gift?"

"My birthday gift—"

He thought for a moment. "Do you mean from when I first came to Heartland Metro Hospital? The cookout for your birthday?"

I nodded.

"You hadn't opened it before now?"

I shook my head.

"That's a bit odd."

"Why did you pick that book?"

"What, *Jane Eyre?* I do have to say I was very surprised to find a poster of it in your room. But, um, I guess you reminded me of Jane."

"*I* reminded you of Jane? And more importantly, you've read it?"

"Don't get too excited. It was a college assignment, but it wasn't bad."

"Please don't give me more reasons to want to stab you," I said, and he threw his head back with laughter.

"Okay, it was good. Happy?"

"No. Not even a little. You still haven't told me why I reminded you of Jane. I'm nothing like her. She is small, and I am super tall. She's plain and simple, and I'm more of a fiery, in-your-face kind of a presence, or so I've been told."

Hector chuckled. "Well, you are right on all accounts. But you are also otherworldly, like Jane. You can't be from this planet. You are so . . . rare. Mainly though, if I remember correctly, Jane was Rochester's equal, as you were—are—mine. No one else could understand either of them on a deeper level, but they didn't have to even speak to know what was in the other's heart."

"For someone who only read it for a college assignment, you have a pretty good understanding of the novel. I read it once a year—at *least*."

Hector gave me a side-glance but didn't comment further.

"What about the last seven years?" I asked him.

"What about them?"

"There hasn't been anyone in your life in that time? A St. John—if you will?"

"No." Hector shook his head. "I dated, especially those first few years. I was trying to forget you, but nothing ever got serious. It's hard to try to grow feelings for someone when you know your soul mate is elsewhere."

I scoffed. "We are scientists. How can you believe in soul mates?"

"I didn't use to." Hector cupped my hand in both of his and pressed it to his chest. He kept a grip on it, not letting me have my hand back. "But I'm not exaggerating when I say *everything* changed with you."

A long stretch of silence followed as I thought of what to say next. I wasn't sure why I was back here. I only knew I had no freewill to stay away.

"What about you?" Hector asked after a moment.

"What about me?"

"It killed me to think of you with Ramiro or with someone else all these years. It was excruciating not getting on a flight and claiming you as mine."

"Really?" My anger was rising again. "It always comes back to this. What is it with you and Ramiro? He is family. Always has been, always will be."

"So, you never got together with him after I left?"

"No!"

Hector let out a breath he had been holding.

"If you must know," I said. "In the last seven years, Ramiro has had two great loves. Neither of whom was me. Now, he is very happily married, and very much still someone I consider family."

"And there hasn't been anyone else?" he asked.

"Like you, I dated some, but nothing ever came of it. I was too focused on work, and most men can't handle a schedule as busy as mine."

Now that my sight had adjusted to the dark, I could make out Hector's face as his nostrils flared.

"I want to kill, just thinking about you with anyone else," he admitted.

"Don't be a hypocrite. You just told me you dated as well."

"And how did you like hearing that, baby?"

I shifted in my seat. I hadn't liked it one bit, and immediately wanted to know names, how long they had lasted, and all the sordid details. But I wasn't about to admit that to him.

"Are you back to stay the night with me, Carolina?"

My body answered before I could, and I found myself nodding. He stood and helped me up from the sofa. He then took me by surprise and lifted me off the ground. My legs wrapped around his waist, and my arms clutched around the back of his neck. It was amazing that he could carry me—I wasn't a light little feather like Sara, but this man was *strong*.

He kissed the tip of my nose before speaking again. "I won't be able to take you leaving again. It will drive me to insanity. Please tell me you are here to stay."

"I think I am," I said.

"At least promise you won't get mad at me again for the remainder of the night."

"You know I can't promise that."

Hector squeezed my ass, and I squealed. "Could you at least *try*?" he asked.

I nodded, and my jaw dropped when he carried me all the way upstairs and into his room without so much as a grunt.

Once in his room, he pressed me up against a wall, and my legs unfurled away from him, my feet finding the ground once again. I took his shirt off over his head, and my hands explored his upper body.

His shoulders and arms were massive, and his chest was firm, but his abdominal muscles weren't too obvious. I'd never really understood the fascination most women have with a six-pack. Hector was slim at the waist. An understated shadow hinted at the muscles beneath his tanned skin, but there were no overly pronounced striations.

But what really made my mouth water was the v-cut line of muscles that peeked out from above his pajama bottoms and pointed downward like a beacon leading me to my prize.

He flipped me over, and I gasped with the surprise of his sudden movements. I held onto the wall for balance as he slowly drew down the zipper of my dress. The soft caress of his fingers followed the trail of the zipper sliding down my back.

Damn it. Hector was taking too much time. I needed him *now*. I pulled off the rest of my dress from my upper body with urgency and turned around, not caring that I hadn't worn a bra. He raised his hands in surrender as I untied the string of his pajama bottoms. He chuckled at my desperate movements, the bastard.

"Here," he said, and carried me to his bed. He threw me on the mattress unceremoniously and peeled off the rest of my dress and pantyhose. He stepped back to look at me, and I suddenly became aware that I was splayed out in front of him in only a black thong. "Carolina," he said with a hoarse voice. "You are so fucking beautiful."

I shot up with his words, sitting on the edge of the mattress.

I hooked my fingers to the waistband of both his bottoms and boxer briefs, helping him out of both.

He sprang free, and I gulped at the sight of his erection, facing me and pointing upward. He didn't say anything as I explored him. I placed a hand around his shaft and squeezed gently, feeling his girth. Hector drew in a breath at the touch, and a small drop of pre-cum escaped him. I rubbed it with my thumb around the head and brought my thumb to my mouth, licking it. The flavor of him in my mouth quickened my breathing.

My intention was to draw him into my mouth, I wanted to taste him, but he pulled out of my grip before my tongue reached its desire.

"Tsk, tsk," he said. "Not yet. I won't be able to last if you do that, and I want to devour you, baby."

I swallowed, even as I was denied what I wanted most. Still, his words stirred inside me, and I felt my pussy contract in response.

He pushed me gently by the shoulders until I lay back onto the bed. He was on top of me in no time.

When he kissed me the second time, it was different. This was not the exploration of tentative lovemaking, full of sweetness like his kiss earlier in the night. This kiss—it was all desire and hunger. He made good on his promise and devoured my mouth. His lips crushed mine, and his tongue played roughly with mine like he couldn't get enough, making me squirm under him.

His cock rested on me, his shaft nestled gently between the seam at my center, and my hips raised forward, searching for the head, wanting him inside me. He let out a deep chuckle at my desperation, and I could have killed him right then and there.

"My eager little Carolina," he said, admonishing me. "We have all night. What is the rush?"

"The rush," I said in a breathy voice, "is that we have been waiting a decade." I circled my hips, rubbing my clit against the shaft of his cock, seeking my pleasure.

His eyes darkened, and I was almost afraid of what I saw in them—almost. He looked wild, like a starving savage.

His mouth trailed down my body as he pinned me to the bed by my shoulders. He let go of his grip when his mouth reached my pubic bone, and his hands found themselves on my thighs, spreading my legs even wider.

With his index finger, he pulled my thong to the side. There was a gentle caress, teasing at my entrance, and my body writhed at the touch.

"What do you want, Carolina?"

"I want you." Damn it, I wanted him *now.*

"Say it, baby. What do you want from me?" His stubble scratched my inner thigh as his finger continued to toy at my entrance, not giving me what I wanted. I was about to cry.

"I want your mouth," I said.

"Like this?" He slid his finger deeper in me and gave me a gentle kiss on the outside of my pussy. I groaned.

"No. I want your tongue on me."

"Oh, you mean like this?" He licked at the outer lip of my pussy, as his finger twirled inside me.

"Hector, damn it! I want you to lick my clit!" I surprised myself at how loud I had said it, but my bluntness was rewarded. He chuckled as the tip of his tongue circled my clitoris gently.

He made a soft *mmmm* sound, and the sound vibrations were unlike anything I'd ever felt. He was unreal.

"Oh, Hector." My eyes rolled back with pleasure. He flicked his tongue a little faster and slid a second finger inside me, sending me reeling. I grabbed a fistful of fabric from the bedsheets and held on for life. My thighs clenched, and he pulled his fingers out of me to stabilize my legs wide and open like he wanted them.

"No!" I protested, the emptiness leaving me nearly in tears.

"Then, don't close your legs for me, got it?"

I nodded rapidly, wanting to be rewarded. What the hell? Where was the polite and respectable Hector Medina? This Hector was all teasing and power and hunger. I fucking loved it. While I didn't want him calling the shots in my career, I definitely didn't mind him calling the shots when he had his way with me.

He returned his attention to my pussy, and this time he plunged three fingers inside me, stretching me further. I was so wet by that point, there was no pain at the extra width of the fingers inside.

His tongue rolled once again over my clit, this time picking up speed, and his fingers went in and out of me more rapidly each time. When he curled his fingers slightly upward, finding that spot, I couldn't take it anymore.

"Hector, No! Please stop, I'm going to come." I didn't want to. Not yet. I wanted his cock inside me when I came.

"Yes, baby. Come for me. I want you dripping down all the way to my wrist," he said and pushed his fingers deeper inside me.

A familiar tension coiled in my core, and bursts of white lights set off behind my eyes as my body answered him, giving him what he commanded.

My orgasm came in waves, and my abdominal muscles spasmed with the pleasure. My pussy clenched around his fingers. And his mouth left me.

"Oh, Carolina," he said hoarsely at the sensation around his fingers.

He stood, and I momentarily panicked. "Where are you going?"

"I'm just going to the dresser. Need to grab a condom."

"Wait," I said. I couldn't look at him, but I needed to ask. I wanted to feel him, and not between a layer of latex. "I'm on birth control. I have an IUD," I said. "And I'm clean. I'm sure of it. Would you want to . . ." I trailed off, not able to finish my thought.

Shit. What the hell was happening? Where was the confident and assertive Carolina Ramirez? Being naked with each other had seemed to reduce both of us to repressed personality traits we avoided in our everyday lives and careers.

"Carolina, you are my every dream come true," Hector said and finished peeling off my thong. I welcomed him with open thighs as he found his way back on top of me.

One of his hands went to the back of my head, holding me in place for a kiss, just as he had earlier in the night. The tip of his cock played at my entrance, and I writhed beneath him, trying to get him deeper inside me. I groaned in his mouth, and my reward was another inch of him.

He pushed in slowly, stretching me inch by inch in the most gentle way. I was so wet that there was nothing but pleasure, and just when I didn't think he could possibly go inside me any deeper, he thrust in another inch, and then another.

I hunkered down, taking in his cock and adjusting to the size. I'd never been with a man this big, and I thought it might be painful when I first saw him, but it wasn't. It was the most delicious stretch of my life.

"Are you okay?" he asked between kisses.

"Yes," I said, and my legs wrapped around him, my ankles pushing on his ass so I could have him deeper.

"Yes, ma'am," he said teasingly, and pulled out of me almost entirely, then drove in again with force.

I screamed his name and cursed in the same breath, and he was amused by all of it. He was paying close attention, finding my eyes even when I tried to look away. He was studying me.

He wanted to know what my body reacted to—what I liked. Hector Medina was conducting research on my body.

He pulled out again, this time staying away, with only his tip inside me. "Please, Hector, *please* come back," I begged.

His mouth found me first, and he drove his tongue in my mouth before he drove his cock deep inside again. I moaned into his mouth, my eyes shut tight, and that coil started building again.

My legs tightened around him, and I dug my fingertips in his back—luckily, like all doctors, I had short nails and didn't scratch him. Or at least I didn't think I had.

I took my mouth away from him, gasping for air, and my head rolled back as the second orgasm hit. My pussy tightened around him as I came, and it only made him thrust harder, sending me over the edge again.

He was wild now, his eyes darkened like a sinister, other-worldly being as he pounded into me. My pussy was still contracting from the orgasm when he plunged deep inside me and remained there. A groan that escaped from deep within him followed as he came shortly after I did. I realized he'd been trying to hold out until I came again—like a gentleman.

He pressed his forehead to my collar bone and tried to catch his breath. My arms embraced him around the neck, and I couldn't help running my fingers through his hair.

"I'm never letting you get away again," he said between breaths and while he was still inside me. He kissed my left breast and looked up at me. "But more importantly, I'll never again give you a reason to want to go."

MORNING AFTER

The house was quiet, but the sun rays flooding through the window warmed my skin. I felt a tickle at my nose, and my eyes fluttered open. I had fallen asleep on his chest, and his thick chest hair tickled my face awake. I smiled when I realized his chest hair matched the salt and pepper hues of his thick mane.

I slept like the dead, though I didn't imagine he could have been very comfortable. I had his arm pinned under me, and nearly half of me was on top of him, my legs wrapped around his right leg.

As I rubbed the sleep from my eyes, he shifted under me. "You awake?" His voice didn't sound hoarse or groggy.

"Yeah. How long have you been awake?"

He caressed my shoulder. "An hour," he admitted.

I pushed myself away from him, horrified. "I'm so sorry, Hector. You should have woken me so I could move. You must have been so uncomfortable."

Hector only tightened his grip, pressing me to his naked body. "Come here. I wasn't uncomfortable. Actually, it was heavenly. You looked so at peace, I didn't want to wake you."

"Well, thank you," I said with doubt.

"Not that I could wake you up if I wanted to."

"What's that supposed to mean?"

"It means, my love, that you sleep like a log. I don't think a freight train could wake you up. And don't let me get started on that cute little snore of yours—"

"I do not snore!" I tried wiggling out of his grip, but who was I kidding? It was only a threat. I wasn't going to willingly separate my skin from his. I settled back into the warm nook of his body, and I couldn't remember the last time I'd felt that safe—or if I ever had.

I covered my mouth for a yawn, preoccupied with my morning breath. "That was a yummy sleep," I admitted and brought my hand back to his chest. I gathered some of his chest hair between my fingers and started twirling the locks around. This man was *mine,* and I couldn't believe it. As I played with the curls, something caught a ray of sunlight from within the chest hair and glimmered. I pulled my hand to my face and realized it was on my finger.

I shot up into a sitting position and grabbed the bed sheet to cover my breasts. Hector remained calmly lying down and drew circles on my naked back with the pad of his finger.

"Hector, wha-wha-what is this?" I held my left hand to my face and pushed aside the strands of hair obscuring my view. I was sure my locks were suffering from a severe case of sex hair, but I couldn't worry about that right now. On my hand, staring back at me, was a classically cut round diamond on a sleek and simple platinum band.

"That's your engagement ring, love. Guess I'm lucky you sleep like you do, or I would have never managed to get it on you without waking you."

Love? He had gone from *baby* to *love* in one night. "How did you get—"

"I've had it for a while now," Hector said.

"How long is *a while*?" I asked, looking at him now.

"That ring has been here, in this house, for eight years."

"What?" My eyes bulged to saucers. It was possible I was dreaming or still so groggy I hadn't heard him right.

"I was only renting at first, but when you came over, you mentioned you liked the house, so I bought it."

"You bought a house because I mentioned I liked it?"

"Yes." Hector sat up in the bed and scooted me back toward him so we could both rest our backs on the headboard. He took my left hand in his and kissed it. "I bought it for you—for us. I told you, love. I fell in love with you back then, and I was ready to propose, but you were so damned mad at me, and well, you know what happened after that."

"And it has been here this entire time?" I stared at the ring again. It was sizable and looked expensive, but it wasn't too much. It felt elegant and classic on my hand, even to my untrained eye.

"Waiting for you. That ring was going to be on your finger one day, or it would never get to feel the skin of another human. The poor thing," he teased.

"Would have been such a waste," I teased back.

"The worst," Hector said.

"And you kept the house empty? All this time?"

Hector nodded. "I couldn't bear to sell it. Doing so would have been like admitting I was giving up on us, and I never did. Not even when I tried to convince myself it was over. In the back of my mind, I always knew that I'd come back once your career was established, once I could be in your life without simultaneously destroying it."

He had been right last night when he'd asked whether I wouldn't have done the same thing he had. I was starting to understand the sacrifice of his restraint. He waited seven years for me to make a name for myself and risked me moving on with someone else. It would have killed me, but I couldn't lie to myself; I would have done the same thing if I'd thought I was ruining everything he had ever worked for.

It wasn't like he stayed away so I could keep a job. He loved medicine as much as I did and understood that losing a love like that would have all but killed me. Because he was right. I would have chosen him at the risk of my career, and if I had lost the ability to conduct research, it would have slowly killed me and taken its own particular toll on our relationship.

I dropped the sheets from my body and pulled them away from both of us. The contrast of his tanned skin on the white linens was astounding in the morning light, and I couldn't stop myself from fucking him with my eyes as I raked my gaze up and down his body.

So much had been missing last night in the dark. He had fucked me hard, with hunger and desire and longing, but it was all touch and sounds. The glory of his body was missing from the limited senses lacking vision in the night.

I smirked when his erection made its presence known, but then my pussy contracted. I was sore and swollen from what we had done not too many hours ago. He looked bigger in the clarity of daylight, and I winced.

"As much as I love you devouring me with your eyes," Hector said, "I was hoping you'd actually touch me."

"We have the rest of our lives. What's the rush?" I threw his words at him and bent over his body.

I gripped the shaft of his cock and moved to make him think I was going to have him in my mouth. But this was payback for all the teasing from earlier. He would pay.

I leaned to kiss his inner thigh and dragged my tongue from his knee to his thigh on one leg, then the other, stopping each time before reaching the spot where he wanted me.

"I shouldn't have teased you last night, should I?" Hector asked.

"No, darling. You *really* shouldn't have." I was mainly teasing him as he had done, but I was also exploring his body again, this time with my eyes. I scooted up, and my tongue trailed the thin strip of hair that led to his bellybutton, and I nipped at the skin of his stomach.

"Damn it, Carolina," Hector said, his voice hoarse. "I swear I'll never tease you again if you stop."

I withdrew from him and studied his expression as I licked my lips. "You want me to stop?"

"No! Agh! That's not what I meant. *Please* stop teasing me."

I understood now why he had done it. Him begging, saying my name, pleading drawn-out *pleases,* was like a prayer for me. It was so goddamned empowering and so fucking hot.

Rewarding the prayer offering, I bent again and gripped his shaft, pumping once, then twice. Still, I wanted to savor him, so I only licked, first along his shaft from root to head. I let my tongue linger there and circle the head, finding the saltiness of us from the night before.

Hector was still half-sitting up against the headboard, and he gathered my hair in his hand so he could watch me—I wanted him to see what I was doing to him. I drew the tip of his cock into my mouth and sucked only there, at the very edge, and he bucked his hips, trying to go deeper, but I was in control now.

"Tsk, tsk," I said as I let him out of my mouth. "This is my show now."

"I'm sorry," he said. "*Please* get back here."

"Are you going to be good?" I sat up, giving him a full view of my body, and circled my nipple with my finger. I drew my hand down, tracing a zig-zag pattern from my breast down to my clit.

"Yes, I'll stay still, just *please*—" He tried reaching for me, but I was just out of grasp. I moaned as I toyed with my clit, high on the look in his eyes as he watched.

"Please, Carolina. You've made your point. This is cruel."

I bent over him again and kept my balance on one hand so I could keep playing with myself with the other while I sucked him. I took him deeper into my mouth the second time, and he growled—he actually *growled*—and I etched the sound in my mind so I could take it with me for the rest of my days.

"Stop, Carolina," he ordered, and I couldn't stop myself from obeying, his power over me from last night lingering somewhere in the recesses of my brain.

I crawled up toward him and found his mouth, letting him taste what had been on my tongue, morning breath be damned, because this was so hot. I used his shoulders for support as I came up over him and slid down over his cock slowly—so slowly.

The girth of him sent a stretch of pain to my core as I slid down around his length. My mouth parted from his. I gulped some air to ebb the pain away, but he noticed my wince.

"Are you in pain, baby? We don't have to, we can stop if you are too sore." His body stilled like he wouldn't dare move a muscle lest he hurt me.

I shook my head.

The thing was, there was a pain where we joined, but also so much pleasure, and there was no way I was stopping now. I circled my hips gently as I took the rest of him in, and he groaned.

"I'm okay," I promised. "A little sore, but nothing I can't handle." I slid down further until there was nothing more to take in and rode him for all that I was worth.

Hector grabbed onto my hip bones, encouraging my rhythm. He helped me up his shaft and brought me down forcefully. His fingers dug into my skin, but the pain was masked under the pleasure of his fullness inside me. The way it felt to be with him had never been close to this with anyone, not even remotely.

He sat up fully and took my mouth in his. I moaned into his

tongue, and he rewarded me by pushing me until I fell on my back. He rolled up over me in an instant, never once disconnecting from my body. Grabbing my right leg, he placed it over his shoulder, and the stretch felt divine.

"Oh," I moaned with the surprise of this new position. I tried bucking my hips, but too much of his weight was on me, and I was powerless. "Hector," I moaned.

"I'm here, baby," he said, claiming my lips once again.

He picked up speed as he drove into me over and over, and when I couldn't take it any longer, I clenched around him as I found my release. My center convulsed around him, and his body stilled. The morning light splayed across his forehead, and I could see a vein making itself known over his taut skin as he came inside me.

After we both came undone, he rolled off me. We lay next to each other for a long moment, panting. The sweat from the heat of us started to cool over my body, and I curled to his side, seeking his warmth.

We both lay there for a moment as we brought down our heart rates and our breaths. After a long moment of coming back to, Hector broke the silence.

"So I take it that was a *yes?*"

SIX YEARS LATER

THANKSGIVING DAY

❧

*H*ector stood in front of the fireplace mantel with all the family pictures, our five-year-old daughter in his arms. Marisela's long legs dangled nearly to his knees, and already we could tell she would grow up to be tall—just like her parents.

She wore a deep blue dress with grey wool leggings and looked positively adorable in her daddy's arms. Though physically she looked most like me, her attitude, brain, and mannerisms were all Hector Medina.

When our daughter was born, Hector had wanted to name her after my mom, but Marisela came into this world with my face—my mother's face. I couldn't handle looking at her *and* calling her by my mother's name day after day. Instead, I suggested we name her after *his* mom. Hector had grinned as he let out a tear. Marisela, who had been in her dad's arms swaddled in the tiniest bundle I had ever seen, caught the tear with her forehead.

Grammy Marisela, as we all now called her to differentiate between grandmother and granddaughter, wasn't joining us this holiday season. In her seventies, she didn't like leaving her home in Mexico to travel any longer, but we had promised to visit in the spring.

"Daddy, this is my brother," Marisela said, pointing to the picture of Jake my dad had added to the mantel.

"Yes," Hector said. "That's your older brother Jake."

"He's in heaven," she told him matter-of-factly, and the words sounded like my father's counsel.

"Is he now?" Hector asked like she had all the answers.

"Yeah!" Marisela said with a confidence not unlike her father's. "Grammy Consuelo takes care of him there." And *that* explanation definitely had Dad written all over it. Hector chuckled, and Marisela didn't notice her dad's eyes misting over, but I caught sight of it when he turned his face slightly away from her to take a deep breath.

Dad placed a hand on my shoulder. I was standing, leaning against the door frame that led to the living room, watching my family. "You know, *Mami* would be so in love with her grand-daughter," I said as I clasped Dad's hand on my shoulder.

"She *is* in love with her," said Dad. I wasn't sure I believed that, but it was still comforting that *he* believed it, and he believed it enough for the both of us. "You have a package," he said. "It's on the table."

I went into the kitchen where Sofia and her daughter Audrey were smearing *masa* onto dry corn husks and helping Dad roll *tamales*. I grabbed the small box from the table so it wouldn't be in the way of their work.

I watched Audrey work diligently, her tongue poking out to the side as she concentrated on getting the perfect *tamal*, and I laughed. She was twelve now and growing into a beautiful young woman. Her dad and Sofia were going to have a heck of a time with boys real soon.

"*Tía*," Audrey said, looking up at me. "Is *Tía* Sara coming to dinner with the boys?"

"Yeah, why aren't they already here *helping*?" Sofia asked with mock-disdain.

"No, Mom!" Audrey said. "My *tía* Sara doesn't come until the food is ready."

Audrey made the accusation so seriously, Dad, Sofia, and I all roared with laughter. Hector and Marisela joined us in the kitchen, asking us what was so funny. Hector joined in with laughter when I repeated Audrey's matter-of-fact statement.

"Yes, sweetie," I told her. "Sara is coming, but it's better if she comes when dinner is ready, or do you want her tornado boys here while we try to work?"

"No!" she said with horror, and we all laughed again. Audrey returned her attention to the *tamal* she was rolling. She feigned disinterest when she spoke again, but I didn't miss her cute little rosy cheeks reddening crimson. "What about *Tía* Mandy? Is she bringing Lulu?"

Why was my niece asking about Mandy's son Lucas? I knew they were almost the same age and went to the same school, but the redness in her face amused me. I tried not to show it as I answered her. "No, sweetie. Lulu is in Spain with his other grandparents for the holidays. He'll be back after the new year."

Audrey shrugged, and I changed the subject to prevent her any embarrassment if anyone else caught on. I still had her back. I just hoped there wasn't payback from Sofia when Marisela became a pre-teen and started thinking about boys.

Hector lowered Marisela to the ground, and she ran to her grandpa who had a ball of *masa* waiting for her to play with. She rolled the dough in her hands and sank her fingers into it, giggling at the sensation. She ran to the living room with it still in her hands.

"What's the package?" Hector asked.

I had forgotten about it and looked down at the small box still resting on my lap. "I don't know. Hand me the kitchen scissors?"

"Is your dad coming to dinner, Audrey?" Hector asked as he handed me the scissors.

Audrey's little face fell, and she bit her lip just like her momma.

"No," Sofia said when Audrey didn't answer. "He's in Germany working, but he'll be back by Christmas, right, honey?" Sofia ran her fingers over Audrey's bangs, pushing them away from her eyes.

"Right," said Audrey, more cheerful now.

Opening the package, I found an assortment of Mexican candy, and I smiled. I knew exactly who these were from. The box was filled with tamarind-covered candy, my favorite watermelon lollipops, banana bubble gum, and several *cajeta* and *dulce de leche* candies. I opened the card, recognizing the familiar handwriting that found me every holiday season.

For the doctor who gave me a fighting chance,
Thank you for saving my life.
Much Love,
Valentina Dennis

"It's from a patient," I said. Hector hovered over me, looking inside the box. His hand reached toward my lap for a piece of candy, but I smacked it away. "That's *my* candy, Dr. Medina," I said.

"Is that right, Dr. Ramirez?" Hector put his hands on his hips in warning just like he did when he was attempting—and failing—to be stern with our daughter.

I sprang to my feet, opened the door to the backyard, and ran as I clutched the box in my hands. I only barely heard Hector's footfalls on the grass as he followed me, but I knew he wasn't far behind.

He caught me and gripped my waist with one hand as he tickled me with the other.

"No, daddy!" shouted Marisela, now next to us. "She is going to drop the candy!"

I wiggled in his grip. "Stop! Stop!" I pleaded through the laughter.

Hector stopped long enough for me to hand my daughter the box. Marisela's eyes widened at the sight of all the candy, and she ran with it back inside the house to show her grandpa.

"Dr. Ramirez," Hector said. "Half of what is yours is mine."

"Everything except for candy." I grinned at him, and he tackled me to the ground.

Dad hadn't raked the yard yet, and I laid on a bed of yellow and orange leaves. Hector's weight pinned me to the ground, and he dipped his head to kiss me gently—just one chaste little peck would do for now, until we got home and put Marisela to bed.

As he looked at me with that smile of his, I thought of everything we had created together and how beautiful it all was. Nothing we had ever done together was ever short of remarkable.

I had come from a tiny family, just Dad and me, but I'd slowly but surely grown it. First, with Ramiro, then Sara, then all my girlfriends, and finally, all my nieces and nephews. We had filled this house with a huge family and a lot of laughter.

I lay there, looking up at my husband, feeling the crisp autumn air nip at my skin, incredibly grateful for the family we had made.

FIN

BONUS CHAPTER

Would you like to read a free bonus chapter from *Remission*? To get Hector's point of view when he first meets Carolina, go to: ofeliamartinez.com/freebooks

In the meantime, are you ready to start on Valentina's story? Keep reading for an excerpt from the second book in the Heartland Metro Hospital series, *Contusion.*

CONTUSION

CONTUSION EXCERPT

CHAPTER ONE

It's either the machine or me. *You are going down*, I telepathically warn the vending contraption holding my Pop-Tart hostage. I've never had a Pop-Tart in my life, but I haven't eaten all day, and *hangry* Valentina Almonte . . . well, let's just say even inanimate objects wouldn't want to meet her. "I train with two-hundred-and-fifty-pound men, so you better give it soon," I mutter under my breath as I think about my coach, Chema. Chema, who didn't know where I was and was probably worried. Two-hundred-and-fifty-pound Chema, who I have only been able to wrestle to the ground once. I should call him today, but not until I eat. Chema isn't fond of hangry Valentina either. I shake the vending machine as discreetly as possible.

I'm getting ready to start kicking the thing when someone clears their throat nearby to grab my attention. I turn and am faced with a red-headed, freckled man who has about four inches on my five-foot-five frame. I stare with surprise at the handsome stranger with piercing green eyes. His nose and cheekbones are chiseled like a Roman marble statue. I've never seen a red-headed person this close before, and I've always been a sucker for bearded smart guys. He wears glasses, so he has to be smart. That's the rule, right? Yet there is something manly about him, starting with his short beard and solidifying with a surprisingly deep voice considering his slender frame.

"Here," he says, extending two dollar bills my way.

"Um, it's okay," I say, self-conscious about the last remnants of my Spanish accent that I was never quite able to shake off.

"Please," he insists. "I'm afraid for its life." He points to the vending machine and smirks as he extends the bills my way again.

I cock my head to the side, unsure I should accept—my brain misfiring at what to say to this handsome stranger—when he sweeps past me to insert the bills into the machine. His arm brushes mine, and I jump back like I am dodging a strike from my opponent.

"What was it?" he asks and smiles broadly.

I point to the lopsided pastry package dangling from a corner caught on the claw of the feeding coil. "The Pop-Tart," I say. This is so embarrassing. I finally meet someone in the U.S., someone handsome, and he is buying out my hostage snack.

When the snack drops, he bends down to grab my prize, and I don't check out his ass. Not one little bit. But if I had, which I didn't, I'd have to admit it is quite a fine ass in that light-colored denim.

"Are you waiting for family?" he asks, handing me the Pop-Tart.

I look around nervously at the nearly empty waiting area. I'm not ready to tell anyone, even a stranger, so I shrug and change the subject instead. "Thanks, um—what's your name?"

"You betcha. I'm Rory," he says, and his smile extends to his eyes. He offers his hand, and I take it in mine.

"Valentina. Nice to meet you."

He adjusts the backpack strap over his shoulder, and I wonder if he is a college student because he has to be in his early twenties. "Valentina," he tries out the name in his mouth. "That's pretty. I don't think I know any Valentinas."

Except for the salsa, I think. "It's Mexican," I say abruptly.

"Is that where you're from? Mexico?"

I nod. "Well, thanks again for the snack. I appreciate it."

I'm walking toward my spot in the waiting room when he calls out after me. "Anytime. And take it easy on the equipment, tiger."

Sitting in my chair, I track the fiery-haired Rory as he leaves the waiting area. I slump back in my seat and open the silvery package—my stomach groans at the sound, and my mouth waters. I had seen Pop-Tarts on American television many times, but by the time I was old enough to travel north, I was already in training.

My rigorous training included a strict food plan that was gluten-free, sugar-free, dairy-free, and all the other trendy '-frees' that coach Chema could throw my way. I had fought it at the time, but he'd refused to train me if I wouldn't agree to follow his rules to a T.

Chema is a coveted mixed martial arts coach, and I wasn't about to pass up the opportunity to train with him, so I promised I would stay on the food plan if he would train me. He has coached me since I was sixteen, and after eight years of training, he's more like an older brother than a coach.

If he could see me now, about to eat a gluten-full, sugar-full, dairy-full atomic snack, I'd be doing push-ups for days in punishment. I smile and take a healthy bite. My face contorts, and my nose scrunches up. Maybe I should have taken baby steps with the sugar after eight years without.

Yes. Eight years with no sugar. It wasn't a sacrifice. Well, it had been at first, but it was one I was more than willing to make if it meant I could one day get to the UFC.

I only manage to eat half of one Pop-Tart before I have to throw it out, completely *empalagada,* and I wonder what the

English word is for that sickening over-sugared nauseous sensation. The search engine on my phone has no answers, and I let it go.

"Valentina Almonte," a young woman calls out, and I follow her through two sets of doors until we settle in a small office.

"Please take a seat," she says with a warm smile.

This woman has to be close to my age, and I find myself relaxing a little at the familiarity.

"I'm Amanda. You can call me Mandy. We spoke on the phone."

"Yes. I remember. You did the eligibility questionnaire when I first signed up for the clinical trial."

"Exactly. I'm Dr. Ramirez's research assistant." She smiles again and splits her attention between my face and her computer screen as she reads my medical chart.

"I have to confirm information you have already given."

"Okay," I say. I squeeze my hands into fists and relax them, repeating the motion several times. I follow my calming technique with deep breaths as I prepare for what's next.

"Please state your full name."

"Valentina Almonte."

"Age?"

"Twenty-four."

"City of Residence."

"Well, it was Mexico City, but it will be Kansas City for the duration of the treatment as well as six months of follow-up care."

"Any changes in symptoms?"

"No symptoms other than the slight back pain I already reported."

"Has the frequency or intensity of the back pain changed in any way?"

"No. It's the same."

"I know when we spoke on the phone, you hadn't received any treatment, but have you received any treatment since?"

"No cancer treatment. No. I only take over-the-counter pain medication sometimes for my back, but not every day."

"Thank you," Mandy says. "I know it's weird because you gave all the information already, but I want to prepare you. Many doctors, nurses, and even hospital staff will have you confirm a lot of the same information over and over. Please be patient with us. It's hospital policy."

I smile reassuringly at her. "Sure," I say. "No worries."

"I do have a few concerns about your eligibility," Mandy says, and my stomach drops.

No. She can't turn me away now. This is my best shot. The only one I want to take. I can't be kicked off the clinical trial before I've even started. My mouth dries up as I try to focus on her words. I picked this trial—and Dr. Ramirez—because it is the most aggressive cervical cancer treatment anywhere, and I want to be as aggressive as possible.

"You're a very special case, and Dr. Ramirez agreed to make some exceptions for you, but I want to reiterate that this process will be very difficult. Are you sure there isn't any support system you can count on? A friend, perhaps? You'll need someone to care for you after hospitalizations and drive you when you are too sedated after appointments."

"I'll be able to hire help as needed. That sounded really stuck-up. That's the American expression, yes? Stuck-up?" Mandy nods. "I just mean I have family in Mexico who is paying for my treatment and resources while I'm here. I'll be able to hire nurses and drivers as needed, and besides, my apartment is only two blocks from here. I wouldn't compromise my eligibility into the trial. If it's money you are worried about, I understand none of my treatment is covered under the trial. Since I don't have medical insurance, I've given deposits already, but if you want, I'm happy to pay in full in advance."

Mandy's eyes soften, but I don't mind it as much as I would anyone else's sympathy. I couldn't stand Mom or Dad looking at me like that. I definitely couldn't stand Chema or my sister Pilar looking at me like that, so I keep it all to myself.

"It's more than that," Mandy says. "You'll want some emotional support."

"I don't want anyone to know. Not unless they absolutely have to—if the treatment fails."

"Okay. I'm following protocol, making sure you are going to have all the support you will need. But I'll take your word for it that you have it figured out."

"Thank you. I appreciate that. And I do. Really," I reassure her.

"Okay, then. Are you ready to meet Dr. Ramirez?"

I nod, and Mandy walks me to an exam room. I wait, shivering in the hospital gown Mandy provided before she left, until Dr. Ramirez announces her presence with a knock at the door.

"Come in," I say.

In walks a stunningly beautiful Amazon of a woman. I press my lips together to avoid gawking at her. She is tall and has muscular legs I would kill for—I can tell even through her scrub bottoms. I'm only a flyweight at one-hundred-and-twenty-five pounds, but I bet she is a bantamweight, or maybe even a featherweight, if she were a fighter. She wears a white coat over her blue scrubs. Her hair is up in a ponytail of straight dark-brown tresses that almost hit her waist, and she has the most expressive eyebrows I have ever seen on a woman.

"*Hola Valentina. Soy la doctora Ramirez. ¿Prefieres español?*"

"English is fine."

Dr. Ramirez smiles with what seems like relief. "Good. I'm Dr. Carolina Ramirez. It's a pleasure to meet you," she says. Her amber eyes hold my gaze, and I can't help but smile back. I'm already at ease.

Dr. Ramirez grabs the chair in the corner and rolls it over to sit in front of me. "I've gone over your chart, and it sounds like your case is an excellent fit for the trial," she says.

I let out a breath, feeling more reassured that I have done the right thing by coming here and seeking her out.

She finishes my physical exam and pelvic exam, and I sit up to close the gown once again. I wrap myself in the flimsy cloth that does nothing to warm my skin.

"We're retaking some images. So long as there is no change, we will be able to start treatment this week as part of the trial."

What she means by 'change' is if the cancer has progressed further. There's still a chance this could go the other way, but I nod because Dr. Ramirez's presence is somehow reassuring, and I'm feeling calmer than I thought I would.

"It's part of the trial protocol, but I have to ask again," she says. "Are you sure you understand the trial treatment is more aggressive than the standard of care, which is still an option for you at this point? This trial will take a toll on you."

"I know, doctor. I want to be as aggressive as humanly possible."

"There's one last concern I have," she says. "I'm sorry, I must insist, you are so young and with no children. You understand the radiation will more than likely render you unable to conceive naturally?"

"Yes. Mandy went over all my pre-trial plan options."

"I'm willing to wait a few weeks if you want to freeze your eggs."

"Won't we risk the cancer spreading further?"

"That is a risk. Yes. But if having children at some point is important to you, I want to make sure I'm also advocating for what you'll need to have a happy life."

I smile. She wants to make sure that if she saves my life, she's not leaving me with a miserable one. "Look," I say. "I've never given any thought to children. I may one day want children, but I don't need that child to be biological. There are many children in the world in need of good parents." I don't say that I have chosen family I love more than bloodline family. "I'll be very happy with adoption if children ever become important."

"Okay, then. Let's do this."

Four hours of waiting and several scans later, I finally get to leave the hospital. It was all cold metal, shivering, and waiting in exam rooms, but it's not my first rodeo. I already went through all of this in Mexico when I first received my diagnosis.

I stand in front of the hospital, unsure of my next steps. Less than twenty-four hours in Kansas City, and for what is probably the first time in my adult life, I don't have a schedule to keep.

Pulling out my phone, I call a car with my car service app. I ask the driver to take me to any street with multiple car dealerships, and he drops me off in front of a Ford dealership. I look down the busy boulevard, flanked by dealerships, feeling daunted at all the options. I shrug. *When in Rome . . . or in this case, America.* I walk into the Ford dealership, and a nice old man hooks me up with a used but reliable Ford sedan. I could probably afford new, but I don't want to take advantage.

I had ordered furniture to be delivered to my apartment, but it won't show up until tomorrow. Realizing I need essentials, I pull up the navigation app on my phone and roll away in my new pre-owned car. The salesman was adamant it isn't 'used.'

After shopping, it takes three trips to get all of my supplies into my new barren apartment. I was shocked at how expensive rent is in the U.S., but being close to the hospital was a priority. I opted for a two-bedroom, thinking if it came to it, I could rent out one of the rooms to offset some of my expenses. I could only ask my sister for so much money before she got suspicious. Not that she wouldn't give it in a heartbeat if I told her what was going on, but I'm not ready to tell her.

I plop on the cream duvet over the white carpet, not sure I will be able to sleep on the floor—first time for everything, I guess. Once chemo and radiation start, wine will be off-limits, so I went to town at the grocery store's liquor section.

Uncorking the bottle of merlot, I sip straight from the bottle as I sit in my dark apartment. On the second floor, the apartment faces the busier side of the street. Two restaurants and a small used bookshop sit directly below, and I wonder if they call the books 'pre-owned' too.

The coolness of the glass in the floor-to-ceiling windows soothes my skin as I press my arm against it to look down the street. There are a few bars, and it's late enough that people are starting to go inside with broad smiles and flirty looks.

It's a beautiful city, and I wish I had come here under different circumstances. Now all I will have as souvenirs will be the bitter memories of cancer treatment.

I take a long pull from the bottle of wine, not caring when some of it spills from the corners of my mouth and down my chin, splattering over the white duvet. I'll get a new one tomorrow. I press my forehead to the glass and hug the bottle to my body while I look at the lights of the city night.

My phone is on silent mode, so I don't hear it when it rings, but the bright glow in the dark apartment signals the incoming call. I block the light with one hand as I grab the phone with the other. *Pili* is displayed on the screen—my nickname for my older sister Pilar. I've called her Pili since I was four-years-old, and she's hated it ever since.

"Tini?" I hear on the other end when I pick up. I hate her nickname for me as much as she hates mine for her. We would both benefit from a truce, but we are both too stubborn.

I roll my eyes. "Hi, Pili. How are you?"

"You promised you would call me when you landed yesterday, and I never heard from you," Pilar whines.

"I'm sorry. Been busy with training and all. I was actually about to call you—"

"Sure you were," she huffs. "Well?"

"Well, what?"

"How's it going? Are you settled in? How's the new coach? Give me an update!"

I suppose as my benefactor, she deserves information. "I just got here, but yes, everything's fine," I lie. "I got my apartment keys yesterday, furniture comes tomorrow, and I've been training all day."

"Furniture tomorrow?" She yells, appalled, and I pull the phone away from my ear for a second after her shriek. "You should have stayed in a hotel until then. Do you need more money?" she asks.

"No. You've given me more than enough. Don't worry." A million dollars should cover treatment and living expenses in the U.S., shouldn't it? I couldn't ask her for more. I just couldn't, not even knowing she could spare five times that amount without batting an eye.

"You sound tired."

"Yeah, training right after a long day of flying can really take it out of you, you know?" I never lied to my sister before my diagnosis, and I am surprised at how easily it all rolls off my tongue.

"And when are you going to tell Chema?"

I wince. "Soon. I need to find the right time to—"

"The right time was when you were here. *In person*. I hate to tell you this, Tini, but you are a little shit for not being upfront with him. He deserves to know you got an agent and a new coach. You basically just ghosted him."

She isn't saying anything that isn't true about me being a shit, though nothing about the agent or coach is true—that's my cover. I rub my temples. "I know. Trust me. I know. I'll tell him soon."

"I miss you," she says.

"Me too." Guilt washes over me for leaving her alone. My brother-in-law doesn't allow her to go out with her friends, and

I'm one of the few people he does let visit her. I've left her more isolated than ever. He wouldn't have allowed her to come with me for treatment. Of that much, I was sure. Not unless he could come too, and if there is a last person in the world I wouldn't want to see, it is Felipe Conde, followed closely by Dad. "I'll call more often," I promise.

"Good night."

"Night, Pili."

Half of the bottle of wine is gone, and I pour the rest down the sink before bedtime. I lay down on my makeshift sleeping bag next to the window and stare at the smooth ceiling. Taking deep breaths, I repeat my intentions over and over into the echoes of the empty apartment, exactly as I would do before any fight.

"Get back to fighting."

"Beat the shit out of cancer."

"Get back to fighting."

"Live."

CONTUSION EXCERPT

CHAPTER TWO

Nothing appetizing takes up space in my fridge. After extensive research, I bought groceries to pack on the pounds. My one-hundred-and-twenty-five pounds are all muscle, and I know I'll lose weight once chemo and radiation start. I need to gain some weight before I start treatment. I'll have a hell of a time fattening up after an entire adulthood of balancing food to keep muscle up and fat down. I bought all the things the internet suggested, all high in calories, proteins, and fat, but low in volume. I look at the eggs, olives, butter, peanut butter—why are there so many butters?—avocados, and whole milk. None of it seems to go together, so I close the fridge and hit the shower to go out to breakfast instead.

The furniture delivery service won't arrive until after ten, so I have time to explore the neighborhood and grab a bite. I hardly slept a wink as I thought about my web of lies, but I didn't want to waste any more of my precious time sleeping.

～

Kansas City is flat. At least compared to the tall buildings of my home city. None of the structures in this neighborhood are taller than a few stories, except for the hospital that reaches a whopping seven floors and sticks out above everything else on this street. Also, unlike my home city, greenery flanks almost every road.

I'm surprised when I find a gym not too far from my apartment. I look through the window, itching to go in, but what's the point? I can't get a membership. It's not a fighting gym of any kind, but it would be better than nothing. I watch men and women go in, and I get a few friendly hellos. Maybe I could get a week's membership and just come to lift weights until the treatment starts? I'm getting ready to open the door when I hear a voice behind me.

"Don't even think about it." I turn like the kid caught with my hands in the *masa* to find Dr. Ramirez and Mandy staring at me. Dr. Ramirez's arms are crossed over her chest, and one of her brows is arched in warning. Mandy is pressing her lips together, suppressing laughter at this exchange.

"I-um, I wasn't going to go—"

"Yes, you were," says Dr. Ramirez.

I hang my head with shame. "Yeah, you're right."

"You're supposed to be softening up and trying to gain as much weight as possible this week."

"I know. I know. I just don't know how to not do what I was born to do." I smile lamely at the women, and we all ignore my eyes misting over.

"We're just going for breakfast," Mandy steps in just in time to avoid my tears spilling over. "You're coming with us." She isn't asking. She grabs my arm and laces hers through mine, tugging me away from the first place that has looked like home since I got here.

∼

"Are you going to work today?" I ask as I sit in front of the two women looking at their menus.

"Yes," Mandy says. "We grab breakfast together Monday mornings. You're welcome to join us."

"Thank you, I might do that," I say, relieved to have someone to talk to besides a bottle of wine.

"So, are you really a UFC fighter?" Mandy asks with interest and much too loudly.

"Mandy," Dr. Ramirez scolds. "I don't think Valentina wants to talk about that."

I look between the two women who couldn't be more different. Mandy is short and has unruly wavy hair in a chocolaty dark brown shade. It's almost witchy as the tresses stir with her movements. Her skin is a smooth, cool-toned light brown. Her rectangular face meets in a square jaw, and she has one of the widest smiles I have ever seen. She is almost my height and definitely much shorter than Dr. Ramirez.

It's not just their physicality that is polar-opposite either. Dr. Ramirez moves with grace and sits with impeccable posture, while Mandy looks a bit frumpy and slouches in her seat, making her seem that much shorter. But what she lacks in physical height, Mandy makes up for in volume. Mandy is *loud*. So loud it's almost embarrassing, and I can't help but look at the other diners when she speaks.

I take a deep breath and answer Mandy. "No. I wasn't a UFC fighter *yet*. I was starting to get close—before—well, before everything happened."

"I'm sorry, *amiga*," she says and reaches across the table to grab my hand.

I smile at her choice of words and hope she is sincere because, lord help me, I'm going to need a friend.

When the waiter comes to our table, Dr. Ramirez snatches the menu from my hands, and my brows knit together.

"I'll be ordering for her," says Dr. Ramirez. "She'll have two fried eggs over-medium. Hash-browns, Texas toast with butter, two slices of bacon, and one biscuit on the side with gravy, if you have it."

"And for you, ma'am?" the waiter asks Dr. Ramirez.

"I'll have the spinach-egg white omelet with avocado slices and half a grapefruit," says Dr. Ramirez.

I blink at her, and Mandy throws her head back with a roar of laughter so magnified, several rows of tables turn to stare at us. I sink in my chair.

The heaping plate of food set before me doesn't look even a little appealing. I tug the plate, and the mountain of food jiggles. "Do I really have to eat this?" I ask.

"As much as you can, within reason," says Dr. Ramirez.

I turn my attention to a glob of something white that seems to have bits of sausage in it. "What is *that?*" I ask. It looks revolting, and despite my hunger, my stomach churns at the sight of it.

Mandy laughs again. "That's biscuits and gravy," she says with a bright, toothy smile. "Welcome to America."

"There's no way I'm eating that," I say.

"Fine," says Dr. Ramirez. "But eat as much as you can of the rest. Have a milkshake later, if you can, for a snack. When you find it hard to eat in volume, you'll be glad you can drink some calories."

"It's true," Mandy adds. "A few weeks from now, you'll be sending me on an errand to get you this very breakfast, and you won't be able to keep it down."

I take the fork and knife, one in each hand. *You can do this, Vale.* I pep myself, and Mandy roars with laughter again. My glare rises to her, and she presses her lips together.

"It's not so bad," says Mandy. "You'll see."

And it really isn't. It's greasy, and I'm not used to it, but I stop when I'm comfortable, and Dr. Ramirez nods with approval at the amount I manage to devour.

"Well, ladies," she says. "I have to get to work. Mandy, why don't you take the morning off? You haven't used any vacation time in a while."

"Thanks, boss," Mandy says, between mouthfuls of the pancakes she ordered, before Dr. Ramirez leaves us alone.

When we ask for our checks, the waiter informs us that both our tabs have been taken care of.

"Dr. Ramirez is generous like that," says Mandy. "Sometimes too generous. People tend to want to walk over her."

"Don't take advantage. Noted."

As we make our way outside, I ask Mandy something that crossed my mind during breakfast. "Hey, is it okay for us to socialize outside the hospital?"

"Not with Dr. R. Today was fine, but she won't be hanging out with us on the regular. She needs to keep a line drawn between her personal life and her patients. But I'm cool."

"You won't get in trouble?"

"No. I don't handle patient care or anything like that. The hospital won't have a problem if we're friends, if that's what you're worried about."

We are on the sidewalk, and Mandy stands in front of me. "So, what would you like to do? Seems I'm free this morning."

I shrug. "I was just planning on exploring the neighborhood a bit."

"That's great." Mandy starts to rattle off suggestions on which direction we should take when I see the glint of red hair walking in our direction. The man in front of him walks into a shop, and I can clearly make out Rory—the guy who saved my Pop-Tart. He is looking at his phone and hasn't seen us yet, and for some reason, I don't want him to.

"Let's go there," I quip and grab her arm as I haul her across the street and into the used-book store. I look out the window as Rory passes by, swallowed in a crowd of people.

When we are safely inside the bookshop, Mandy flashes me a funny look. "Okay, weirdo. What was that?"

"Just this guy I met the other day—"

"Oooh, a guy? Which one is it?" She cranes her neck after the group of people crossing the street. "Is he cute?"

"Doesn't matter. I can't really date now, can I?"

"No, but enjoy your sex-drive while you can. Trust me. It's going to take a bit of a vacation once you start treatment. Everyone handles it differently, but your body will change a lot. Sex will be the last thing on your mind."

I'm so stunned at her directness, I change the subject. "Well, I have to get back. I have furniture deliveries today."

"Oh, I'll come with. I can help move things around."

"You really don't have to."

"I want to." And just like that, Mandy invites herself over.

As we walk to my apartment, it dawns on me I don't know her full name. "What's your last name?"

"In case you have to give the cops a description?"

"What? No!" I laugh. "I just—I like to know my friend's names."

"Gomez. Amanda Gomez."

When she walks into my apartment, Mandy whistles. "This is nice," she bellows but stretches the word 'nice' into two sylla-bles. "I knew you were rich, but this is . . . I think only surgeons live in this building."

I stiffen. She already knows the trial requires patient insur-ance or upfront out-of-pocket deposits for treatment and hospital stays. This shouldn't be a surprise to her.

"I'm sorry," she hastens to apologize. "I'm working on my filter. It's not very good yet."

"How old are you?" I ask.

"Twenty-eight."

"Twenty-eight? You don't look it." It's hard to believe she is older than me. I laugh nervously. "And no worries about the filter, but no, I'm not rich. My sister is. She's bankrolling my treatment." *Without her knowledge*, I think, but don't offer Mandy that information.

"Oh yeah? What does she do?" Mandy walks around the apartment on a self-led tour as we talk. She grins when she sees the kitchen with its marble island and brand new appliances. The white subway tile backsplash particularly catches her eye. Then she walks from room to room, making sounds of appreciation at each one.

"Nothing. That sounds bad. I don't mean 'nothing.' She's a homemaker."

"Nothing wrong with that," Mandy says with a wide, toothy smile that is growing on me. She pops a piece of gum in her mouth and talks through the chewing. "My mom is too. She's amazing. So your sister, she married money or something?"

"Sort of. I mean, she did. Her husband owns a company in Mexico, but she has her own money."

"From what?" Mandy asks.

Geesh. She wasn't kidding about the filter. Is it common for Americans to talk about money like this? "From her dowry," I say like it's the most natural thing in the world, but I know it isn't.

"Her *dowry?*" Mandy's jaw drops, flashing me the pink bubblegum in her mouth. "Like Jane Austen and shit?"

I laugh. "Yeah, Mexico had colonizers too. They brought their dowry ideas with them."

"No shit?" she says and plops herself on the floor as she leans on the wall for a back-rest.

"No shit," I say.

"Will you get one too?" she asks.

"What?"

"A dowry."

My nose crinkles, and I shake my head. "Nope. Don't think so. There's a clause Dad has to approve of my husband-to-be, and to Dad, it means he gets to pick him out."

"So your Dad has money?"

I side-eye her. "Yeah. He does," I say with resignation.

"So I was right before. You're a rich girl."

"I'm really not. I was starting to get sponsors and handle my own money that *I earned* before I got sick."

"Hey, I didn't mean anything by it. I'm honestly just curious. I don't give a shit one way or the other."

"You say 'shit' a lot."

"Yeah. I like to cuss when I'm not at work or at home because it's the only time I can."

"Why can't you cuss at home?" I ask.

"I have a thirteen-year-old baby brother."

She lives at home? At twenty-eight? That can't be right, but I'm not comfortable asking such personal questions. "You know he's probably cussing already."

"Oh yeah, he says shit way worse than me. But my parents still think he's a sweet little innocent angel."

"Got it."

"Where'd you go?" Mandy snaps her fingers in front of my face when I stay quiet too long.

I'm now sitting next to her on the floor, and I know I checked out of the conversation. "Sorry. Just thinking about what's ahead."

"Hey, don't worry. Dr. Ramirez is amazing. You are going to be fine."

"How do you know so much? I mean, you mentioned about the food and drinking calories and then the sex drive thing. Do research assistants usually know so much about the trials?"

"Yeah. I also keep the database of adverse events. If any trial participants experience side effects, they call me, and I add them to the database. Expected side effects are par for the course, but if they are unexpected, we have to monitor those closely."

"I see."

"Can I ask you something?"

I side-eye her. "I have a feeling you will even if I don't say yes."

Her toothy grin spreads, but then her face turns serious. "How come you didn't tell any of your family or friends?"

I think about that for a moment, trying to find the right words. "I don't want this to define me. I was a rising star in my field, as *fresa* as that sounds. Everyone in my life has a perception of me as the strong one. I can't now be the sick one."

The doorbell rings, ending our conversation, and I'm glad I don't have to keep explaining something I'm in the process of trying to understand myself. I make my way to the intercom, and a man's voice fills the living room. "I have a delivery for Valentina Almonte."

"That's me." I buzz them up.

Three muscular men trickle in and out of the apartment as they bring in all the furniture I could possibly need. I even ordered a second bed for the guest bedroom. When I'd shopped online, I'd opted to buy entire showcase rooms from the website because I've never been good at putting together home decor. Pilar would have loved to help, but the less she knew, the better. I didn't want to slip up and have her get suspicious.

Feeling more in the way than helpful, Mandy and I press our backs against the living room window. A few of the pieces of furniture require assembly. One man goes into the bedroom to start on that while a second crouches in front of us, putting together the sectional.

"I'm so glad I came," Mandy says. I look at her to find a twinkle in her eye. It's amusing until her intentions become clear. "Go talk to him," she says in a hushed tone.

"What? No!"

"Remember what I said about the sex drive? He is so hot. Do it."

I panic because even though we are whispering and the living room is large, he is right there, and I'm sure he can probably hear us.

"Fine. You're too slow. I'm calling dibs."

"What? Mandy!" I warn, but she only puts her hand on her hip and tussles her hair over one shoulder.

"Hey," she calls toward the man. "What's your name?"

The tall, dark, and handsome man looks up at us with a bright smile. He had introduced himself to me when I opened the door for them, but Mandy was at the other end of the room. "Chris, ma'am," he says.

Mandy walks toward him. "None of that 'ma'am' business. I'm Mandy." Chris stands to stretch out his hand, and their hand-shake connection lingers for a beat too long.

Chris is much taller than Mandy, allowing me a view of the amusement in his eyes from her flirting. She finally lets go of his hand and starts rummaging through her purse. I see the corner of a piece of paper that she pulls out and hands to him. "I have a solo art show soon. You should check it out." She gives him what I assume is a flyer. "Hold that," she says and keeps rummaging through her purse.

Chris smooths out the flyer in front of him and looks at it. His mouth forms up into a smile. "An artist, huh?"

"Yeah, I'm a painter. Landscapes and portraits mostly. Here." She stretches her hand out so he'll give the flyer back, and she starts writing something on it. "My number," she hands back the flyer to Chris. "You know, if you want a sneak peek before the show." Mandy turns and starts walking back to me. She continues to ogle Chris as he works and brings more furniture in, both of them smiling like fools the entire time it takes the three men to get my apartment furnished.

"Ma'am," the man who seems to be in charge calls after me, a clipboard in his hands. "Could you please sign here that you received everything you ordered?"

"Sure." I sign, and the men leave. Mandy looks out onto the street as she watches them go.

"You are shameless," I say to her jokingly.

She turns and winks at me. "I'm so tapping that ass," she says, and I laugh.

There's not much moving around I want to do, so Mandy and I try out the sectional.

"So, you're an artist?" I ask.

"Yeah. I'm an RA, and I work the information desk at the hospital so I can have health insurance, but one day I'll make a living just from my painting," she says as she stares dreamily into space.

"I'd love to go to your show too."

"Well, duh, you are going," she says and rolls her eyes. "I have to go. Still have half a shift I have to cover."

"Thanks for everything, Mandy. It's nice to know someone here."

Mandy smiles at me. "I'll see you soon, okay? And hey, think about what I said," she says while turning the doorknob.

"About what?"

"Have a sexathon tonight, then let your body rest the last two days before treatment starts."

I throw one of the sofa cushions at her, but it only hits the door after she is on the other side.

After she leaves, I try to remember when was the last time I got some. I've been so numb and in shock since my diagnosis. Sex has been the last thing on my mind. I'm lucky not to have some of the more embarrassing symptoms many women in my situation have. Maybe a night of reckless abandon will help me feel alive again. *I'm not dead yet*, I remind myself. And the furthest thing from the act of dying is the act of lovemaking.

I've never had a serious long-term relationship. I mostly

lived at the gym. Luckily, Chema's gym is full of hot men to pick from, and I have a deep bench of booty-call friends I call on when I need to scratch the itch or just relax after hefty training.

I sigh because I have to admit it has been too long, and that bench is oh so very far away in Mexico City. Maybe I could offer to pay for one of them to come here?

No. Not only was that too desperate, but I would lose a day or two before they could get here, and treatment starts in three days. Not to mention a disrespectful use of my sister's money when she thinks she is sponsoring a future UFC titleholder. Looks like the bar it is.

In the evening, I shower and throw on a pair of faux-leather leggings with a navy-blue silk camisole. My breasts are on the small side, so I feel comfortable skipping a bra and showing a bit of cleavage. I hate wearing high-heels and instead opt for black moto boots that I leave untied and slouchy.

The one girly thing I do enjoy is makeup. I don't get to wear it often because I'm always training, but now seems like the perfect opportunity to wear it.

I opt for a smokey eye with charcoal-black eyeliner. For the lips, I wear a kissable nude shade just a few shades darker than my tanned natural color to give my face some life.

Standing in front of the mirror, I look at my full figure. Taking in those slim, toned muscles I worked so hard to perfect sends me into an emotional state I wasn't expecting. I look great, and I know I won't look this way again for a long time, or maybe even ever. I can't even begin to imagine the many ways in which my body will change and am so grateful Mandy suggested this so I could enjoy my body—this version of it—one last time. I blink away the tears before they get the chance to ruin my makeup.

Not wanting to take a purse with me, I place my ID and credit card in my back pocket. I secure my apartment key into my boot laces, and I head outside.

I have several options to choose from as I walk down my street. For some inexplicable reason, I walk toward the hospital instead of away from it. I hadn't noticed the bar precisely across from the emergency room entrance. *Smart location*, I think.

The door's sign is in a simple font with white LED lights that reads *La Oficina*. Looks like I found my bar.

CHAPTER THREE

It's early, and the bar isn't even at quarter capacity. It's easy to find a space at the bar, and I pull out my credit card to open up my tab.

A bartender so beautiful I find it hard to formulate words comes over to take my order. She has the body of a model, and I can't tell what race she is. She has an other-worldly face, fair skin, and a perfect black bob hairstyle. Her beautiful full lips move again, and I replay what she just said in my head. *What can I get you?*

"Um—sorry. Whiskey sour, please."

She takes my credit card and comes back with my drink a few minutes later.

"Here," she says. "I like your accent."

"Thanks." My face grows hot, and it's not the whiskey.

"*¿Hablas español?*"

My head snaps up to her in surprise. Her Spanish is impeccable. "*Sí,*" I say. We switch back to English after that. "Where are you from?" I ask.

"I'm Chicana. Mom's Mexican, and dad's Chinese. It throws

people off. I know." She laughs easily as she says this. "I haven't seen you around here. You work at the hospital?"

"No. New in town," I say.

"I'm Sofia," the bartender says and stretches her hand out to me. "I own the place."

I shake her hand and smile. "Valentina. Nice to meet you."

"Welcome to KC. Let me know when you want another one, okay?"

"Thanks."

Sofia walks away to flirt with two customers a few seats down the bar. Poor suckers don't know she is playing them so that they buy more drinks. I smile. I like this woman.

Sipping on my cocktail, I scan the room for a potential one-night-stand. Someone muscular and handsome who won't need to ask for my phone number after. Someone alone, and more importantly, someone single. Nothing on the menu is appetizing yet, so I order a second drink and nurse it as I wait for the place to fill up.

A few guys come up to hit on me, but they aren't my type. I don't feel any attraction physically, and if Mandy is right and this is my last hurrah for a while, then I want something yummy. I mean, someone yummy. Fuck it. Men objectify women all the time, so I have exactly zero qualms about objectifying them just this once. They would be doing a humanitarian service, I decide. Would they go for it if I sold it as some sort of make-a-wish-for-adults service? No. That would probably kill the mood.

A third man walks over to hit on me, clearly inebriated. I resist the urge to roll my eyes. Could he even get it up, as drunk as he seems to be? Probably not. I smile and do my best to be nice to him—though I hate that's my impulse.

He sways a bit, but it's enough for me to notice. His black hair is slicked back with gel, like this is the nineties or something. "Can I buy you a drink?" he asks.

I point to my glass, showing it's half full. "Got one. Thanks, though." I smile curtly and divert my eyes from him, hoping he takes the hint.

"Oh, I like your accent. Where are you from, *señorita?*" he asks.

I do roll my eyes this time and take a sip of my drink. "I'm from Mexico. Where are you from?" I ask pointedly, though I probably shouldn't engage him any further.

Sofia looks at me with a question in her eyes. I roll my eyes and shake my head as if to say *I got it, thanks*. She tips her chin, and I know she'll throw his ass out if he gets rowdy. Hopefully, I can get him to back away without having to make a scene. I am here to catch a big fish, after all. I won't have a bite if I come across as drama before the night even starts.

"I'm from this here, the U.S. of A." He grins, and it feels eerily like he is about to pound his chest with his fists like a Neanderthal. He is somewhat handsome, tall, black hair, blue eyes. If he wasn't that far drunk, and he hadn't opened his mouth, I may have considered him as my boy-toy for the night. "I'm Doctor Keach," he adds. When he says *doctor*, I take it I'm supposed to be impressed.

"I'm actually waiting for someone, so if you don't mind . . ." I trail off, hoping he gets the hint this time.

"Oh, come on. You look so exotic, like a spicy Latina." He says Latina with a mocking accent that I can only assume is meant to mimic my own. My nostrils flare, and I count to ten.

This idiot doesn't realize I could have him on the ground and begging for his mommy in less than ten seconds flat. *Don't use your power on civilians, Valentina.* I remind myself of Chema's anger management lessons. Leave it for the cage. *Never out in everyday life.*

"We can have a good time, honey," he slurs.

"Sorry, buddy, she's with me." A voice much too deep for the body it came out of turns both our attention. I do a double-take when I see Rory, who is in the process of placing his hand on the small of my back. He doesn't make contact with me, though, and instead lets his hand hover over my backside. He wants drunky here to believe it, and he is selling it good.

"Like I said," I tell Dr. Keach, "I was waiting for someone."

"All right, all right. No harm done." He raises his hands in surrender as he walks backward, stumbling on a few people before he turns to face the opposite direction.

"Thanks," I say to Rory.

"No problem. It didn't look like you were having fun."

"I wasn't, but I had it under control."

"I don't doubt it," says Rory. "But I thought maybe I could save you some time."

My gaze sweeps his body from face to shoes. He is wearing jeans and a grey t-shirt, but the outfit is polished. His short, reddish beard is expertly kept, and he looks fresh like he just got out of a shower. This will do nicely. Very nicely indeed.

"That's the second time you saved me this week," I say.

"I thought you looked familiar."

"The vending machine?" I remind him. "You bought me a Pop-Tart."

"That's right. That was you." His eyes squint like he is trying to place my face in that scenario.

"In your defense," I offer, "I look much better tonight."

He smirks, accepting my awkward flirting. God, I'm so bad at this. My booty-call bench is so much easier. All I have to do is text one of them, at random, so no one's feelings get hurt, and ask: Free to fuck tonight? Somehow I don't think that methodology will go over well with Rory. "Can I buy you a drink?" I ask.

"Um—" he looks toward a group of men sitting at a table in the corner of the bar.

"Hey, don't worry about it." My heart sinks a little, but I keep smiling. "I just wanted to thank you for the Pop-Tart and for coming to my rescue tonight. Let me buy you the drink—no strings. You can take it over and enjoy it with your friends."

"No, that's not what I—um, just, let me go say bye to them, and I'll be right back."

My heart flutters, and I don't understand this new sensation. It must be the whiskey. "Sure. I can order in the meantime. What's your poison?"

"A beer?"

"You got it."

I order his beer, and Sofia has it ready for him before he gets back. I swivel in my barstool to look at him standing near the table with his buddies. They roar with laughter, and one of them pats him in the back. His fair complexion makes the reddening of his neck glaringly obvious, and I smile. He palms the back of his neck as if he can feel the heat there. It's cute, really.

Rory is nerdy and slim and oh so very handsome. I hope he'll let me take him home tonight. If this fails, I have to make a mental note to hit the nearest adult toy store first thing in the morning.

He grins as he takes the barstool next to mine. "Thanks," he says as he grabs his beer and takes a long pull. He is nervous and buying time. It's adorable.

"It's the least I could do," I say, opening up the conversation for him. He seems lost for what to say next, so I speak again. "Are you from Kansas City?" I ask, starting with a safe topic I hope will engage him.

"No," he says. "I'm from Minnesota." His entire face brightens when he thinks of home, and I know I've chosen the right topic. "Here for work. I've been here a few years now."

"I'd love some advice on what to check out. It's only my second night in Kansas City. Sofia?" I call her attention, and she looks over right away. She smiles knowingly as she looks between Rory and me, and I point to my empty drink.

"Oh, KC is great. You'll really love it," says Rory.

I start on my third drink, and Rory falls silent. His brows crease like he is thinking of something and he is unsure if he should say it. "Well?" he asks finally. "What are we waiting for? Let's go."

"Go where?" I ask.

"I'm going to show you Kansas City."

"*Tonight?*" I set my drink down and wipe my mouth with a napkin.

"No time like the present."

I cock my head to the side. Is this man serious? *No time like the present?*

"Come on. You are wearing walking shoes. Let's do this."

"Can I at least finish my drink?" I ask.

"Yeah. Sure. The night is young."

I almost spit my drink. Does he only speak in clichés? "Did you just say that?"

"What?"

"*The night is young?* That's such a cliché," I inform him.

"It's going to take a lot to impress you, isn't it, Miss Valentina, um—what's your last name?"

"Almonte. And are you trying to impress me, Rory . . . ?"

"Dennis," he says. "And, yes. Maybe I am trying to impress you."

I bite my lip as I lock eyes with him, and his jade-green eyes darken. The third drink is plunging me into tipsy territory, and I push it away. As I stare deep into his eyes, I realize even his eyes have freckles.

"What are you looking at?" he asks.

"Your eyes have freckles. These little flecks of brown swimming in the green."

"Ah, that." He takes another swig of his beer. "Yeah, my mom used to tell me it was poop."

"What?" I almost yell as I ask, my eyes wide with surprise.

"Yeah, when I was a kid, she had me convinced the little pieces of brown were tiny flecks of poop floating around my irises. Said it was because I was so full of shit." He smirks and drinks from his beer bottle again.

I throw my head back with laughter. This man is funny. "Your mom sounds like a badass," I say.

"She really is."

We are both laughing and relaxed. I don't remember feeling this way with anyone on a first date. "I don't think I'll be finishing my drink after all," I say. We both stand, and I press my hand to his chest. It's firm, and my body heats at the feel of it. "Rory," I say with a breathy voice.

"Yeah?"

"If we go out tonight, I hope you understand I intend to take you to bed before the date is over. Don't leave with me if you are not interested in that."

His eyebrow arches, and he pushes his glasses further up his nose so he can better look at me. His jaw slackens, and I know his brain is misfiring. I walk out of the bar without looking back but hope he is right behind me.

I step into the warm night and take a deep breath of air. Not even three seconds pass before Rory is at my side.

"Sorry," he says. "You kind of caught me off guard there."

"You're here, so I take it you are interested?"

He nods. "You're very forward, aren't you?"

"Not really, but I don't have any time to waste," I say plainly because it is the absolute truth.

**Valentina's story is releasing September 17, 2021.
Order your copy of *Contusion* today!**

ACKNOWLEDGMENTS

I want to thank all the women in my life who inspire me with their strength, grace, and love: My namesake, the O.G. Ofelia, Lety, Alma, Aida, Crystal, Andrea, Melissa, Aubrey, Anny, and Liz. You've all taught me what it is to lift each others' crowns. There are no words that could adequately describe how much I love you.

Also, much gratitude to my beta readers without whose feedback this book wouldn't exist: Claudia and Chris. You are both the best!

Big thanks also due to the editors at Midnight Owl Editors. Your amazing team saved this manuscript.

Lastly, to my partner and best friend, Robert. Though you never understood the dream, you fueled it with your encouragement and love. Thank you for setting up my writing space, keeping my technology alive long enough to finish this book, and providing the snacks and chocolate when I was buried in deadlines. But most importantly, thank you for being a prince among men and giving me my happily ever after.

Ofelia Martinez is a Mexican-American author. Originally from the Texas border, Ofelia now resides in Missouri with her partner and their dog, Pixel.

This is Ofelia's first book.

She loves good books, tequila, and chocolate. She proudly shares a birthday with Usagi Tsukino. When not writing, you can find Ofelia making visual art.

Visit OfeliaMartinez.com to learn more.

facebook.com/OMartinezAuthor
twitter.com/OMartinezAuthor
instagram.com/omartinezauthor